CONFETTI OVER BLUEBELL CLIFF

DELLA GALTON

Boldwood

First published in Great Britain in 2022 by Boldwood Books Ltd.

Copyright © Della Galton, 2022

Cover Design by Debbie Clement Design

Cover Photography: Shutterstock

Every effort has been made to obtain the necessary permissions with reference to copyright material, both illustrative and quoted. We apologise for any omissions in this respect and will be pleased to make the appropriate acknowledgements in any future edition.

A CIP catalogue record for this book is available from the British Library.

Paperback ISBN 978-1-80280-887-2

Large Print ISBN 978-1-80280-883-4

Hardback ISBN 978-1-80280-882-7

Ebook ISBN 978-1-80280-880-3

Kindle ISBN 978-1-80280-881-0

Audio CD ISBN 978-1-80280-888-9

MP3 CD ISBN 978-1-80280-885-8

Digital audio download ISBN 978-1-80280-879-7

Boldwood Books Ltd
23 Bowerdean Street
London SW6 3TN
www.boldwoodbooks.com

For Mum & Keith

1

TOGETHER WITH THEIR FAMILIES

Olivia Lambert
& Phil Grimshaw

INVITE YOU TO THEIR WEDDING

AT 2PM ON 7TH AUGUST
AT BLUEBELL CLIFF HOTEL
BALLARD DOWN, DORSET

RECEPTION TO FOLLOW

Ruby Lambert held the white, gilt-edged, incredibly classy-looking invitation between her finger and thumb and gave a deep sigh. Not because she wasn't thrilled to bits her sister, Olivia, was finally marrying the man of her dreams. Phil was definitely one of the good guys and the pair were clearly made for each other. It was just that the arrival of the invitation which had plopped onto the mat just now made the whole thing incredibly real. Not to mention incredibly close. Seventh of August was just four months away!

Ruby had known the date for ages, of course. She'd been one of the first to be consulted. The sisters had always got on well. They'd become even closer since Ruby had given birth to her unplanned, but much-loved son, Simon, who was named after his great-uncle and was now six months old. Ruby had been delighted and honoured when Olivia had asked her to be chief bridesmaid. But therein lay the problem. The two sisters might be only five and a half years apart in age, Ruby was thirty-five and Olivia was forty, and they might love each other to bits, but they had pretty much nothing else in common.

Olivia was a glamorous, willowy, dark-haired actress, often mistaken for Alison King who played Carla Connor on *Coronation Street*. She never put on an ounce of weight, despite the fact she also owned a business called Amazing Cakes and regularly sampled her own products.

Ruby was a curvy, English rose blonde, with the emphasis on curvy – she'd had a cleavage since she was fourteen and a sweet tooth for as long as she could remember. Like all mums, she had put on some baby weight when she'd had Simon, who was currently on his morning snooze, bless the gorgeous bones of him, while his mother agonised over the wedding invitation.

'Baby weight soon comes off.'

'You'll be so busy you'll be thin as a reed in no time.'

'Breastfeeding makes you thin.'

These and other clichéd wisdoms had been regularly trotted out by her friends and family and Ruby had relied on them being true. But they were not! Although she was still breastfeeding and lived in hope.

She had to admit she hadn't been paying too much attention to her weight anyway – she'd been far too happy. She adored being a mother, she'd embraced motherhood with a gusto that had surprised even her, and she'd adored returning to her roots and creating art instead of selling it. She was a high-profile, very successful art dealer with a London flat she used as a base when she was in the city and a lovely four-bedroom Tudor-style house, overlooking fields on the outskirts of Weymouth where she spent the rest of her time.

But for the last six months the selling side had taken a back seat and she'd spent her time looking after Simon. In between taking him to Baby Rhymetime, Baby Yoga, and Buggy Keep Fit for her (although she'd given that up quite quickly), she'd spent her time wafting around her huge studio in the loft conversion at the top of her house in floaty pinafore dresses and roomy dungarees. Fortunately, her mum was a very hands-on granny and she came round three times a week so that Ruby could work remotely. Technically she was on maternity leave, but her business could tick over without her working full-time as long as she didn't take on any demanding new clients.

All of this meant she could stay in blissful denial about the two stone she'd put on. In fact, it might be more than two stone. She wasn't sure.

Ruby frowned. The delicious scent of cinnamon and vanilla filled her kitchen from the selection of Danish pastries cooking in her oven. They were the type that came loose, uncooked and frozen from the farm shop, which meant you could cook them individually – rather than have to cook a whole pack, which you'd then be tempted to eat. Not that she did cook them individually. It seemed pointless turning the oven on just for one. Oh my God, they smelled gorgeous. She had got into the habit of having a couple, mid-morning, to keep her energy levels up.

She peeked through the glass door of the oven. They were just about ready. She retrieved the hot baking tray and set it on the side. Her mouth watered as she stared down at the two almond croissants that had risen in perfect gold crescents of deliciousness. The cinnamon swirl and the apricot Danish looked amazing too. The latter was new to the menu and Ruby was taste-testing it for her mum, who had a penchant for them.

Who was she trying to kid? It was just an excuse to stuff more sugar into her mouth. Making a supreme effort of self-will, Ruby made a bargain with herself. She would find out how much weight she'd put on and if it was more than two stone, she wouldn't eat today's pastries. She would go and weigh herself. Right now. Every instinct she had screamed, no, no, no!

Yes, yes, yes, she told herself firmly and ran upstairs, which wasn't as effortless as it used to be, she had to admit. The scales were in the guest bedroom en suite. She'd moved them out of her own bathroom a while back and had felt less guilty immediately.

She pushed open the door of the bathroom, which was one of the few places in the house not cluttered up with baby stuff, and located the scales, which were covered in dust. They were the electronic kind that also recorded BMI, by way of a handle that you had to grip firmly and hold out in front of you. She positioned them in the middle of the bathroom and switched them on. With any luck, the battery would be flat.

It wasn't flat. They hadn't had much use lately.

Ruby kicked off the comfy slip-on pumps she'd taken to wearing, took a deep breath, gripped the handle, held her stomach in for good measure and stepped on.

The scales flickered evilly, and the digital display showed her current weight compared with her previous weight from the last time she'd used them. No way. She couldn't possibly be thirty-eight pounds heavier. That was more than two and a half stone.

Remembering that she usually weighed naked, she stepped off quickly and peeled off the dungarees she was wearing. They had to weigh at least half a stone. She took off her nursing bra – that was padded and probably heavy too. Finally, she unhooked her Apple watch and the three strands of funky wooden yellow and blue beads that Simon loved playing with – they were quite chunky and probably weighed loads.

Then she repositioned the scales in case they were on a bad bit of floor – Ruby seemed to remember that could make a difference – and switched them on and off to reset them.

Holding her breath, this time through fear, she stepped back on. The display showed only three and a bit pounds less than it had just now. Oh crap. This was bad. Far worse than she'd even dared to imagine. She'd been ten stone before she'd got pregnant with a perfect BMI of 22 and she was now twelve and a half stone and her BMI, according to the scales, was 27.5. Ruby's heart was pounding and her hands felt damp as she got dressed again slowly. She felt like bursting into tears.

She stole a glance at herself in the bathroom mirror. That was another thing she'd avoided doing lately – looking in mirrors. But now she had a good long hard look. She had never been willowy like Olivia, but she had once had a defined waist and hips. And that jelly belly. Mmm, not a good look. She twirled slowly. No way had her bum been that size. Two and a half stone extra would be hard to carry off if she'd been tall. She winced. Five foot seven was not that tall. OK, so she had been through the trauma of pregnancy and birth, not to mention the trauma of discovering her baby's father was an adulterous scumbag who wasn't interested in his son, but it was time she moved on. She knew she hadn't been eating properly lately and she'd done virtually no exercise. She'd been too tired.

She turned away from the mirror with a small sigh. At least she now knew the facts. When you knew the facts, you could act on them. Living in the solution, as she had always called it, was part of the strategy that had made her the very successful art dealer she was. It was a wonderful wisdom, which basically meant identify the problem, identify the solution, then list the steps you need to take to transform the problem into the solution.

Well, that was simple enough, Ruby thought, as she walked downstairs with considerably less enthusiasm than she'd bounded up with. Her problem was that she did not want to be an overweight chief bridesmaid. She wanted to be a slim and very beautiful bridesmaid and make her sister proud. And herself of course.

She pictured the wedding photos. Beautiful Olivia, standing beside her best friend, Hannah, who was the only other bridesmaid and very slender, on the gorgeous lawn of the Bluebell Cliff Hotel, then herself alongside them. In all of Ruby's fantasies, she was fabulously slim too. But this wasn't going to happen by itself. Ruby set her chin determinedly. She had the impetus now and she needed to make the time. The steps she'd need to take to transform problem to solution were also simple and could be summed up in one word. *Diet.*

* * *

Not one to hang around once she'd made a decision Ruby told her mother her plans when she came round at lunchtime to look after Simon so she could do some of the necessary work to keep her business ticking over. Simon was her first grandchild and Marie was utterly besotted with him, showering him with love and spoiling him rotten. He adored his granny too.

'You don't need to diet, love, you look lovely.' They hugged and Ruby breathed in the gorgeous Lancôme scent her mother always wore and managed a smile. 'And you've just had a baby.' Her mother headed for the highchair and bent forward so her bobbed fair hair fell forward too and tickled her grandson's face, which made him giggle. 'Hello, my little man. Hello, 'ello, 'ello...' She sounded like an old-fashioned policeman. 'You look more scrumptious every day,' and she was off into baby talk, which Simon loved and responded to with gurgles of gahs, goos, guhs and toothless smiles.

Ruby waited patiently until they'd finished communing before saying, 'I had a baby six months ago and I'm getting heavier not lighter.'

'Are you? I hadn't noticed.'

This was probably true. Marie Lambert wasn't particularly observant when it came to day-to-day life. As well as being the world's greatest grandma, she was also an archaeologist, as was Ruby and Olivia's father, James Lambert, and the pair of them were known for being total authorities on the far distant past, whilst managing to miss a great deal of what was going on right under their noses.

Since Simon had come along, things had changed considerably. At least they had in the sense that Mum had amazed her entire family by giving up archaeological digs and moving back into the family house so she could help out with childcare, for which Ruby was very grateful. She might have taken a sabbatical from her own work, but looking after Simon was all-consuming. Especially as she was a single mum. Simon's father, who'd turned out to be a liar with no integrity – he'd neglected to mention he was married – was firmly off the scene. His name was on the birth certificate, but that was it.

When Ruby looked back to the time before Simon, it seemed to her that having a baby had been like dropping a bomb onto a peaceful, suburban neighbourhood. It had blown life as she knew it to pieces. When the dust had settled and the shockwaves had worn off, things had settled back down again quite nicely, but one thing she knew for certain was that nothing would ever be the same again.

Aware that her mother was looking at her curiously and clearly expecting her to comment on the whole dieting thing, Ruby said, 'I want to look good for Liv's wedding and I won't if I'm bursting out of a peach satin dress.'

'I didn't know she'd changed to peach.' Her mother looked surprised.

'She hasn't, it's a figure of speech, Mum.' The bridesmaid dresses were in fact a rather classy dusky rose pink, but they might as well have been peach in that they were clingy and pastel enough to highlight every last lump and bump. When they'd been choosing them, Ruby had felt like some great pink blancmange in too small a dish in every dress she'd tried. Ruby knew their mother would never understand – she was a size ten.

'The invitations look great, don't they? Did she tell you that she's thinking of leaving the hotel in a hot-air balloon?'

'No way.' Ruby stared at her mother in amazement.

'It was your Aunt Dawn's idea. She offered to pay for it too. She thought it would be something the pair of them will never forget. It seems the Bluebell Cliff are happy to accommodate a balloon.'

'Wow!' Ruby shook her head. 'Why not, I guess.' Olivia must have liked the romance of the idea – she and Aunt Dawn had always been really close.

'They'd need to have the right weather of course,' her mother added thoughtfully. 'So I'm guessing a backup plan is in order.'

This led on to some more discussion about the wedding plans – things were hotting up now it was closer – and then Ruby escaped with her laptop while her mother took charge of Simon for the next couple of hours. Ruby hadn't gone back to work properly yet, but work had begun to press in on the edges of her mother-and-baby world. There were important contracts with clients that needed her attention. She couldn't avoid work for ever. Neither did she want to.

A couple of hours later, Ruby emerged from the art world – an old client wanted her to sell a Damien Hirst for him – and went to say thank you to her mother. She found her looking at the baking tray of pastries that Ruby had put back in the oven earlier. Out of sight, out of mind.

'Did you forget these, love?'

'Um, no. I had a change of heart.'

Now her mother looked concerned. 'Don't be too hard on yourself. There's plenty of time to lose a few pounds. Don't go believing the stuff you read in those glossy magazines about those celeb wives fitting into their size six jeans a week after they've given birth. It's not true.'

Ruby swallowed. 'I know it's not. Thanks, Mum. And thanks for keeping Simon entertained.'

'You know that's my absolute pleasure. See you on Thursday.'

They went together to the front door, with Simon in Ruby's arms.

'Weight Watchers,' her mother said absently as they parted company. 'That's supposed to be good. You just count points and when you've run out you stop eating.' She waved a hand.

'Thanks,' Ruby said.

She might have inherited her mother's English rose colouring, but her mother had never had a weight problem in her life. She was also brilliant at maths. Not that you probably needed that much maths to do Weight Watchers. Or any other diet. It was a simple enough equation: food eaten got converted into calories. One cancelled out the other, so if you ate more calories than you'd expended, you put on weight, and if you didn't, you burned them off and lost weight. Ruby couldn't actually see why she wasn't doing the latter. She felt pretty tired all the time.

'They're all over the place,' her mother continued. 'There's one at the church hall in the village, I believe.'

'One what?'

'A Weight Watchers. Or it might be the other one. Slim Land.'

'Slimming World,' Ruby corrected automatically. She had tried so many different diets in the past, she was pretty well versed on them all. 'I'll look into it,' she promised.

'Not that you need to lose too much. Maybe you could have a word with your sister. Choose a slightly different colour for the dress. A more slimming colour. Is it too late to change the colour?'

'Yes, Mum. I think it probably is.'

Sometimes she thought that her mother was still only on nodding acquaintance with reality, even now she had emerged from the Jurassic period!

Black was a nice slimming colour, Ruby mused, waving goodbye from her front door, with Simon tucked on her hip, as her mum turned her car in the gravel drive and just missed driving over a clutch of golden narcissi that were blooming in a flower bed. But she was pretty sure her sister wasn't going to want her entire colour scheme changed to black.

2

Over the next few days, Ruby did some research. Now she had decided to embark on a weight-loss regime – that sounded a lot less terrifying than the word 'diet' – she wanted to make sure she chose something that would be sustainable.

She quite liked the idea of one of the fasting plans because that meant you didn't have to do it every day and could have days off that involved eating as many almond croissants and cinnamon swirls as you fancied. But her rational side, which was bigger than her wistfully hopeful fantasising side, told her this probably wouldn't do her any good long term. She needed to make some serious sustainable changes.

Like, for example, having a proper breakfast. Every single eating plan she investigated was adamant that eating a healthy breakfast was the best start you could make. Ruby wasn't a great fan of breakfast. She'd got out of the habit when she'd got pregnant – her morning sickness, which had lasted all day, had always been at its peak around breakfast time and so it had been easier to skip it.

She decided to change that and eat fruit for breakfast. A bowl full of berries should do it. That was easy and she lived near Eco-

Cow, which was a great farm shop – the same one the pastries came from – it was simply a matter of avoiding the freezers and sticking to fresh. 'Fresh not freezer,' Ruby decided would become her new healthy-eating mantra.

Ruby was about to go to Eco-Cow one morning, complete with a teething Simon who'd been grizzling ever since he'd woken up, not to mention half the night, when Olivia turned up. Her sister looked bright-eyed and happy and bounced in through the front door with an energy that Ruby dreamed of regaining.

'Hey, sis, how's it going?' She spotted the piles of baby paraphernalia piled up by the front door that seemed to be necessary on even the shortest of car journeys. 'Oooh, have I come at a bad time?'

'No, of course not, but we were just going to Eco-Cow. Fresh not freezer is my new mantra and I've run out of fruit.'

'Would you like me to go? I could nip up if you like? Or I could babysit my nephew for half an hour?' She eyed the baby, who was already strapped into his car seat, with affection. 'Hello, my little sweetheart.'

Simon, who had been grizzling quietly, stopped when he saw his Aunt Olivia, who he adored, and held out his chubby arms. 'Gah,' he said. 'Gah, gah ooh.'

'It would be great if you'd babysit for half an hour. Are you really sure, Liv? He might not be good company. He's teething. Do you need anything?'

'No. I only came round to drop this off.' She held out a glossy brochure and Ruby spotted the heading.

Bluebell Cliff Booty Busters
Lose weight and get fit the easy way with YouTube sensation, Saskia York, and celebrity chef, Mr B, at the stunning Bluebell Cliff Hotel on Ballard Down.

Olivia's eyes were warm. 'Mum mentioned she spoke to you the other day and you were planning a diet and this is about to start – so it seemed like synchronicity. Chuck it away if you don't want it. And take your time at the farm shop.'

Ruby nodded and stuffed the brochure in her bag.

Half an hour later, having done her shopping – it really was much quicker and more peaceful not having Simon in tow – she loaded the bags back in her black SUV again, sat in the driving seat and retrieved the brochure to read properly.

The premise was that you did a combination of especially designed fat-busting workouts led by Saskia and followed a menu sheet designed by Mr B. There were various levels of membership: bronze, silver and gold. Ruby turned straight to the gold membership. She didn't believe in doing anything by halves.

Gold Plan – renewable monthly
1. Motivational introductory talk with YouTube sensation, Saskia York, and celebrity chef, Mr B.
2. Freshly prepared calorie-controlled lunches and dinners delivered to your door (weekly hamper).
Weekly workout with Saskia York at the Bluebell Cliff.
3. Weekly weigh-in with Saskia York.
4. Downloads of Saskia York's fat-busting cardio workouts to be done as often as you like in the comfort of your own home.
5. 24-hour online support for slimmers who experience a wobble.
7. 100 per cent success rate guaranteed if you follow the plan.
Money-back guarantee. Plan can be cancelled at any time.

Ruby suppressed a smile at No 6. That was unfortunate wording. You surely wouldn't need to be on a diet unless you had already experienced a wobble!

The gold plan was eye-wateringly expensive. Not that this put her off. If it was expensive, she was more likely to stick to it, and it did sound good.

She glanced at the other plans. There was quite a bit of difference in price between gold and bronze, but that appeared to be because no meals were provided on the bronze (although they were on the silver). On the bronze plan, you had to cook everything yourself from the menus that were provided. Ruby was definitely not up for doing any cooking. So the bronze plan was out.

She checked out the silver plan and discovered it provided lunches only and the dieter cooked their own dinners. This was billed as the plan for the nine-to-five office-based dieter who needed a grab-and-go solution for lunch but had more time in the evenings to cook.

Ruby discarded this too. She was busy enough being mum to Simon and keeping abreast of the admin she still needed to do to keep her business ticking over. It would be nice to just pop a healthy calorie-controlled meal in the microwave for herself. It looked as though the meals were freezer-ready and could all be cooked, or more to the point, heated up in the microwave.

Ruby had heard excellent things about Saskia York, too. You'd have needed to be on a different planet not to have heard of Saskia. She was a fitness guru and influencer whose online workout sessions had attracted a couple of million followers on YouTube and she was regularly interviewed on Breakfast TV.

Ruby had also heard *not* so excellent things about Mr B, who was the Bluebell Cliff's eccentric chef.

Phil Grimshaw, Olivia's intended, had been maître d' at the Bluebell Cliff Hotel before he'd got his big acting break. He was currently playing a heart-throb villain and filming away. He still did the occasional shift at the Bluebell and his relationship with Mr B had always been turbulent. The tempestuous chef and the theatrical Phil had a love-hate relationship based on years of pranks and wind-ups – some more far-reaching than others. Mr B and Phil had, according to Olivia, reached a truce when Phil had asked Mr B to be best man at his and Olivia's wedding. He'd been so honoured that he'd promised faithfully never to play another prank on Phil as long as he lived. Ruby had a vague memory of Olivia telling her that he had not honoured this promise for very long, but she could have been wrong. She hadn't yet met Mr B.

On the plus side, she did know that Mr B was an amazing chef, so any diet menu he was involved in was likely to be very tasty. Her spirits lifted as she stuffed the brochure back in her bag and headed for home. Maybe there was light at the end of the tunnel after all!

* * *

Olivia and Simon were playing pat-a-cake on the kitchen floor on his play mat when Ruby walked in. Simon was a little bit young for this game as he couldn't really sit up yet but he loved it – he was propped up against his auntie's knees and squealing with delight. They looked the picture of happiness.

Ruby felt a brief flicker of jealousy and then felt quite ashamed of herself. She was delighted they got on so well. Just because her son had been grizzly with her all night, it didn't mean he shouldn't have fun with his auntie. He didn't see her all day every day. There was the novelty factor.

Olivia caught her gaze and glanced up. 'Hey, you were quick.'

'It's definitely easier without Lord Lambert here.' She heaved the box of fruit and veg onto the side. 'I may have got a bit carried away on fresh not freezer. Squashes were on special offer so I got

four. I don't even know how to cook squashes, but there are virtually no calories in them. Are you stopping for coffee? Shall I put the
machine on?'

'Yes please. I don't know how to cook squash either. Ask Aunt
Dawn.'

'I will.'

They sat on stools at the breakfast island to drink their coffee.
Olivia had Simon on her lap for a cuddle – and Ruby got out the
brochure and put it in front of them. 'I didn't know Mr B was a
celebrity chef?'

'Oh, he's always been a celebrity chef in his own eyes. At least
that's what Phil says. I don't think he's ever actually been on television. The man has an ego the size of a planet. Saying that though,
he is very good – and Saskia's a superstar, isn't she?' She hesitated
and her eyes softened. 'I think you look great, Rubes, but Mum said
you wanted to lose weight. I hope you don't think I'm trying to poke
my nose in.'

Ruby swallowed, feeling touched. 'Of course I don't and thanks
for being so lovely, but we both know I've put on a lot. I got on the
scales the other day and I was shocked how much.' She shook her
head. 'But at least I have a plan and, yes, this does sound fun and a
bit different from your run-of-the-mill diet. When does it start?'

'The introductory spiel is this Monday coming,' Olivia replied. 'I
can babysit Simon if Mum can't.'

'Perfect timing. I should be able to lose two and a half stone in
just under four months, shouldn't I?' She felt suddenly vulnerable.

'You will absolutely smash it,' Olivia said. 'I have no doubt about
that. Look at how much you've achieved. Your high-profile London
clients, not to mention jet-setting off to see New York billionaires.
You've built up all that on your own. You are the most motivated
and disciplined person I know.'

'I haven't been very disciplined lately. I haven't been doing any jet-setting either. I've been enjoying myself, slobbing about and acting like an art student. You've always been more disciplined than me when it comes to exercise. It's about time I got back into a better routine. Anyway, enough about me, I'm boring myself. What's the latest on the wedding plans?'

'Doves,' Olivia said, and rolled her eyes. 'That was Mum's idea, not ours. She read somewhere that it's popular in the States. They're brought to the venue in a box and released by the wedding couple – us – by pulling a gold cord. The doves are supposed to represent harmony and peace.'

'I knew someone who went to a wedding where they did that,' Ruby offered. 'It didn't go well. Just before it flew off, one of the doves crapped on the mother of the groom's head. That wasn't harmonious or peaceful, I can tell you.'

'I bet.' They both giggled and then Olivia's face sobered and she added, 'I'm not sure how ethical it is, either, using animals as part of our ceremony. What happens if the birds don't make it home?'

'True. And it certainly wouldn't be a great start to life with your mother-in-law. I mean, if the doves got caught short. Have you spoken to her lately? I bet she's getting excited.'

'She is, bless her. She's quite an extrovert – I can see where Phil gets his theatrical side from. Her sisters are quieter. Did I tell you Phil had a couple of aunts as well? They're coming, of course. They're staying at the Bluebell. He's getting them family and friend rates.'

'There are definite advantages to getting married at the place where you work... *Used* to work,' Ruby corrected herself.

'There are.' Olivia's eyes went a little dreamy. 'Honestly, Ruby, I have to pinch myself some days to believe this is all happening. Me marrying the man of my dreams and starring in *Nightingales*. Being on-screen on prime-time television every week still blows me away.

If you'd have told me a year ago that either of those things would be happening, I wouldn't have believed you.'

'You totally deserve to be where you are. My God you've worked hard enough.' Ruby hesitated, not sure whether to mention Olivia's other big dream – the dream of having her own family, but Olivia must have picked up on her thoughts because she said lightly, 'All we need now is for me to get pregnant.'

As she spoke, Simon squealed and Ruby said, 'Yes, and look he's agreeing with you. He wants a little cousin he can boss about.'

They both knew it wasn't quite as simple as that. Olivia and Phil had fertility issues and the chances of them conceiving naturally were slim, but at least they had options.

'You're definitely not going down the adoption route then, Liv?' Ruby asked.

'Not yet. We've got our name on the list for IVF. The list is quite long, but at least we're on it and once we've got the wedding out of the way, we can focus on that.' She bounced Simon up and down and he squealed with excitement. 'Blimey, listen to me, I sound like getting married is something to get out of the way and I'm really excited. Your Auntie Liv is really excited,' she told Simon, and then in an aside to Ruby, 'I think he needs changing, would you like him back?'

'Are you sure you don't want to get in some practice?' She laughed at the look of alarm on her sister's face. 'It's OK, I'm kidding. You'll have plenty of time for that. Hand him over. He's probably ready for a nap too.'

* * *

The sisters said their goodbyes soon after that and Ruby got changed into her painting smock and beads and took Simon up into the studio to finish the canvas she was working on, but she didn't feel as relaxed as she usually did when she painted. She felt restless and she knew she couldn't put this down entirely to Simon's fractiousness – he'd started grizzling again not long after Olivia had left. Maybe they were sparking each other off.

'It's OK, sweetheart,' she soothed, snuggling him in her arms and pacing the length of her studio – it spanned the entire length of the house. 'It's OK, my darling little boy. It won't hurt for long.' She got him his Tommee Tippee teether, spread some soothing tooth gel on it and gave it to him.

He quietened as they paced, soothed by the rhythm of her walk, and Ruby's mind was free to roam. It had been amazing being totally focused on painting and motherhood and she was in a rather lovely routine, but she could feel the winds of change. Its cool breath was on her neck. In some ways, she was surprised – she had planned to spend the first year of her baby's life enjoying motherhood, focusing on nothing but the two of them, building an unbreakable bond with her baby. But in another way, she wasn't surprised she felt restless. That she felt as though something was missing.

Since her late teens when she'd been at art college, the entire focus of her life had been art. She'd built up an incredibly successful career. She loved the adrenaline of making a deal, going to auction, getting a good price for her client. Not to mention the schmoozing, the wheeling and dealing and the status of being a highly successful woman in a man's world. She loved it all. In some ways, it was amazing she'd stayed away from it this long. It was definitely calling to her and she had always known she would go back to work.

She blinked away these restless thoughts. She was not going to go racing back to work. There was no need, it wasn't as if she couldn't afford childcare, but she did want to make some changes and the first one was to get back into shape.

* * *

When Simon was asleep that afternoon, Ruby dialled the number on the Booty Busters brochure and it was answered by a very helpful-sounding young woman, who Ruby quickly realised must be Zoe, the receptionist at the Bluebell Cliff Hotel. Olivia had mentioned how nice she was before.

'I'd like to reserve a place on the Booty Busters club starting on Monday please.'

'Hold the line a moment please and I'll see if there's availability. I think we're almost full.'

Ruby held her breath. Having decided to join, she would be really disappointed if she was now told she couldn't.

'Mmm,' Zoe said. 'Which plan were you thinking?'

'The gold plan, if possible.'

There was another pause.

'It does look as though it's fully booked. There's limited availability on that one.' Ruby could hear her tapping away on a keyboard. 'What did you say your name was again?'

'Ruby Lambert.'

'Are you Olivia Lambert's sister?'

'I am, yes.' Ruby crossed her fingers that this would make a difference.

'Just bear with me a second, please.' Zoe's professional voice had gone a few shades warmer. 'I'll check with my manager.'

Ruby drum-rolled her fingers impatiently on the breakfast island where she was sitting, one eye on Simon who was asleep in his travel cot. Maybe it would help to have a connection with the Bluebell.

It clearly did, because Zoe came back almost immediately. 'We can squeeze you in.'

Ruby suppressed the urge to make a joke about being squeezed in to a weight loss club. 'Thank you so much. That's fantastic.'

'You'll be in very good hands.' Zoe sounded as thrilled as she was. 'Saskia York is amazing.' She lowered her voice and said in hushed, star-struck tones, 'She's actually in the building right now. She's just arrived. She and Mr B are in the restaurant discussing the fine details ready for Monday – they're going to be the ultimate dream team.'

At that precise moment, Ruby thought she heard the sound of raised voices in the background, a woman's and a man's.

'In my opinion they're total zounderkites...' That was the man's voice. 'Ninnyhammers, the lot of them.'

But then the phone went silent and Ruby realised she had been put on mute. Had she heard that right? Ninnyhammers and zounderkites? She amused herself by looking up zounderkite on her phone while she was waiting for Zoe to come back and discovered it meant bumbling idiot.

She was just about to look up ninnyhammer when Zoe came back on the line. 'I do apologise – we had a bit of a customer altercation in reception.'

'I hope it wasn't Saskia and Mr B?' Ruby joked.

'Of course not.' Zoe's voice had gone back to ultra-professional again, although she did sound slightly rattled. 'Please could I take your credit card details, Miss Lambert?'

When the phone call was finally finished, and Ruby had parted with much more money than she'd planned – she'd signed up for fifteen weeks, which would take her to a week before the wedding – she felt a mixture of relief and excitement. She wasn't entirely a subscriber to the maxim you get what you pay for, but one thing she did know was that having paid so much money upfront, she was now going to make absolutely certain she didn't fail. Bring it on.

3

On Monday evening, just after six thirty, Ruby parked her SUV in the Bluebell Cliff car park and realised she was incredibly nervous. The leather steering wheel felt damp beneath her fingers and her Apple watch showed her heart rate was so fast it figured she was in the fat-burn zone already.

This was crazy. She was starting a fitness regime, not negotiating some million-pound deal. Ironically, she'd have felt much more in her comfort zone doing the latter. Still, at least it had been a scenic drive over. Forty-five minutes through the stunning countryside and pretty villages, past Corfe Castle, originally built by William the Conqueror, but now an ancient ruin high on a hill, and then along the road to Swanage, where every so often she had glimpsed the dazzle of the distant sea.

Ruby loved spring. There had been clumps of wild bluebells growing by the roadside, as well as being visible in gaps between the trees, turning the floors of the woodlands into vivid violet carpets of blue.

The Bluebell Cliff Hotel, which had itself been named after the bluebell wood alongside it, was set up on Ballard Down, a headland that overlooked the English Channel. It had the most fabulous views across Old Harry Rocks, three giant chalk stacks that jutted out into the sea and were a local landmark. The hotel gardens ran down to the South West Coast Path, which in turn threaded six hundred miles along the Jurassic coastline from Poole in Dorset to Minehead in Somerset.

There was even a decommissioned lighthouse, which formed part of its fabulous accommodation and which Olivia and Phil had booked for the first night of their honeymoon.

The Bluebell Cliff, Phil had once told Ruby proudly, was famous for being the hotel where people went to make their dreams come true.

This was part of its ethos. Back in the sixties, it had been a health spa – sea air being a fabulous restorative – but a few years ago, it had been bought and refurbished by an eccentric million-airess who'd formerly been a world-famous concert pianist and had turned the hotel into a place built on dreams and aspirations.

Ruby had been on a whistle-stop tour once with Olivia and Phil. She had seen the state-of-the-art recording studio and the music room that converted to a wedding venue. She'd also heard about its spacious art and writing rooms. Presumably one of those would be used for Booty Busters.

Her email confirmation said the introductory session would last an hour and would include their induction and first weigh-in – but not the fat-burn workout. The first one of those was tomorrow and then weekly for the next fourteen Tuesdays. After tonight, the weigh-ins were weekly and on Tuesdays too.

Ruby took several deep breaths of the salt-scented air as she crossed the car park and started to feel better.

'You've got this,' she told herself, without being aware she'd spoken aloud until a man, walking in front of her – he must have just arrived too – turned and said, 'Excuse me?'

'Sorry,' Ruby said, embarrassed. 'I was, er, talking to myself.'

The man, who was very tall – six foot five at least – and with shoulders wider than a rugby player's, said, 'I do that sometimes, too.'

'Do you?'

He had dark eyes which had a definite twinkle in them and a high forehead. Ben Affleck with slightly less beard was Ruby's first impression.

'Yep. I find at least then I get a sensible answer.' He was wearing a casual jacket, black with a North Face logo, and she caught the scent of an expensive cologne on the sea air.

She felt an immediate affinity with him and they fell into step alongside each other as they strolled round to the main entrance.

In the vanilla-scented foyer, he gestured for her to go ahead of him to the desk and she liked him even more.

There was a man on reception today and Ruby wished suddenly that she didn't have to ask him where Bluebell Booty Busters was located as she got out her paperwork and shunted it across the desk discreetly so as not to say the name aloud.

He glanced at it, then pointed to the stairs. 'First floor for the Booty Busters,' he bellowed.

Ruby winced. Did he have to shout it out loud like that? He should get a job in a doctor's reception.

'That's where I'm going too,' said a voice from behind her and Ruby shot a glance over her shoulder. It was Mr Twinkly eyes. She hadn't expected that. She hadn't expected any men to be on the plan at all. Slimming clubs were largely the domain of women in her experience. There wasn't time to feel too awkward though, because before she had the chance to say anything else he held out a hand. 'I feel as though I should introduce myself. I'm Harry Small. Small by name, but unfortunately not in stature. Although I can hold my stomach in for quite a long time.' That twinkle again.

This time, she smiled back at him. 'Me too,' she said. 'I've had years of practice. And I'm Ruby Lambert.'

He eyed her appraisingly, but he didn't say anything smarmy like, you don't look as though you need to diet, and for that she was grateful.

They headed off in the same direction and by the time they reached the first floor, both of them were puffing slightly. It was now obvious where they were supposed to be. A sign on a stand directed them to an open doorway, beyond which Ruby could hear a buzz of chatter.

In the light and airy oblong room, there was a table along one wall on which stood several glasses and napkins and some jugs of water which had ice and slices of cucumber floating in them. There were also bottles of sparkling water in a cool box. Ruby longed for a cold glass of wine, but it was obvious the only drink on offer was zero-calorie water – a choice of sparkling or still. She reminded herself she couldn't have wine anyway while she was breastfeeding. Tonight, she had gratefully passed the baton of Simon's bedtime routine and some expressed milk over to her enthusiastic mother.

A group of people were crowded around a table at the other end of the room and Ruby glimpsed a woman wearing an electric blue Lycra outfit that moulded perfectly to her slender outline. Saskia York. Ruby felt star-struck. This feeling was intensified as she edged closer and realised the other end of the room had mirrored walls so Saskia's perfect figure was reflected from all angles. It must be a regular gym studio. There were also a few rows of chairs in front of a microphone, some of which were already occupied.

Harry Small had already headed in the direction of the chairs and Ruby followed suit. There were about twenty-five people here.

To her relief, most of the women were either bigger or a similar size to her, so she didn't feel too out of place. Harry was the only guy and now she'd had time to study him discreetly, she could see he was carrying a fair bit of extra weight too, more than she'd first thought because he had the advantage of height. She wondered if he really had been holding his stomach in. He certainly didn't look supersized. Maybe he just planned to nip things in the bud before he got any bigger. Very sensible.

She found herself standing beside a very pretty woman of about her age, who introduced herself as Becky. Within a few minutes, they'd established they were both here to get rid of their baby weight – Becky had given birth to her daughter, Maisie, just five months before Ruby had had Simon.

'You're keen,' Becky said, when they compared notes. 'Although, actually, I wish I'd joined a slimming club before I got this big.' She patted her ample tummy and sighed. 'I fell for the line that the weight would fall off once Maisie arrived. But it didn't.'

'Me too,' Ruby said, pleased she had another ally.

'My hubby's treating me to this so I can get bikini-ready for our holiday,' Becky confided. 'Was that your husband you came in with?'

Ruby blinked. 'Oh – gosh, no.' She glanced across at Harry. 'We only met in the car park.'

'Men don't normally come to a diet club by themselves,' Becky mused. 'I wonder what his motivation is.'

They were interrupted by someone tapping the microphone and Ruby saw that a woman in a gorgeous sunshine yellow suit was trying to get their attention. She guessed it was Clara, the Bluebell's general manager, who she'd heard about but had never seen. Beside her was a very tall, but definitely not overweight man – if anything he bordered on skinny – who she recognised from his photo on the brochure as the infamous Mr B.

Clara was smiling. Mr B, on her left, wasn't quite frowning but he looked imperious and Saskia York, on Clara's right, looked serene.

'Good evening, everyone,' Clara began. 'Please do take a seat.' She waited for them to comply and then cleared her throat. I'm Clara King, manager of the Bluebell Cliff, and it's my very great pleasure to welcome you here tonight. As you may already know, the Bluebell Cliff's mission statement is, "We're here to help you make your dreams come true," and I sincerely hope that our new venture, Booty Busters, can help you to make your weight-loss dreams come true.' There was a smattering of enthusiastic applause. It was impossible not to warm to Clara – she was beaming so widely, she exuded warmth.

'I'm now going to leave you in the capable hands of our very own Mr B – who is one of the best chefs in Dorset.'

'The best,' Mr B corrected, as he stepped forward and gave a small and rather formal bow.

Clara paused only momentarily to accommodate the uncertain clapping before going on, 'And, of course, no introduction is needed for the fabulous and delightful Saskia York, who has single-handedly helped 2.1 million people get into shape via her incredibly popular YouTube channel.'

Saskia stepped forward with her trademark gesture of welcome, which was a spreading of her arms wide to welcome her audience and a beam that lit up the room. She was a very good advert for her fat-burning workouts. As well as being slender, she was incredibly pretty, blonde-haired and fresh-faced, with skin that glowed with health. Her white teeth had a little gap in the middle that gave her an endearing look. She put Ruby in mind of a younger Kylie Minogue, the archetypal girl next door.

This time, the applause was much louder. As Ruby joined in enthusiastically, she stole a surreptitious glance at Mr B and saw that he was scowling. Wow, he clearly wasn't keen on Saskia getting the lion's share of the attention. Her mind flicked back to the argument she'd heard in the background when she'd made her booking. Zoe had insisted it was a customer altercation, but Ruby would have put money on it being Mr B and Saskia and she envisaged fireworks ahead.

Still, that could liven things up and take their minds off the diet and exercise bit.

Saskia launched into her motivating induction speech. 'The workouts are very simple,' she began in her smooth-as-velvet voice. 'They are designed for the complete beginner.' She was English, but there was an exotic edge to her accent that made her sound incredibly sexy. Her guided workouts were reputed to be as popular with men as they were with women and Ruby could see why. 'There is no need for anyone to worry. There is absolutely no pressure.'

Ruby drifted off a bit as Saskia went on to say that she had received all the pre-workout forms they had filled in and was therefore totally in tune with each person's specific requirements and issues.

Ruby wasn't the only one who had zoned out. She saw Harry Small stifle a yawn with his hand. But then suddenly she realised that Saskia was looking her way with an expectant expression. She must have just asked her a question and Ruby had no idea what it was.

The room had fallen silent as though waiting for her answer and Ruby felt her face flame.

'I do apologise. Would you mind repeating that?'

'Please do not worry. I was simply asking if anyone would like to share their motivation for being here tonight.'

Ruby wished the ground would open up and swallow her. Her heart felt as though it would pound out of her chest. She pulled herself together. 'Er – yes, OK. Well, I put on some baby weight when I had my son and I'm keen to get back into shape.'

'Great answer.' Saskia began to clap and the rest of the room joined in.

Ruby's heart slowed a fraction. That would teach her not to pay attention.

'Would anyone else like to share?' Saskia asked, her friendly gaze flicking around the room.

A young woman near the front put her hand up. 'I started comfort eating after I lost my mum to a car accident. The weight just piled on.'

There was a sympathetic murmur from the rest of the group.

After that, the answers came in thick and fast. Everyone seemed to want to share their reasons for being here. Everyone except Harry, Ruby noticed, who was keeping very quiet. Saskia didn't push him.

When it was clear that no one else wanted to speak, she leaned forward, her face serious. 'Thank you, everyone, for opening up to the group. That was very brave. It takes courage to make positive changes in our lives. And you have all shown that tonight in bucket-loads, simply by coming in the door. You have taken the most important step. Well done, everyone. Let's give ourselves a great big round of applause.'

Everyone clapped once more. At this rate, they'd all have sore hands by the end of the evening, Ruby thought and berated herself for being cynical. It was great that Saskia wanted to motivate them. That was, after all, half the battle. She became aware that the fitness guru was speaking again.

'I promise you that knowing your reasons for wanting to make changes will stand you in very good stead.'

The room had gone silent again, hanging on to her every word. She really did have a mesmerising voice.

'I would now like to hand over to Mr B, our fabulous chef, who is going to tell you about his side of the programme.'

'Which is by far the most important side of the programme,' Mr B said, stepping forward.

Ruby sneaked a glance at Saskia, but her smile held.

She was a lot more diplomatic than her co-host. Throughout Saskia's introductory spiel, Mr B had been looking bored. In fact, at one point, Ruby had noticed he'd been tapping his foot, but now he was in the limelight, his mobile face became animated.

'I will be very brief,' he said, drawing himself up to his full height. 'Because my recipes are all self-explanatory. A ten-year-old zounderkite could follow them.' There was that word again. It had definitely been Mr B and Saskia arguing. 'But one thing I would like to say is that no one ever lost weight through exercise alone. For example, the average person would need to run several marathons in order to burn off the calories consumed by eating a single banana.'

'Wow,' Becky said under her breath. 'That explains a lot.'

'I don't think it's several marathons,' Saskia interrupted. 'Although I agree with the principle that it is much harder to lose weight by exercise alone. But the more calories you burn, the more you will lose.'

'One marathon – a dozen marathons.' Mr B waved a hand as if there was hardly any difference and added silkily, 'As you say, it's the principle I'm talking about.' He turned back to the audience, 'Which means that my part of the plan is by far the most important. Stick to the menus and eat nothing else – no alcohol, no sugar-laden fizzy drinks, no snacking on anything – and you will lose pounds in the most healthful of ways, even if you don't do so much as a toe wriggle of exercise. If you cheat, you will only be cheating yourselves. Now, are there any questions?'

Harry Small's hand shot up. 'I noticed there were no breakfasts included in your menu plans. Does that mean we have to add the calories consumed at breakfast into our overall count for the day?'

'There is no need to eat breakfast,' Mr B replied, which caused a little ripple in the room. Ruby guessed that she was among seasoned dieters and like herself they'd probably been on a lifetime of plans which proclaimed that a healthy breakfast was an essential part of any diet regime.

Harry Small raised his eyebrows. 'Really, I'd always thought...?'

'Empty your mind of all previous misconceptions – I can assure you that breakfast is quite unnecessary. Lots of people don't like breakfast, myself included, there is no need to force yourself to take in unnecessary calories.'

Saskia looked as though she wanted to say something else, but before she got the chance, Mr B held up a fan of bronze-, silver- and gold-coloured folders and waved them at the group.

'In my hand, I hold the secret of slimming success. Do make sure you pick up your pack before you leave for your weigh-in.'

The weigh-ins were held in a section of the studio that had been partitioned off with a couple of room dividers so they were private. Ruby was relieved to discover they went in one at a time and could hear only muted voices from the other side of the partition, so no one could overhear any embarrassing truths.

She was sandwiched between Becky and Harry in the queue. Becky came out looking depressed and Ruby gave her an encouraging smile. Then it was her turn – but at least she knew what to expect – having done the 'nasty surprise' bit at home. It was also a relief to find out the Booty Buster scales were an exact match to the ones in her bathroom when it came to her weight. Although it was still unpalatable to see the figure replicated on the scales. But it did give her the extra motivation she needed, she decided, as she collected her belongings and made for the exit.

Ruby was walking back downstairs hoping to catch up with Becky – she planned to ask if she wanted to exchange numbers so they could support each other and maybe their babies could meet for play dates – when Harry caught up with her.

He wasn't smiling either. The twinkle had totally disappeared. Ruby felt compelled to say something to cheer him up. 'Don't worry. The way I see it, this is the heaviest we're ever going to be. Every week from hereon in, we'll be a bit lighter.'

'Yeah. That's a good way of looking at it. I was just...' He shrugged and broke off. 'I was just thinking I'm probably not going to make the deadline.'

'For what?' She frowned. 'I didn't realise we had a deadline. I thought that we just lost as much as we could in the fifteen weeks.'

'Yeah. Yeah we do. I was talking about my own personal deadline.' He hesitated, clearly caught in a dilemma. 'I, er, didn't want to say this in the group, but I'm here because my wife gave me an ultimatum. I need to lose four stone by the end of July or...'

'Or what?'

'She leaves me.' His face darkened.

Ruby was sure he was going to follow up this statement with some light-hearted remark. But he didn't. For a second, there was something in his eyes that was incredibly vulnerable. Then he swallowed, his Adam's apple bobbing, and turned his head slightly. Clearly this was no joking matter.

She felt a rush of emotions. Amazement, empathy, anger at his wife – what on earth was going on there? Wanting to make him feel better, she said, 'I have a personal deadline too. My sister's getting married and I don't want to be an overweight chief bridesmaid.'

'I'm sure you'll succeed,' he said seriously.

'You will too. It'll be fine. Men usually lose weight quicker than women.'

'Yeah. Cheers.' He gave himself a little shake as if already regretting sharing his story. 'Like they said back in there – we've taken the hardest step. The rest of it is just simply sticking to rules – right?'

'Absolutely,' Ruby agreed. 'We've got this.'

4

As Harry Small climbed into his silver two-year-old Lexus IS Sport, he felt an urgent desire to bang his forehead on the steering wheel. What had possessed him to blurt all that out to that lovely girl? Good grief, no wonder his wife, Annabel, accused him of opening his mouth before he edited his thoughts – she was right. Restraint of pen and tongue, his father would have said. Now he felt hopelessly disloyal.

Yes, it was true that Annabel had given him an ultimatum. 'What do I have to say to prove I'm serious, Harry? Diet or divorce? Is that what it would take to make you listen?' Her eyes had flashed fire. 'Well, I'm saying it. Lose four stone by the end of July, or I'm out of here.' But it was also true that Annabel only ever wanted what was best for him. She didn't just issue ultimatums for no reason, as she frequently pointed out. They were meant to inspire and motivate and they shouldn't be taken out of context.

They were usually a little less heavy-duty though, like, 'Snoring is unreasonable behaviour, Harry. Find a way to stop or you can sleep in the spare room.'

That one was carried out regularly.

Or, 'Untidiness is unreasonable behaviour, Harry. Pick your socks up from the bedroom floor or they're going in the bin.' She'd done that a couple of times too. His favourite cashmere socks, one of life's little luxuries.

The weight thing was different and he wasn't sure how serious she was being until she'd presented him with a brochure for an exclusive diet club that she'd already signed him up for with his credit card.

He was pretty sure the ultimatum about her leaving was an idle threat – he knew she loved him, but he certainly planned to give the diet his best shot. After all, his wife did have a point. He'd had a medical recently for the company insurance and his cholesterol was a tad high, as was his BMI. He'd found out today that he'd need to lose more than he'd thought to get down to a healthy BMI, although not quite as much as four stone.

Annabel had warned him ages ago – just three months after their wedding, to be precise – that he would need to watch his weight if he didn't want to drop dead of a heart attack like his father had.

'I've only got your best interests at heart,' she had said, stroking the sleeve of his suit, tipping back her blonde curls and standing on tiptoe to look up into his eyes. 'You do know that, don't you, darling. I want you to be around for a very long time.'

Harry had hugged her and said that he wanted that too. Of course he did. Annabel was stunningly beautiful and sexy as hell. Looks wise, she reminded him of a young Kate Winslet with her gorgeous lips and wavy blonde hair, except Annabel had blue eyes, not brown, and she had a slightly more elfin face than Kate. She was also very smart – she was a solicitor – and, deep down, he'd always had an inkling that she was way out of his league.

Kindness and tact had prevented him from pointing out to her that his father hadn't died because he was overweight. He'd been reasonably trim. He had, however, had very high blood pressure, due to the stress of taking over the family business, Gargantuul, passed down to him by his own father.

Gargantuul, which meant, rather aptly, very high numbers, was a software business that sold its products to massive clients, like the MOD and the NHS.

The selling gene had skipped a generation unfortunately. Stephen Small, Harry's father, hadn't inherited the love of selling at all. He'd have been much happier working in an outstation on the moon than he'd been schmoozing clients. Harry, however, had always taken after his grandfather, both in stature and temperament. He had far more in common with Grandpa George than he'd ever had with his father.

Things would probably have worked out much better if Grandpa George had passed Gargantuul directly to his grandson when he'd died six years ago instead of to his reluctant son, who had passed away one year later. That way, Harry wouldn't have lost both his relatives before he'd hit the age of thirty-two, but that wasn't the way things were done in his family. Consequently, Harry had been forced to grow up fast. He'd inherited the major shareholding in the company and had been rocketed to the position of CEO when he was just thirty-three years old.

He was now thirty-seven and an incredibly wealthy man. For a while, he'd felt a certain amount of survivor's guilt about that, but as his emotionally very astute mother, Elise, had pointed out at the time, he shouldn't feel too guilty. Two dearly loved relatives had had to die to give him the privileges he had today and it was his duty to make the most of them. It was also his duty to restore the company's brilliant reputation – his father's reign had been relatively short but damaging – and to have sons or daughters to take over in their turn from him.

The first part had been easy. Harry had worked in the family business since he'd graduated from university with a First in economics and he loved it. He was a born salesman and a natural leader. Last year's profits had soared into the stratosphere.

Unfortunately, he wasn't doing so well on the heirs front. He and Annabel had been married for a few months short of two years and she hadn't yet fallen pregnant.

She had told him recently – although not in so many words – that the main reason for this was because of the excess weight he was carrying.

'Weight isn't good for a man's fertility. That's another reason you should shed it fast.'

Harry had promised to do his best, knowing she was right and cursing his sweet tooth and penchant for the sugar-loaded snacks that fuelled the long hours he worked.

However, he wasn't entirely in agreement with her. The main reason she hadn't yet fallen pregnant, as far as he could see, was because they rarely made love.

He snapped his thoughts back to the present as he reached the long-gravelled driveway that led up to his property. It was in a hamlet on a reasonably new development not far from Studland Bay. You could see the sea from the upstairs windows, which he loved, and there was a swimming pool in the garden. Annabel had insisted that he install a hot tub too when they'd married, which he'd gladly done.

The hot tub was in a glass-walled extension that he'd had built especially at the back of the house. It had sliding doors that opened out to the garden, but it was basically inside, which meant it could be used all year round. They'd used it a lot last year on warm summer evenings with the glass doors open to the garden. There was nothing quite like sitting in a hot tub with the jacuzzi setting on full and sharing a bottle of bubbly.

'Bubbles and bubbles,' Annabel had coined it with a squeal of delight. The name had stuck. Harry was hoping it would soon be warm enough for bubbles and bubbles again. Not that they couldn't have used it in the winter too, of course, but Annabel hadn't seemed so keen lately.

There were four other houses in the hamlet, but they were so far apart that you could have gone a year without seeing your neighbours if you so desired. At the end of the driveway, the electronic gates of Studland Views swung back to admit him, alerted by an automated call from his car, and he drove in and parked beside Annabel's BMW.

For a few seconds, he paused to look up at the chalet bungalow, which was painted white, with a Mediterranean-style pillared terrace around the front door. He loved this place. He had bought it outright with a bonus he'd earned a few years after he'd started working at Gargantuul. It had been the location that attracted him and the space. There were four bedrooms, even though back then he'd only needed the one. There was a big, state-of-the-art kitchen which Annabel had insisted was made even bigger so she could have a breakfast island installed and still have room to 'swing a cat', as she put it – if not a full-size Siberian tiger. She'd also wanted the old Aga upgraded to an eight-burner commercial range oven. He'd never been quite sure why she'd wanted this – neither of them were great cooks, unless you counted popping Marks & Spencer ready meals into the oven and setting the timer.

That was probably another reason he'd put on weight. They didn't eat many meals that were cooked from scratch. The meat and two veg that he'd been brought up on was a thing of the past. Annabel was a fan of Thai curries, creamy stroganoffs and pizza if she was in a hurry. She didn't have a big appetite herself and often skipped meals, but she loved to feed him. He'd been happy to comply with whatever she wanted. He adored her. He still did and he still couldn't quite believe that of all the men she could have married, she'd chosen him. Coming home to Annabel after a hard day's work was like coming home to a breath of fresh air. No matter how stressful a day she'd had, she always looked and smelled gorgeous. Harry knew he was a very lucky man. OK, so she was fond of issuing ultimatums, but he could handle that.

He put his key in the front door. He had high hopes for tonight. Annabel was bound to be in an especially good mood now she knew he'd done what she'd asked. He'd gone straight to the Bluebell Cliff Hotel after work. He whistled as he strolled down the long hall, turned right into the kitchen, shrugged off his jacket and called her name. No reply. That was odd – the house felt empty too. She hadn't said she'd be late too, had she? Maybe she was on a case – she occasionally worked longer hours when they were needed. He'd have preferred her to work fewer. It wasn't as though they needed the money, but at the same time he respected her need to be independent. Contrary to what one or two of his less charitable mates had said, Annabel had definitely not married him for his money.

There was no note anywhere as far as he could see, although he could smell that food had been recently cooked – perhaps she'd come in and gone out again. She clearly hadn't driven herself.

Harry plonked the gold Bluebell Booty Busters folder on the table with a sigh. What he'd have liked most was to sit down with his wife with a cool glass of wine – maybe half a glass for him as he knew alcohol was high calorie – and chat about the days they'd had. He was sure he could make her laugh telling her about Booty Busters and the improbable partnership between the internet influencer and the skinny chef. Wasn't there a saying, 'never trust a skinny chef'? Although, in these circumstances, that was probably a plus point rather than a minus.

Harry picked up the brochure and looked inside. There was a plastic folder that contained the first week's menu. It was printed in a swirling, difficult-to-read font and it took him a few moments to decipher it.

Day One
Lunchtime
Main: Buttered breast of chicken, served with creamy
mash, parsnip puree and celeriac gratin.
Dessert: Chocolate profiteroles.

*

Evening
Main: Beef bourguignon, served with tiny roast
potatoes, and roasted Mediterranean vegetables.
Dessert: Strawberry gateau

Harry did a double take. None of that sounded like diet food to him. He'd been expecting rocket salad with a plain fillet of chicken if he was lucky. Maybe they'd put in the wrong menus. Or perhaps they'd just started with a more generously calorie-counted meal to ease you into the diet gently.

He flicked to the next one.

Day Two
Lunchtime
Main: Lamb fricassee, served with crispy courgette
fritters and avgolemono sauce.
Dessert: Mr B's world-famous brownies.

*

Evening
Main: Slow-cooked fillet steak with creamy peppercorn sauce, served
with skinny fries, grilled tomatoes and garlic mushrooms.
Dessert: Tarte au citron.

Crikey O'Reilly, some of those dishes sounded superb. Surely most of those things were sky-high in fat though. Then again, Mr B was a very clever chef from what he'd heard, so he must know what he was doing. Perhaps the trick was to serve up very small quantities of top-quality food. Quality not quantity. Yeah, that made a lot of sense. Harry was sure the chef had mentioned that.

The gold option package he had signed up for certainly hadn't been cheap. Perhaps this was what you paid for. It sounded a hell of a lot more appealing than 'as much rocket salad as you can eat'. His mouth watered as he put the menus back on the worktop. It looked as though this whole diet and exercise routine wasn't going to be such a drag as he'd feared.

He was still disappointed that Annabel had gone AWOL, but reading the menu had lifted his spirits. He was now seriously looking forward to the next day's delivery of his first week's supply of meals.

* * *

Ruby had thought exactly the same thing when she'd read the menus, which had been when she'd got home last night.

It was now Tuesday morning and her first week's supply of precooked meals – they only needed to be heated up in the microwave – had just been dropped off by the Bluebell Cliff's delivery van. Ruby couldn't wait to see what the lunch for Day One tasted like. It hadn't occurred to her that the menus might be calorie-controlled because you got miniscule portions. She'd assumed that Mr B would be making some serious ingredient swaps.

All good 'diet' cookery books relied on ingredient swaps. She'd read enough of them in her time to know that was how it worked. Sugar was replaced with sweetener, full-fat versions of everything high calorie were replaced with half-fat or, better still, fat-free versions. The taste element sometimes suffered in the process, but if you knew what you were doing, you could compensate with clever use of herbs and flavourings. The whole thing was an incredible faff and, in her experience, it could easily go wrong if you weren't a brilliant cook already. There weren't really any substitutes for fat and sugar. However, Olivia had mentioned that Mr B had won awards and that it was down to him that the Bluebell Cliff had two rosettes. He was in the perfect position to produce an amazing range of diet meals.

Ruby's mouth watered as she took out the lunch for Day One. They were in sealed recyclable containers, but they were carefully labelled. She transferred a large chicken breast and the generous portion of creamy mash onto a plate, along with the other veg and popped it into the microwave.

Her doorbell rang just as it pinged to say it was ready.

Her visitor was Olivia. 'Hey, sis,' Ruby exclaimed with pleasure. 'I wasn't expecting you. I thought you were going back to Bristol this week for filming?'

'I am. I'm on my way, now. I just popped in to say goodbye.' Olivia looked carefree and happy. Her shiny dark hair was loose around her shoulders. She usually wore it tied back and her eyes were sparkling. 'Filming doesn't actually start until tomorrow, but I'm meeting Phil for dinner tonight in Bristol.'

'What's he doing in Bristol?'

'It's a long story, but it's something to do with a future audition. His agent's up there.' They went into the kitchen and Olivia sniffed the air. 'Hey, something smells good. What are you cooking?'

'Heating up, not cooking. That's one of Mr B's creations. I'm on day one of my diet.'

'Fantastic. That's another reason I called – to see how that was going? Have you met Saskia York yet?'

'I have. Last night at the induction. She seemed really nice. We haven't actually done any workouts yet, the first one's tonight, but I've started the diet plan. Or I'm just about to start.' She took the steaming plate out of the microwave and put it on the breakfast island where she'd already laid a knife and fork. 'Check this out.'

Olivia's eyes widened. 'Wow. That looks amazing. I wouldn't mind that myself.'

'Hands off. This is diet food. For dieters.'

Olivia raised her hands palm up. 'Don't let me stop you. Where's Simon?'

'Mum's taken him to feed the ducks at the village pond. He loves going there. It's his favourite place. His first word is probably going to be duck.'

'Aw, bless him. I'm sorry I won't get to say goodbye though.' She hesitated. 'The other thing I came to say is the bridal shop rang. They're wanting to pencil in dates for fittings. There's one a week on Friday, which Hannah's going to, but I figured you might want to put yours off for a bit?'

'I sure do. There's not much point in me going for a fitting when I plan to be three sizes smaller by August.'

'That's what I thought. Shall I tell them to just reserve you a particular size?' Her eyes were uncertain and Ruby nodded.

'Yep, tell them to reserve me a size twelve.'

'I will.'

Ruby took a mouthful of the mash, which was so light and creamy it seemed to melt on her tongue. 'This is awesome,' she said when she'd swallowed. 'Did you say Mr B is doing your catering?'

'Yes, he's also Phil's best man, presuming they don't fall out. They're still playing ridiculous pranks on each other.'

'What kind of pranks? I thought their paths hardly crossed any more.'

'Mr B phoned Phil up the other day pretending to be his producer and told him they were filming the next three episodes he's in on location in Romania. Phil nearly fell for it – there's been talk of doing some location episodes for a while.'

'When did he find out it was a wind-up?'

'Not until Mr B phoned him and confessed later in the day. He was worried Phil might actually go and buy plane tickets. He was on the verge of it too – there was a really good Ryanair deal on, which, of course, Mr B knew about. That's what gave him the idea.'

Ruby would have laughed if she hadn't had her mouth full.

'I think he's just about forgiven him. What's the chicken like?'

'It's divine. I think I could forgive Mr B anything if he can cook like this. It certainly doesn't taste like diet food.'

'It doesn't look like it either.' Olivia eyed the plate with suspicion. 'That mash looks really creamy.'

'You should see the dessert. Chocolate profiteroles. They're in that tub by the microwave.'

Olivia got up and went to look. 'Blimey, they don't look very fat-free either. A big portion too. They look exactly like the ones Mr B usually makes for his afternoon teas.'

'They can't be, though,' Ruby said. 'He must have done something clever with the ingredients. Unless there's been a mix-up.' An awful thought had just struck her. 'Do they do any other meal deliveries?'

'No, I don't think they do. According to Phil, this is a brand-new venture, set up by Saskia, Mr B and the Bluebell Cliff and each party is taking a share of the profits.' She blinked. 'Fill your boots. I almost wish I was on a diet now too.'

5

Harry's usual work lunchtime routine was to grab a couple of baguettes from the deli opposite his Swanage-based office. Ham or cheese with creamy coleslaw. They did a great home-made coronation chicken too. There was nothing dry about their baguettes. They also did the most awesome Danish pastries. He'd got into the habit of picking up one of those too and having it with his afternoon coffee.

Maddie, the silver-haired lady who owned the deli, was so nice. She always picked out the largest pastry with her tongs – there was often banter about him being a big man so needing a big pastry. He towered above Maddie, who couldn't have been more than five foot and was slender as a silver birch. How did that work? How could you spend all your time in a place that sold awesome food and never put on an ounce? He'd felt bereft when he'd told Maddie he wouldn't be in for a while as he planned to lose a few stone.

'Don't lose too much,' she'd warned and fluttered her eyelashes. She flirted with all her customers. It didn't matter what age they were or what gender. 'You can carry off a bit of weight, great big, hunky bloke like you.'

'I promise you, Maddie, I will be back.'

'Maybe I'll think about putting some low-calorie baguettes on the menu for when you are.'

'I'll look forward to that.'

Harry decided to go home for lunch. Annabel had promised to be there too. So they could eat together. She had finally come in at nearly ten p.m. last night, full of apologies. 'We've got a big case. Nick asked me to stay on and help.'

Nick was the senior partner in the family law company where she worked.

'I'm so sorry, Harry. I thought you'd be late too. I did text.'

When he'd looked at his phone, he'd discovered she had. It was still on silent. He must have forgotten to turn it back on after the Bluebell Cliff.

It was only later when they were in bed – she'd said she was too tired to make love and had rolled over and gone to sleep – that he remembered she must have come back from work and cooked herself tea before returning to the office. Surely it would have been easier to work on through, not to go back and forth. She hadn't taken her car back either. That was a bit strange. But then the thought had been sucked into the whirl of other inconsequential thoughts that so often swirled in his head when insomnia overtook him and had been forgotten.

He was feeling tired today too – it had taken ages to get to sleep last night – but he was looking forward to them having lunch together. It was something they'd done a lot before they were married, but it rarely happened now.

Annabel was in the kitchen when he got home. He heard the clatter of cutlery before he got there. One of her endearing character traits was that despite her diminutive size – she was only five foot four – she could never do anything quietly.

'Hi, darling.' He went into the kitchen and hung his jacket over the back of a stool. Annabel was emptying the dishwasher, her back to him, her white-blonde hair piled up in its usual chignon.

'Don't put it there,' she said without turning. 'Hang it on a hook.'

'Sorry,' he said, automatically doing her bidding and then going across to kiss her. 'This brings back memories, doesn't it?'

'Kissing?'

She raised her perfect half-moon eyebrows and he looked into the stunning blue of her eyes and said, 'No. I meant eating together in the middle of the day. I feel like I'm bunking off.'

'That's a perk of being the boss, isn't it?' She yawned. 'Sorry. I'm tired. It's full on at work. I can't stop very long.'

'Thanks for coming back.'

'I said I would, didn't I? Besides, someone has to keep an eye on you. Make sure you stick to your diet.'

'Well, you can relax on that score.' He went to the fridge and retrieved the plastic container that was marked up Day One. 'I don't think I'm going to have any trouble sticking to this menu plan. The meals look amazing.' He paused, one hand on the open fridge door, the cool air hitting his face. 'What are you having, love?'

'I'm fine with coffee.'

'Are you sure? You should really have something. I don't want you keeling over.'

'Harry, I'm fine. Really. I'll sit and watch you.' There was a touch of impatience in her voice and he shut the fridge door feeling discomfited. He'd thought today was about them having a nice lunch together, not her rushing in to check up on him and then not even eating.

'There's probably enough to share,' he quipped, as he transferred the not insignificant chicken breast and large portion of mash onto a microwavable plate. He didn't even really need the parsnip puree, but it was included, so he put that on too.

Annabel shot across the kitchen. 'That's the meal on the plan?'

'It is. Yes.' He met her eyes and was surprised to see a flash of annoyance there.

'You've got them mixed up. That will be dinner.'

'I haven't. I—'

'You must have done. No way is that a midday meal.' She whisked the plate away from him.

Calmly and without fuss, he showed her the label.

'In that case, *they* must have got it mixed up.'

There was no answer to that. He stared at her, bemused, and his stomach rumbled loudly. He'd forgone chocolate biscuits with his morning coffee. He'd even forgone milk. As well as the diet menus in the folder there had been strict instructions that no other food but the meals on the plan should be consumed. Permitted drinks were black coffee, taken without sugar, water and other non-specified calorie-free drinks.

Harry had only managed to do all that because he knew that he would be having an amazing lunch. And now it looked as if he was going to be denied even that.

Annabel was now pacing around the breakfast island. She pounced on a second container and read the label aloud, 'Chocolate profiteroles?' She managed to make the word profiteroles sound like something you'd step in. 'What the...?' She pulled back the lid and gave one of them a poke.

There were four, Harry saw with an ache of longing. What he would have given to eat just one of them. Even a half of one would have done. He was getting some serious sugar withdrawals. His mouth watered madly and his stomach gave another loud rumble. Annabel glared at him.

'This is not a diet menu. Any fool can see that. You're not eating it. I'll phone the club and put in a complaint. Where's the number?'

'I'll speak to them.' He could see from her face that this was the only way he was going to stop her from carrying out her threat right now.

'You wouldn't have done though, would you? If I hadn't been here. You'd have just sat on that stool and munched your way through that immense pile of calorie-laden junk. That, Harry, as I'm sure you'll agree, is unreasonable behaviour when you're supposed to be dieting!' She shook her head and, before he could react or even formulate a sentence, she spun around and stalked out of the room. A few seconds later, he heard the front door slam behind her and he was left wondering what the hell had just happened.

One moment he'd been anticipating a lovely luncheon with his wife and the next they'd been in the middle of a row. No, not a row – he'd hardly got a word in edgeways. It had been more of a tirade. The injustice of it all stung. But it wasn't the injustice that was hurting the most. It was the look she'd given him. Pure disgust. She had never looked at him like that. No one had ever looked at him like that.

Still in shock, he walked down the hall and opened the front door to see if she was perhaps still here. He half hoped he would find her sitting in her car on the gravel frontage, regretting her outburst. She'd said she was tired and it might well be her time of the month too. That would explain a lot. He could forgive an irrational outburst if there was a good reason for it. But, no, her car had gone and the gates were closed. She hadn't hung around at all.

He went back into the kitchen and looked at the chicken and mash still plated up on the side. The suddenness of the row had stolen his appetite. Oh, the irony.

On the other hand, there was no way he was throwing good food in the bin. His father, who'd been something of a puritan, would have turned in his grave. He'd have turned in his grave at the price of the gold plan in the first place, Harry thought, with wry amusement. He put the plate in the microwave and set the automatic timer.

When it pinged and he retrieved it, feeling only slightly guilty, a delicious fragrance hit his nostrils – chicken, with a hint of rosemary if he wasn't mistaken. His tastebuds tingled and his appetite was right back on course again.

He savoured every mouthful. The parsnip dish was divine. In for a penny, in for a pound. He heated up the celeriac gratin and ate that too. He'd always been a fan of celeriac. Then he washed up his plate and slipped it back into the inbuilt rack in the cupboard. No sense in deliberately winding up Annabel by leaving his dirty crockery out.

Finally, he turned his attention to the profiteroles. Should he or shouldn't he? That was the question. He felt pretty full already. Maybe he should take them back to work. He could have them with his afternoon coffee instead of a Danish pastry. He was entitled to them after all and it wouldn't make any difference when he ate them.

Making a decision which felt slightly mutinous, he picked up the plastic container and took it with him. He also grabbed his sports bag and packed it with a towel and the new workout gear he'd bought online. Tonight was the first fat-burner workout with Saskia York. Frankly he'd rather have boiled his head in oil than show up for that, but he'd made a commitment to stick to this plan – no matter what Annabel seemed to think – and he intended to follow through. He could ask about the menus too. If there had been a mix-up, then sorting it out face to face would be better and more constructive than trying to do it on the phone. Harry was a firm believer that more things were solved by being calm and constructive than they were by losing your cool and complaining. The whole ethos of his company was based upon it.

* * *

Ruby was not looking forward to the first fat-burn workout one little bit. She'd been half hoping her mum would phone and say she was sorry but something had come up and she couldn't babysit Simon after all. Maybe Dad had popped back unexpectedly and wanted a quiet evening. Not that this was very likely. He was on a dig somewhere up near Loch Ness. Digs always seemed to be miles away.

Her mother actually turned up early, complete with a new toy for her grandson – a fluffy green two-foot-high Tyrannosaurus Rex with the name Simon spelled out in red felt letters down the side.

'Isn't he marvellous,' her mother crowed, waving the toy excitedly under Ruby's nose. 'I thought he'd be a great reminder of the kind of family he's been born into.'

'Like he doesn't have enough of those already,' Ruby protested, breathing in her mother's trademark Lancôme scent, thinking of the selection of fluffy dinosaur toys her son already owned, not to mention the tiny toy trowel for digging up fossils, the latter had been from her father, who'd said it was never too early to go fossil hunting on the Jurassic Coast.

'I love spoiling him. You don't mind, do you?'

Of course she didn't.

'I also thought if his name was on there, it could help him with his reading.'

'Mum, he's six months old. He's only just getting his full depth perception.'

'He's my grandson. He's advanced.'

They both giggled. And Simon was always happy to see his favourite grandma. That much was certainly true.

Fleetingly, Ruby wished that there were more male role models in Simon's life. Her dad had been around a fair bit for the first three months, but he was away on his latest dig and they tended to go on for weeks. Simon's own father hadn't wanted anything to do with him. He'd got off the scene as fast as possible and had only contributed financially because he'd been legally forced to do so. Ruby had been glad of that at the time. His reaction to her being pregnant had made her skin crawl. First he'd asked if she was sure the child was his, then he'd wanted her to have a termination. He'd been terrified his wife would find out, but in the end, it turned out his wife had known about his countless affairs anyway and she'd divorced him and forced him to pay a hefty settlement. His name had gone on the birth certificate but Ruby planned to change it to Lambert by deed poll when Simon was older. Occasionally, she wondered if she was being selfish. Should she have tried harder, for Simon's sake, to get Scott interested in his son?

'So are you looking forward to the exercise class?' her mother asked, breaking into her thoughts. They were now installed in her roomy lounge. Ruby had made her mum a pot of tea and Simon was in his travel cot underneath his sensory panda mobile – another gift from his grandparents.

'Um,' Ruby said, trying to think of something positive to say.

'It'll be fun.'

'No it won't.'

They smiled at each other. Ruby knew her mother felt the same way about classes of any kind as she did – they were both social creatures, but gyms and group workouts weren't their thing.

'It'll be worth it,' Ruby said, bending down to give Simon a kiss and breathing in the gorgeous baby smell of his head. That never, ever got old. 'And the sooner I get there, the sooner I'll be back.' She got to her feet. 'Don't forget bath time at seven p.m. with the Cuddles and Bubbles baby bath. His bottle's in the fridge. See you guys later. Have fun.'

* * *

After the first workout, it would get easier, Ruby thought as she parked reluctantly in the Bluebell Cliff car park just before six p.m.

She wondered who else would be there. She had a feeling that not everyone who'd been at yesterday's induction session and first weigh-in had been on the gold plan. She had a vague memory of being told that there were only eight people on the gold – she had got the last place. Hopefully Becky, the other new mum, would be one of the eight.

Ruby reached for her sports bag from the back seat, which contained an oversized T-shirt, which hid every lump and bump perfectly, and a pair of black Lycra running shorts which held the rest in and had enough stretch not to rip. This, she'd decided, was the perfect combo. She might not be a fan of workout classes, but they were definitely better than the gym. All those pulleys and weights fazed her. At least with a class she could stand at the back out of the way and watch the others. She might have a chance to get some of the moves right. She definitely did not want to be in the limelight.

A silver Lexus had pulled into the car park just in front of her and as Ruby locked up her SUV, she saw Harry getting out. Pleased, she paused to say hi.

'Good evening. Ruby, isn't it?' She felt warmed that he'd remembered her name too. 'How are you doing?'

'I'm feeling a bit out of my comfort zone,' she confessed. 'You?'

'A lot out of my comfort zone. It's OK for you, but I really don't suit sky-blue Lycra at all.'

'Sky-blue Lycra?' Ruby questioned, looking at him in alarm.

'That's what we have to wear for the class, isn't it? Mandatory sky-blue Lycra so we all look the same. It was in the information pack.'

'No way!'

His face which had been serious up until that moment relaxed into a grin. 'Just kidding. But I had you there, didn't I?'

'You did. Oh, thank the Lord it isn't. I'd never have come tonight if...'

'Me neither. Green's more my colour. But you're too young to remember the Green Goddess. I think she rocked up in the eighties. You weren't born then, were you?' He winked, which made the clichéd comment fun and Ruby chuckled.

'I have a vague memory of a woman in a skin-tight green all-in-one. Is that right?'

'Spot on. She had an exercise programme on breakfast TV and my mother recorded them all on VHS. One of my earliest memories is of my mum and my gran on the lounge floor working out to one.' He screwed up his face in mock horror. 'It took me years of therapy to get over that.'

'I'll bet.'

The easy banter had got them to the main entrance of the hotel and Ruby was grateful to him. He was an easy person to get along with. She found herself hoping that his wife hadn't been serious about that ultimatum. Harry Small struck her as an all-round good guy, not to mention a good sport to be coming to an all-women diet club. Mrs Small didn't know how lucky she was.

6

Ruby met Becky in the changing rooms, which lifted her spirits even more.

'I'm so glad you're here,' Becky said. 'I've been dreading this. If it hadn't cost so much money, I'd have legged it.'

'Ditto,' Ruby said, as they put their stuff in lockers and walked back through to the studio where they'd met the previous day. 'How are you getting on with the diet?'

'That bit's amazing. I can't believe it's a low-calorie menu. How do you think he does it?'

'Sugar and fat swaps, I guess.' Ruby shrugged. 'I'm no cook, but it's amazing what you can do.'

'I thought that too. It would be interesting to know what ingredients he uses. I noticed that he only lists the allergens on the ingredient list, but it does say you can ask for the full list.'

'And didn't he say there were recipe cards for the silver and bronze plans. They must list the full ingredients,' Ruby mused.

'I heard they tone the menus down on the other plans. I mean, who's got time to make profiteroles? Mind you, the principle's the same. If he's here tonight, I'll ask him.' Becky lowered her voice,

'Although I wouldn't be surprised if he wasn't. Did you notice that he and Saskia didn't exactly seem to hit it off? Mind you, if you listen to gossip, the chef doesn't get on with anyone that well.'

Ruby decided not to tell her she had inside information on the infamous Mr B from Phil. 'He's a great chef. I suppose that's the main thing,' she said diplomatically, as they walked into the studio.

They were up at the mirrored end of the room today. The chairs had been replaced by a scattering of exercise mats and she saw that Saskia was already in situ and testing out a sound system.

'One two, one two,' she said into a headset mic. 'How is the sound? Are we loud and clear?'

Ruby saw she'd enlisted Harry's help. He was at the other side of the room. He gave Saskia the thumbs up and came back to the front. He was wearing a loose-fitting black tracksuit with a North Face logo. He didn't look that overweight. Maybe a couple of stone, but who was she to judge?

She'd been right about the numbers; she was one of just eight. The oldest woman in the group looked to be in her late sixties. She was very upmarket, with a gorgeous dark bob and a plump cheerful face – Ruby remembered her saying she'd decided to have one more crack at getting slim and fit before she gave in gracefully. She'd just had a new grandchild. There were a couple of women who were a similar age to her, one a lot overweight and the other not quite as much. There were also two girls who she'd guess were in their mid-twenties and looked a little bit chunky but not overly so – Ruby would have happily swapped figures with them. They clearly knew each other. They were whispering to one another behind their hands and giggling. They both had balayage streaks in their hair and were dressed in top-of-the-range designer gear. Ruby mentally labelled them the designer twins and began to wish she'd spent more on her workout gear – she hadn't thought it was worth going too overboard as she figured she'd have to buy smaller leggings before the fifteen weeks were very far through.

'Welcome,' Saskia called, beckoning everyone in the room to the front. 'How are we all doing? Isn't this exciting?' She jumped up and down on the spot and clapped her hands. She was in the same sky-blue skintight outfit she'd worn for the induction. It showed every sinuous line of her fabulous figure. Oh to look that lithe and beautiful, Ruby mused with a little sigh.

Then she thought of Harry's wind-up comments about the sky-blue Lycra and caught his eye across the room. He was clearly on the same wavelength as her – he gave the slightest lift of his eyebrows and she had to look away in case she laughed.

'Now then,' Saskia began. 'The first thing I need you to do is to find a mat. Spread out... that's it... You don't want to be too close to each other.' She had a way of pausing between sentences which made what she was saying sound more meaningful.

Ruby wished there were more of them. She felt very exposed and vulnerable. It was impossible to hide in a group of eight.

'Don't look so worried,' Saskia said and Ruby jumped before realising the exercise guru's comments weren't aimed at her but at the entire group. She was leaning forward, her face intent. 'I've never seen so many worried faces... but I promise you this is going to be fun.' She paused. 'Yesterday, you were brave enough to tell me your reasons for being here.'

Her gaze swept the room, resting briefly on each of their faces. Was it Ruby's imagination or did it seem to linger longer on Harry's who hadn't shared his story?

Perhaps not because Saskia continued fairly swiftly, 'What I didn't tell you... was my own reason for being here... but I'm going to do that now.'

The room hushed in expectation. Ruby half expected a drum roll. Saskia had the most amazing presence. She was one of those people you just wanted to listen to. There was something very genuine and authentic about her. That, combined with her fabulous looks, made it very easy to see how she'd built up her enormous online following.

'I was a chubby toddler, who grew, without ever being aware of it, into an even chubbier little girl.'

She paused a bit longer than usual for dramatic effect, but Ruby was sure that this information was a surprise to no one. It was in Saskia's bio. It did feel different though, actually hearing her say the words aloud to such a select little group.

'I didn't know I was overweight. I had the kind of parents who told me I was beautiful every day of my life. I believed them. No one ever mentioned weight. My parents certainly were not carrying any extra pounds.' She sighed a little wistfully. 'I remember my first day at school. I loved school. I don't even remember it ever coming up then. I wasn't teased. Or if I was, I didn't notice. My parents had given me a precious gift. The gift of total self-belief. In fact, I didn't realise just how much bigger I was than my contemporaries until the day...'

Another pause and she swallowed as though it was painful to recall.

'Until the day I joined a ballet class... Being a ballerina was my dream. I was raised on a diet of ballerina stories – I saw myself as this beautiful ballerina, graceful, dainty, elegant. I had my whole life path mapped out by the age of five. I was going to join the Royal Ballet. I would be a prima ballerina. Famous. Loved. Admired. And then I started ballet school. I was six years old.

'I was so proud and excited to be wearing my first tutu. I was all in pink, like a little fairy princess. I had the most perfect pink satin ballet shoes. I was dancing on air when I went into the studio. And it was amazing. Just as I had always imagined. My mother sat in the viewing gallery with the other mothers, taking a video so we could show my daddy. I adored it all.

'Then, later that day, when Daddy was home, we all sat round to watch the video on our wide-screen TV. I was so excited. I remember sitting there tight with expectation, my little heart going ten to the dozen. And then the video started and I looked at the screen.' She paused again. 'I'm sure you all know what's coming...'

There were a few sympathetic murmurs, Ruby was amongst them.

'That's right,' Saskia went on sadly. 'I watched that video and I fully expected to see a lithe, beautiful pink ballerina pirouetting across the floor and I saw instead this little dumpling wearing my clothes and with my face. And I truly couldn't believe my eyes. It was the biggest wake-up call ever.'

There were more empathetic murmurs and one of the designer twins called out, 'I can so relate, Saskia. I did ballet classes too.'

Saskia beamed at her. 'I have to say that was the first and last ballet lesson I ever did. I look back on it as the first defining moment of my life. There have been others since. I'm sure there will be more in the future. But that was the first. I knew I did not want to be a chubby ballerina. I wanted to become the image of me that I had always carried in my head. I wanted the image and the reality to match.'

The older lady began to clap and everyone joined in. It was a moving story and it was very inspiring.

Saskia basked for a few seconds in their appreciation before clearing her throat. 'Thank you all for being so lovely,' she said. 'I didn't tell you that story for purposes of ego. I told you because I want you to know that I'm not just some effortlessly slim girl who's never known what it's like to feel overweight. Now here's the thing – and this is the bit I want you to listen carefully to – right now, you are probably thinking that a healthy diet and regular fat-burn workouts is the hardest path. But, essentially, it's not. It's the easiest path. I'll say again. It's THE EASIEST PATH. I will tell you why. It's the easiest path because the rewards are amazing.

'Now I want you to remember that. The path you are all embarking on tonight is the easiest path – it might seem harder to eat properly – although I'm sure that isn't the case with Mr B's amazing recipes. I'm already hearing great things about them.'

She paused again.

'But the essence of this programme is that the hardest path is the easiest path. So what path are we on...?' She held out her arms and Ruby realised they were all expected to repeat the words. Oh hell, this was exactly why she hated this kind of thing. Group chanting was not her thing at all. 'Come on – say it with me,' Saskia commanded. 'What path are we on? Say it out loud.'

'The easiest path,' they all repeated it dutifully, although Ruby was pretty sure Harry was just miming the words because she didn't hear his voice. She stole a surreptitious glance at her watch. They'd been here fifteen minutes already and they hadn't done a single fat-burning exercise yet. She had to admit that right at that moment it was beginning to look as though the easiest path was a fast trot towards the door. She forced herself to stay where she was. She had far too much invested in these classes, not just financially, but hope wise. She wanted to look her best for her sister's wedding, but she also wanted to look her best for herself. She was here for the duration.

'Now...' Saskia went on. 'Enough of the motivational stuff. What we will be doing is high-intensity interval training. You can do these workouts up to five times a week. Four at home with the videos and one here with me. They are progressive, so we are always building on what we've done before. So shall we get cracking.' She clapped her hands together. 'You all have a mat – yes. So the first thing I want you to do is to jump purposefully onto your mats. Like so...'

She jumped onto the mat in front of her with an enthusiastic bound and there was a loud, drawn-out farting sound.

The room hushed again, but this time it wasn't the awed hush of admiring devotees but a kind of shocked tension.

The look on Saskia's face would have been comical in other circumstances. Her mouth formed a perfect O as her eyes widened in horror. She stared frantically around as if she was expecting someone to put up a hand and say, 'Sorry.'

But it was crystal clear to them all that the sound had come from her direction.

It was Harry who reacted first. Before anyone else could move, he left his mat, strode up to the front and said, 'I think you may have been the target of a practical joke. May I?' He bent down and lifted a corner of Saskia's mat and, understanding immediately, she shifted so he could peel back the rest. Harry pounced on a yellow circular item that was underneath and held it up so they could all see. 'It's a whoopee cushion,' he said, with an expression that was somewhere between a grimace and sympathy. 'I didn't know you could still get these. Someone with a childish sense of humour, I'm guessing?'

Saskia had gone pink, but she also looked hugely relieved. She didn't reply immediately though, she headed towards the far end of the room at a fast jog. The door of the studio was ajar – Ruby was sure it had been closed when they'd begun. Saskia flung it open and a few seconds later they heard the sound of raised voices. It was impossible to hear it all, but certain words and phrases carried back into the room. 'Unprofessional. Imbecile. Never been so...'

Then the door slammed, cutting off the rest.

Ruby looked at Becky and Harry.

'Bloody hell,' Becky said. 'That couldn't have been the chef, could it?'

'No one in the hotel would be that unprofessional surely?'

remarked one of the designer twins. She sounded very disapproving, and her friend nodded and pursed her lips. 'At the very least it was a waste of our time. I shall complain to the management.'

'It was fairly harmless.' This came from the matriarch of the group, who had a very plummy voice but a definite twinkle in her eye.

Ruby and Becky exchanged glances and Ruby knew they were both in agreement with her. No one could say that there hadn't been a certain amount of light relief in the room after the incident.

'I expect we'll all end up laughing about it one day,' Harry said diplomatically.

The far door swung open again and they all hushed as Saskia marched back across. 'I'm so sorry about that.' She looked around at them. Her face was flushed, but there was steel in her eyes. 'Right. Let's crack on, shall we?'

'Did you find out who it was?'

'Was it the chef?'

'Did he apologise?'

She was subjected to a barrage of questions, which she deflected smoothly with a shake of her head. 'I really would like to put this unfortunate incident behind us. I don't want to waste a single second more of our workout time.'

7
___

'We still had a great workout. And we didn't lose very much time, despite the unconventional start,' Ruby told Olivia when her sister phoned for a catch-up the following Tuesday morning. Olivia was now on her filming stint in Bristol and didn't have time to breathe. Ruby was totally in awe of the long hours and the complete dedication it took to make a top-notch TV programme.

Olivia chuckled. 'I bet it was Mr B. It's exactly the kind of juvenile thing he'd do. It's a miracle he hasn't got himself sacked, but Phil's always said it's incredibly hard to pin anything on him. He's as good at wriggling out of the blame as he is at setting up the pranks themselves. He's got an uncanny knack of being in a totally different place when a prank actually happens.'

'But where's the satisfaction in that?'

'Oh, you can be sure he'll have taken steps to make sure he sees it one way or another. There are plenty of discreet security cameras at the Bluebell. He probably had one of them trained on Saskia's mat. He wouldn't need to be there in person.'

'We heard her arguing with someone outside. I'd assumed that was him.'

'Or some hapless porter who happened to be passing. Although, saying that, the first time I ever met Mr B, he played a trick on Phil and I when he had a ringside view of the result. He'd sealed up some drinking straws so they didn't work. Simple, but effective. He hid in plain sight for that one. He was sitting opposite us but behind a broadsheet, so we didn't know it was him. Phil hadn't thought he was even at work.'

Ruby wasn't sure whether to be impressed or aghast. 'What does Clara think about his shenanigans? Doesn't she mind?'

'I think she turns a blind eye as long as it doesn't get too out of hand or affect the smooth running of the hotel. From what Phil's told me, it goes on quite a lot in the catering industry. Or at least in hotels. I'm making it sound like he's the only prankster in the place. He's not. He and Phil were for ever playing tricks on each other when Phil was there full-time.' There was curiosity in her voice. 'Maybe Mr B has found a new adversary.'

'You think Saskia will retaliate?' Ruby tried to imagine it.

'Wouldn't you?'

'You might be right. I'd think up something a bit more impressive than a whoopee cushion though.'

'Maybe he was testing the waters. Anyway, enough of Mr B. How's it going? Are you enjoying it? Do you think it will work?'

'It better had. I've been doing the exercise videos religiously. Four I've done, so far, so including the one we did with Saskia that's the recommended five and I ache in places I never even knew I had muscles. I've resisted the temptation to weigh myself at home. I decided I'd wait until the official weigh-in. The first one's tonight.'

Olivia gave a non-committal 'mmm...' She obviously knew that already. Ruby suspected that was the reason she'd phoned up today – to wish her luck.

Ruby went on thoughtfully, 'I must admit, prankster or not, Mr B's food is to die for. And I was a bit cynical about the workouts at first – imagine a blancmange in a leotard bouncing up and down on a mat and you'll have a fairly accurate picture.'

'Don't be so down on yourself.'

'I'm not. There are mirrors everywhere and the one thing I'm not is in denial.' She paused. 'Or at least I'm not in denial any more. I think that got smashed the first time I got on the scales and I realised how much I'd gained since Simon was born. Let's face it, I've never been slender like you and Mum. Or Aunt Dawn come to that. Talking of Aunt Dawn, have you spoken to her much lately?'

Aunt Dawn was their mother's sister and Olivia had always been closer to her than Ruby. They had lots more in common. Aunt Dawn had been the reason that Olivia had begun her successful business, Amazing Cakes. She'd taught her to make and ice them – she was a talented baker and icer and she'd ended up working for Olivia when she'd got her big acting break and could no longer run Amazing Cakes full-time. Aunt Dawn, who'd retired from her vintage clothes shop, now did much of the cake design and creation.

'Aunt Dawn is happier than I've ever seen her,' Olivia said cheerfully. 'She's really loving baking again and pottering about on the smallholding and she's uber-excited about the wedding. She's making us the most fabulous cake. It's ambitious even by her standards, four tiers of utter decadence. She likes Phil a lot. I think I've talked her out of the hot-air balloon idea though.'

'I thought you were up for that.'

'I was tempted, I must admit. But there are too many variables. You know Hannah, my other bridesmaid's, a writer – well, she told me that something like seven out of ten balloon rides have to be rescheduled because of the weather. Weddings are stressful enough without that.'

Ruby's radar picked up a thread of tension in her sister's voice and she hesitated. 'Is everything else OK?' she asked gently. 'You and Phil are all right, aren't you?'

'We're fine,' Olivia replied quickly. Too quickly. Then she sighed. 'OK. I thought I was pregnant the other day. I was four days late.'

'Honey, why didn't you say?'

'Because it was four days. And I wasn't. To add insult to injury, I've ended up with the period from hell!'

Ruby knew there was a world of pain behind her sister's forced brightness. 'Oh, Liv,' she said gently. 'That's really crap.'

From the other room, Simon began to wail – he must have just woken up. He was still teething. What crummy timing. Ruby bit her lip.

'Go,' Olivia said. 'Go and give him a hug from his Auntie Liv.'

Ruby ached for her. 'I will.'

'And good luck for tonight.'

'Thanks.'

Her sister disconnected and Ruby hurried in to see to Simon. He put his arms up to her, and then screwed up his little red face for another wail.

'It's OK, my darling. Mummy's here.' She picked him up, her heart swelling with love for him. 'Is it those naughty teeth again? Mummy will get you some gel.'

When she had fallen pregnant with him, she had felt as though it was the worst thing that could ever have happened. She hadn't planned to have children. Certainly not with a man who'd lied to her and deceived her from the start. For a while, she'd toyed with the idea of having her baby adopted. It had been Olivia who'd made her see that it might not be as impossible as she'd thought to raise her son alone. Not in anything she'd said – Olivia wasn't like that – she had just been there, listening and supporting in her non-judgemental way. It was Olivia who'd gone with her to her first scan. And afterwards they'd walked along the beach and they'd talked. They'd talked like they had never talked before and, at the end of it, Ruby had known she couldn't give her baby away. That to give her baby away would be the biggest mistake of her life.

Simon had stopped crying now. He was sucking the tip of Ruby's finger and she felt such an overwhelming rush of love for him that she thought she might weep. She had never imagined there could be so much love. He was her whole world.

Keeping Simon had been the best thing she'd ever done in her life. She just wished that Olivia could be blessed with a baby too. It seemed so unfair. She'd make such a great mum.

Harry was quietly confident about the week-two weigh-in. He hadn't got on his own scales – or rather Annabel's, which were accurate to the gram. He hadn't wanted to pre-empt anything and get overconfident or complacent. But his trousers definitely felt looser. The diet was about the only thing he was confident about right now. Things between himself and Annabel had been tense for a few days. In fact, things hadn't been right since that out-of-the-blue row last Tuesday when his wife had accused him of cheating at the diet and then stormed off. His mind flicked back. She'd been waiting for him when he'd got back from the Bluebell. She'd been sitting in the kitchen on a stool at the breakfast island, her legs crossed and with a weary look on her face, and then she'd said the words he always dreaded.

'I think we need a full and frank discussion, Harry.'

Annabel was a fan of full and frank discussions, a term which he assumed had made the crossing between her career and personal life, but which usually meant she wanted to give him a dressing-down.

He'd braced himself. So she'd discovered the empty containers then, even though he'd washed them up and stacked them in the recycling, instead of leaving them in the dishwasher in a mutinous display. He hadn't been sure which would be more provocative, hiding them or being out and proud, given that he'd clearly done the opposite of what she'd wanted and eaten the contents.

Annabel's gaze met his with a steely directness. 'Go on,' he had said warily.

'I want to apologise, Harry, about earlier. I think I overreacted.'

He hadn't been expecting that. 'It's fine,' he'd said. Totally disarmed, he went across to where she sat, straight-backed. He'd wanted to hug her. He could smell her faint perfume, something gently citrus, and the expensive shampoo scent of her hair. He wanted to do more than hug her. He wanted to scoop her up and carry her up to bed, caveman style. But there was something in her demeanour that had stopped him going any closer.

She'd blinked a few times. She'd looked troubled. 'I'm sorry, Harry. I really thought you were lying to me. I just couldn't believe the chef could be that – I don't know – skilled, I suppose is the word. When I saw those profiteroles... well...' She'd shifted uncomfortably and he'd spread his hands.

'I was surprised myself – at how authentic they looked.' He didn't add, 'and tasted.' He didn't want to rub her nose in it. Instead, he'd met her metaphorically halfway, accepting some of the blame himself. 'I guess I do have form. Cheating on diets when it comes to sweet stuff.'

Once, when he'd promised to diet for one of Annabel's works dinners they were going to – oh the irony! – he'd dutifully eaten the salad Annabel had served up for two weeks while hiding a stash of Jaffa Cakes in his bedside table for when the sugar cravings got overwhelming. He'd got some Jaffa Cakes in the office too, but she had bowled in one morning, gone straight to the drawer in his desk and swooped on them.

'If you catch him eating biscuits again,' she'd said to Victoria, his kindly but brusquely efficient, middle-aged PA, 'please stop him.' Victoria had looked puzzled and Annabel had added, 'It's for his own good. I'm worried about his blood pressure.'

'I'll keep a very close watch on him, Mrs Small,' Victoria had said, catching on. 'You leave it with me. I'll keep him off the biscuits, so I will.'

Victoria McTaggert had been Grandpa George's PA too. She had lived in England for thirty years, for twenty of those she'd worked at Gargantuul, but she still hadn't lost her Irish accent. She reminded Henry of Mrs Doyle from *Father Ted*, and like Mrs Doyle she was very fond of offering people tea and biscuits. But from that moment on, she became the polar opposite. She became the keeper of the biscuit tin, which miraculously disappeared whenever Harry was around.

For several weeks he'd had two women watching him like hawks, instead of one. Was it any wonder he'd had to resort to a secret stash? Which, unfortunately, Annabel had found too.

'I'm not going to cheat this time,' Harry had said when Annabel didn't reply or even smile as he'd hoped she might at the memory of the last time he'd cheated. 'At least I'm going to try my best not to – I'm totally committed to the plan. I promise you that. No cheating.'

'That's good to hear, Harry, because I meant what I said. Cheating is unreasonable behaviour. Don't forget what the doctor said – you need to get your BMI down and I don't want to be married to a blob.'

That had hurt. Instinctively, he'd pulled in his stomach and turned slightly away from her. Was that really how she saw him?

'And you did check with the chef to make sure there had been no mix-up?' she'd asked.

'I did,' Harry had soothed. Technically, he'd checked with the Bluebell's nice young receptionist because Mr B hadn't been available, but she'd been very reassuring.

'I'm sure there is no mix-up. Those are the correct meals. Mr B doesn't make mistakes.'

'Good. So we'll say no more about it.' Annabel had hopped off the stool after that, signalling the end of the full and frank discussion. 'Catch up later – yeah?' She blew him a kiss. 'I need to phone Meggie. She has man troubles.'

Meggie, aka Meg Price, was Annabel's best friend. She always had man troubles as far as Harry could see. The troubles were always the same and could be loosely summed up by the words, selfish and inconsiderate bugger, although the men changed. From what he could gather, there had been quite a few men. But none of them ever lived up to her high standards.

Harry dragged his mind back from the uncomfortable conversation and into the present. Thankfully, things had got back onto a more even keel after Tuesday. Annabel had been her usual sweet self, if maybe a little tense. They'd even made love once this week, although Harry had sensed she wasn't as enthusiastic as he was. He was pretty sure she'd faked an orgasm to speed things up. But maybe that was just him being paranoid.

The fact that they both worked long hours didn't help. Annabel was still busy with the big case – she said Nick couldn't manage without her at the moment – and Harry was busy because he was on the brink of a complicated deal. He was in the office now. It made more sense to go straight to the Bluebell if he was doing a workout, so he'd taken his sport bag to work.

The workouts were the worst part of the programme, he'd decided.

He was seriously considering opting out of the future ones and maybe
going for a jog instead. That had similar fat-burning advantages, he
was sure, and he wouldn't have to do it surrounded by women.

But if he opted out, he'd have to fess up to Annabel and he did
not want to rock the boat. 'Coward that I am,' he told Liam, one of
his sales team as he picked up his sports bag ready to leave.

Liam laughed. 'I don't know what you're complaining about,
mate. I wouldn't mind getting up close and personal with Saskia
York. That girl is seriously hot!'

'She's not my type,' Harry said.

'Yes she is – she's blonde and fit.' Liam had punched his arm.
'What's not to like!' Liam was single and a self-confessed lech.

'I'm happily married.'

'Yeah, I know. But even so – Saskia York!!!'

Harry laughed. 'You should join Booty Busters.'

'I'm seriously considering it,' Liam said, patting his trim
stomach and turning sideways to study his reflection in the shiny
surface of a framed print of a map that hung on the office wall. 'It
might even be worth piling on a few pounds for – what do you
reckon?'

'Trust me, it isn't.'

Harry left him still looking at his reflection. Liam was vain as
well as a lech, but he was an excellent member of the team. Reliable, loyal and generous, a really good team player. Harry would
have forgiven Liam a lot.

He would get through the workouts, he decided. It wasn't so
much the workouts he disliked. Saskia really knew her stuff. They
were cardio-based and he'd felt great after the last one, but it was
hard being the only man. He'd been acutely aware of the women
working out around him, not least because the two younger ones,
who'd been directly in front of him on their mats had flirted outra-

geously – or had he imagined the way they'd wriggled their behinds and slanted glances at him at every opportunity?

They'd both been wearing skimpy outfits and despite the fact they'd joined a diet club neither of them looked particularly overweight. He didn't think he'd imagined the flirting because it had continued after the class. One of them, Cheryl, had come across and put her hand on his arm, fluttered her long eyelashes and asked if he'd mind being in a motivational slimming WhatsApp group she'd set up for the gold members of Booty Busters.

Put on the spot, he'd been unable to think of a good enough reason to refuse, at least without sounding churlish. Only afterwards had he realised there were only three of them in it – himself, Cheryl, and Iris, her mate. The downside of this was that now both of them had his mobile number and they weren't afraid to send him all manner of borderline cheeky messages, which he always deleted immediately in case Annabel ever happened upon them. That was all he needed. He'd thought about blocking them but hadn't yet done it.

But at least he was quietly confident that the diet was working and he had lost weight, Harry thought as he drove to the Bluebell. One of the reasons he felt confident was because, he'd decided to rein in on the puddings. Apart from the chocolate profiteroles, he'd skipped them all. To be fair, he didn't really need them. The main courses were filling enough and all the desserts really did were whet his appetite for more sugar. It was true what they said about sugar. It was shockingly addictive.

8

Harry got to the Bluebell early and the first person he saw was Ruby. They got out of their cars at virtually the same time. She was safe territory. She didn't flirt and she had a great sense of humour. She was the type of woman he'd have liked to be friends with or have as a sister. But he was an only child.

'Hey,' he called, waiting for her to catch up with him. 'How's it going? You had a good day?'

'So far.' She held up crossed fingers and gave him a rueful grin. 'I can't say I'm looking forward to our first proper weigh-in particularly. How about you?'

'I'm expecting a loss. I've stuck to the plan. It's guaranteed, isn't it? A loss in the first week. I'm sure I read that somewhere.' He winked to show he wasn't being entirely serious.

'Nothing is guaranteed when it comes to dieting,' she told him.

'Yeah, I guess that's true. You sound like an expert.'

'Oh I am. I've always had a sweet tooth. And I've never had any willpower. I just can't resist desserts.' She flicked away a strand of blonde hair that had crept free from her ponytail. 'I always end up on a diet sooner or later.'

'But this one's scientifically designed so we can't make any mistakes. Designed by a nutritional expert and created by a master chef. At least that's what it says on my brochure. We can't go wrong.'

'I do hope you're right.' She smiled at him properly now. She had a lovely smile. Warm and open, and he noticed for the first time how pretty she was. Blonde hair that looked totally natural, not a bleach bottle in sight, and that English rose complexion. Interestingly, Liam had been right about him having a type. Blonde was it. But he usually went for polished and sassy like Annabel. Ruby was much more 'au naturel'. For a moment, he imagined going out for a meal with her, imagined them both giggling as they ordered desserts from the menu with extra cream and then enjoyed every delicious forbidden spoonful.

Annabel never ordered a dessert and she disapproved if he did. Had it always been like that? There was a little ache of pain in his gut as his mind flicked back. Yes, he thought it had. Right from the very first meal. Annabel was a food puritan.

Ruby's voice broke into his thoughts. 'Hey, shall we get this over with then? The proof of the pudding is in the eating.' Her eyes danced with amusement. 'If that's not a totally inappropriate metaphor!'

* * *

Ruby found herself wondering if Harry was OK as she got changed, ready for the fat-burn workout which was happening before the weigh-in. For a moment outside in the car park just now, he had looked terribly sad.

Other than exchange pleasantries when they saw each other, their conversation hadn't strayed into personal territory again. She and Becky had each other's phone numbers, just in case they needed to be talked out of temptation and she also had Dana's, the older lady's, because she'd offered it after the first session.

Saskia had told them all it was a good idea to build up a support network when you were embarking on a diet and exercise programme. But Ruby wouldn't have felt right asking for Harry's number. Although she had noticed that the designer twins had asked him and he'd seemed happy enough to share it. She wondered what his wife would think of that. Maybe all men were the same when it came to attractive women. Her mind flicked back to Scott, the father of her baby. Being married hadn't stopped him from flirting with other women. And doing a lot more besides.

There was a world of difference between giving someone your phone number and pretending you were single though. She berated herself for being so suspicious. Harry seemed nice. Not the type to cheat. Not that it was any of her business what some random guy at Booty Busters did anyway.

Becky had just turned up, already changed, and looking breath-less. 'I thought I'd never get away tonight,' she gasped. 'Maisie was being a real mummy's girl. She did not want to stay with her daddy.' She opened a locker and shoved her bag into it. 'How do you manage for childcare?'

'I have a very accommodating mum,' Ruby told her. 'Simon's her first grandchild. She adores him. And, luckily, the feeling seems to be mutual.'

Saskia was already in situ at the front of the room. As was everyone else.

'Sorry,' Becky called, as they took their places at their mats. 'My fault.'

It was interesting how they instinctively chose the same mats as last week, Ruby thought. Or at least the same places. Most of the gold club, including herself, Becky and Harry used the Bluebell's mats, but the designer twins had their own. Ruby had contemplated buying one, but it hardly seemed worth it for the duration of this course. Ruby didn't think she'd carry on with fat-burn workouts once she'd stopped coming here. Or at least not the kind that involved going to a venue.

Saskia's lovely voice broke her thoughts. 'Welcome to Week Two's Fat Burn session. What path are we on? That's right, the easiest path.'

Thank God she didn't seem to expect them to repeat it out loud after her this week, Ruby thought.

Saskia pressed a button and the soundtrack began. The music was pretty cool. A rhythmic beat that began slowly while they did the warm-up stretches, which Ruby was relieved to see were exactly the same as last week's and also the same ones Saskia used in her videos.

Slowly, as the class progressed, the movements built into a high-intensity rhythm alongside the up-tempo music. Ruby felt her watch, which she'd set to 'workout', buzz on her wrist to let her know her heart rate was in the zone.

The exercises were simple: a combination of stretches, knee kicks, side bends, squats and punching the air with their fists. Saskia was also really good at making sure they were all doing the right movements too – and giving them alternatives if she noticed that anyone wasn't keeping up. She wasn't just a good motivator, she was an empathetic teacher who was in tune with her learners.

Ruby had once been to a yoga class where the teacher, Daniella Stretch (Ruby was certain that couldn't possibly be her real name), had demonstrated the moves at the front and then been totally oblivious for the rest of the session as to what her class was doing. In one of her classes, Ruby had got so tangled up that she'd toppled over and pulled a muscle in her back and had barely been able to move for the rest of the class, and Daniella hadn't even noticed. Ruby had abandoned yoga soon after that and had ignored the automated, misspelt follow-up text she'd subsequently received which had begun with the line, 'How can we tempt your back?'

No way was her back being tempted back to any more of Daniella's classes, that was for certain.

Saskia's classes were infinitely better. Ruby was beginning to see why the exercise guru was so revered and respected online. How she had built up so many followers in such a short time and why her new cardio videos went viral as soon as they were released.

She was also the epitome of professionalism. She had refused to be drawn on whether she'd ever found out the identity of the prankster. Despite the fact that the designer twins, Iris and Cheryl, had besieged her with questions.

'Clara King has assured me that the culprit will be suitably punished and I've also made sure that nothing like that will ever happen again.' Saskia had waved a key under their noses with a triumphant flourish. 'This room will be checked and then locked up an hour prior to us having our session. I have the only key. None of our equipment will be tampered with again.'

The designer twins had finally let it go. And so far, Saskia had been right. Tonight the class progressed with clockwork precision.

Ruby focused on getting the exercises right as the class followed the same pattern it had last week, peaking and then slowly getting easier as they approached the final cool-down. She was beginning to see this as her time. While she was here, she wasn't Simon's mum, she wasn't Ruby the art dealer, she wasn't even Ruby the artist. She was Ruby the woman, with nothing else to focus on but her workout session. She guessed this was how Olivia must feel about running. They had talked about it often enough. That feeling of being untouchable by anyone else – just you and the exercise.

So maybe she was finally managing what she'd never managed to do in a fitness programme before. Maybe she was finally getting in the zone. Perhaps this course really would prove to be worth the extortionate fee it had cost after all.

She reminded herself she hadn't had her first weigh-in yet.

* * *

'You're quiet,' Becky said. They'd just finished the cool-down and were heading for the queue for the weigh-in. 'Are you worried you won't have lost any?'

'A bit,' Ruby confessed. 'Are you?'

Becky nodded. 'Although I have been incredibly strict with myself this week. And I haven't eaten anything at all yet today.'

'Really?' Ruby had tucked into chicken and curly fries (Mr B style, of course) for lunch.

'Top tip. Eat nothing on weigh-in day,' Becky said, tapping her nose. 'It's always worked for me.'

'Oh.' Ruby felt a pang of regret. Maybe she should have done that too. She still couldn't quite get her head around how eating two main courses and two desserts a day could possibly lead to losing weight. Even if you did skip breakfast.

Ruby and Becky were last in the queue. Cheryl and Iris were ahead of them, with Harry behind them. Dana had already gone in and had come out with a rueful expression. 'Not quite as good as I'd hoped, but definitely going in the right direction,' she had remarked as she'd gone past them back towards the changing rooms. 'Good luck, ladies. And gent.' Her eyes had rested on Harry.

Cheryl, who was the loudest of the two designer twins, disappeared behind the dividing screen and a few moments later they all heard a shriek.

'That sounds promising. She must have done well!'

'Ooh, I'm not so sure...' Iris began, but before she could finish,

Cheryl burst out of the makeshift weighing booth with a look of outrage on her face.

'No way are those scales right. They've been tampered with.'

'I'm sure they haven't...' A concerned-looking Saskia followed her out. 'I've checked them myself.' She didn't say it aloud, but her face spoke for her. After the whoopee cushion incident, she was taking no chances.

'They can't be right.' Cheryl folded her arms mutinously. 'I'm the same as last week. That's not possible.'

'Are you wearing the same clothes?' Saskia asked.

'Yes. Yes. Of course I am. I'm not stupid.'

Iris leaned forward and said in a stage whisper, 'Time of the month?'

'No, it's got nothing to do with that. It's probably something to do with the same imbecile who thought it would be hilarious to plant a whoopee cushion under your mat.' She spun around in a circle, brushing her hands over herself as though she was expecting to find that some prankster had clipped something heavy onto her skimpy jogging pants. Which clearly they had not.

'Maybe I should try,' Iris said.

'That's a good idea.' Saskia sounded relieved. She beckoned her in.

When the two women had disappeared, Ruby exchanged glances with Harry and Becky, but no one said anything. From the other side of the booth, there was silence. Then all they heard was the murmur of voices.

After about five minutes, Iris reappeared again.

'Two pounds off,' she said, and to her credit, she didn't sound smug. She shot a sympathetic glance at Cheryl, who now looked close to tears. 'It's just a blip,' she said. 'Next week you'll probably lose loads.'

They headed off together.

Harry went in next and a minute or two later he came out smiling. 'Five pounds off.'

'Wow, congratulations,' Ruby and Becky said, almost in unison. As Becky disappeared into the 'moment of truth' room, Ruby swallowed nervously. She really hoped that she and Becky had lost decent amounts too. She didn't know what Becky had done, apart from her starvation stint today, but she had followed the plan religiously. She'd eaten all of Mr B's amazing meals and she'd done six workouts now, including the four at home. She hadn't been sticking to black coffees. She usually only drank it in the morning to get going and she couldn't abide black coffees, but that wouldn't make too much difference, surely. She was a bit worried though. The instructions had been specific. Do not eat or drink anything outside the plan.

Then Becky was coming out. At the door, she put both thumbs up and mouthed the word, 'Yes.'

'A pound and a half,' she told Ruby. 'I'd have liked a little more, but as Dana said earlier, it's a step in the right direction, isn't it?' She glanced at her Fitbit. 'I'd really like to wait for you, but I promised I'd be home pronto as Mark's going out tonight.'

'Don't worry,' Ruby said. 'I'll text you. Well, I will if it's good news.'

'Text me either way,' Becky said and blew her a kiss.

Finally it was her turn. Ruby stepped into the little makeshift room, where there was a desk with two chairs beside it and the weighing scales. They were the kind that had a digital display attached, but it was up high on a pedestal and in big numbers so you could read it easily.

Saskia was standing by the scales. She had a clipboard in her hand and she also had a file, marked Ruby Lambert.

'OK, Ruby, shoes off,' Saskia said. 'And anything else that's heavy.' Her eyes were warm. 'How do you think you did this week?'

'Pretty good,' Ruby said, stepping onto the scales.

She didn't feel as though she could bear to look as the numbers flickered up and down on the digital display and then finally settled. But when she did look, she couldn't believe her eyes. Neither, it seemed, could Saskia, who knew what all their starting weights were because she had them written down on individual cards in their files.

Ruby gave a gasp of horror. That was impossible surely. This Tuesday, she was exactly one pound heavier than she'd been the previous week.

9

Ruby felt the despair crash over her in a tsunami of disappointment. She felt like bursting into tears. She forced them back. It was ridiculous to cry over a number on a set of scales. But she was so bitterly disappointed. And it felt so unfair. How could she possibly have put on weight when she'd been trying so hard to lose it? This was the first time in her life that she'd ever stuck 100 per cent faithfully to a diet.

She had still failed. And the worst thing was she was doing it publicly in front of a woman she both respected and admired.

Saskia's gaze met hers. 'You weren't expecting that?' There wasn't a hint of judgement in her voice.

'No, I wasn't. I don't understand it. I've stuck to the meals. I haven't eaten anything extra. Not one single thing.'

'You haven't been sneaking off to McDonalds?' Saskia was obviously joking – she followed up with a gentle smile.

'Certainly not.' Ruby swallowed. 'I have been a complete saint.'

'And you haven't succumbed to the occasional biscuit or treat?'

'No I haven't.'

'No fruit? Nothing like that.'

'Seriously. I've had nothing extra to eat.' She hadn't even been to Eco-Cow lately. They were probably missing her. She had even given the remaining almost calorie-free squashes to her mother.

'Although… I have had milk in my coffee on occasions. I don't like black coffee. A tablespoon of semi-skimmed at the most. That couldn't be it, could it? I mostly drink camomile anyway.'

'It's highly unlikely,' Saskia said thoughtfully. 'And you don't have a lifestyle that would lead you to graze without really noticing. You have a little one, don't you?'

'I do, but he's not even properly weaned,' Ruby said, catching on. 'I honestly don't know what's gone wrong.'

'Hmmm.' Saskia snapped the file shut with a purposeful look. 'Neither do I. But something clearly has. I had some concerns earlier.' She stood up. 'Different people have different metabolisms, that could make a difference. However, I don't want to say too much, but I don't think it's you. Let me look into it.'

'Everyone else has lost weight, though, haven't they?' Ruby remembered Cheryl. 'Or at least I'm the only one who's put it on,' she amended.

'There are other considerations,' Saskia said ambiguously. 'Let me do a little investigation, OK? Do not beat yourself up.' She compressed her lips and would say no more apart from, 'I'll be in touch as soon as I've had a chance to look into it.'

Ruby had to be content with that.

* * *

When she got home and told her mother, Marie was both supremely sympathetic and refreshingly unconcerned. 'Maybe it takes a little while for the weight loss to kick in, darling?'

'It doesn't, Mum. The first week is usually the best because you lose an amount of water as well. I certainly shouldn't be putting weight on.'

'I really don't know then. How did you leave it with the organiser?'

'Saskia isn't really the organiser, she's the exercise guru. You know the one I mentioned. She's quite famous. She has a massive internet following. Her workouts are legendary.'

'Maybe that's it.' Her mother sounded enthused. 'Muscle is heavier than fat, isn't it? Could that be the answer?'

Ruby's spirits rose briefly, then plummeted again as logic kicked in. 'Yes it is, but I don't think I'll have built up much muscle in a week, and anyway, it's not a muscle-building class. It's all cardio.'

'I guess you'll have to be patient then and see what she comes up with.'

'Not an attribute I've ever had,' Ruby said disconsolately.

* * *

Harry was in a very good mood when he let himself into his house at just after nine p.m. Five pounds off, five pounds off. He felt like singing it from the rooftops. He was smashing it. The ultimatum Annabel had given him suddenly seemed very doable.

It would be great to lose four stone. If he was honest, he'd been in denial about his weight for a long time. Annabel had been right to blackmail him. The end did justify the means, because at least he knew now what was possible if he really put his mind to it.

For the first time, he felt as though he could achieve his target. He could do this. He owed it to himself. And he owed it to their marriage.

'Annabel,' he called, as he reached the kitchen. 'Where are you? I've got brilliant news.'

She wasn't there, but he could hear giggling coming from the hot tub room and the trill of female voices. His heart ratcheted down a notch – Meg must be here. Not that he had anything against Meg, but he'd been hoping for some nice quiet time with his wife. Maybe a glass of wine to celebrate his weight loss.

No, not wine, he caught himself. That wasn't on the plan. But something chilled. A Diet Coke maybe.

He hesitated outside the hot tub room and then decided not to go in. He had a fear of walking in on them naked and being accused of being a peeping Tom. It had nearly happened once when he'd thought Annabel was in there alone. He'd opened the door and Meg had shrieked and grabbed two inflatable yellow ducks to cover her modesty. Harry had retreated hastily. He'd had absolutely no desire to see his wife's best friend in the altogether. It would have felt wrong on so many levels.

So today he stood outside the door and gave a couple of sharp raps. 'Hi, honey, just to let you know I'm back.'

There was a pause. Then, his wife's voice. 'OK, darling. We won't be long.'

She must be in a good mood. 'Darling' was reserved for special occasions.

Harry got himself a black coffee and sat at the breakfast island to drink it. Five pounds. That was brilliant. No wonder his trousers felt loose. He wondered how Ruby had got on. He half wished he'd hung around so he could have asked her. But that would have felt too stalkerish.

His phone pinged with a notification and he picked it up. It was the Booty Busters WhatsApp group.

Admin has added Dana Knight.

Another ping.

Admin has added Rebecca Hunter.

Another ping.

Admin has added Ruby Lambert.

That was interesting. So they must have decided to include the rest of the group after all. He'd wondered why they hadn't done it before. He waited as other names were added and then saw the message:

Admin is typing.

Harry watched with interest. It was clearly a long message because he had to wait some time before it finally came through and when it finally did, he couldn't quite believe his eyes.

Iris and I have had our suspicions from the start, but now we are sure. Foul play is afoot at Bluebell Booty Busters. A saboteur is on the loose. It started with Saskia's mat, but it's escalated. Now our meals are being tampered with at great risk to our health. We urge you to vote with your feet. Demand a refund. We are thinking of approaching local press. If not the nationals. Are you with us? Or against us? Iris and Cheryl. RSVP.

Harry took a deep breath. Wow! He hadn't expected that. Could they be serious? Or was this some kind of joke?

He read the message again. A saboteur sounded a bit over the top. The whoopee cushion had been a childish prank at worst, and as for meal tampering and risks to health, no, he wasn't buying that. He'd been more than happy with the meals. And they'd clearly done the trick. He'd managed to lose five pounds.

He decided to ignore the message. On the basis, least said, soonest mended. The most likely explanation was that the two women, who'd obviously been disappointed with their weight loss judging by their reactions earlier, had gone to the pub, downed a couple of vinos, grumbled about the programme and then talked the whole thing up into a conspiracy.

He was about to put his phone away and forget all about it when he saw that Ruby was typing. He hesitated. She had always struck him as sensible and level-headed. It would be interesting to see what she had to say.

Ladies. These are serious accusations. Could you please tell us on what basis you have made them?

Admin was typing again.

Harry waited. But then the sound of the hot tub room door slamming and voices getting closer alerted him to the fact that Annabel and Meg were done and, moments later, they appeared in the kitchen, both wrapped in towels.

He put the phone away as they appeared.

Annabel blew him a kiss and Meg said, 'Hi, Harry.'

He forced his attention back into the room. 'Good evening, ladies.'

'We'll just get dressed and we'll be with you,' Annabel said. 'You OK?'

'I'm good,' he said, wanting to tell her about losing five pounds but reluctant to do it in front of Meg. That was probably why she hadn't asked him either. She could be quite diplomatic when she wanted to be.

They disappeared, giggling again like a couple of kids, although he couldn't work out what they were laughing about. The kitchen door banged behind them and the room felt void and empty, like it does after a party when all the guests have gone. It was odd, Harry mused, how often he felt alone and the odd one out. Even when he was in his own home and he was with the woman he loved.

It was another hour before Annabel reappeared. Presumably Meg had gone, although she hadn't said goodbye. Harry had got side-tracked with some paperwork he'd brought home from the office to check. He was sitting at the breakfast island, hunched over it, on his second black coffee.

'Are you going to be up late working again?' Annabel stood in the kitchen doorway. She must have washed and blow-dried her hair; it hung in soft blonde curls around her face. She pouted.

'I didn't know you were done with Meg. Sorry,' he said automatically. He glanced at his watch. Ten fifteen p.m. How had that happened. 'Is that the time? I'll come now.'

'Don't rush.' Annabel yawned. 'I've got an early start tomorrow, so I want to get my head down. You had remembered I'm off to London for that conference?'

'Is that tomorrow?' He could have sworn it was at the end of the month.

'Yes, I did tell you, Harry.' A thread of irritation had crept into her voice. 'It's only for a couple of days. I'll be back on Friday. But I need to be in the office at the crack of dawn to go through some last-minute things with Nick.'

'Right.' He wondered if Nick was going along too. Probably not or there'd be no need for Annabel to be there. 'OK,' he said. He'd never have stood in the way of anything she did, career wise. Annabel knew that.

'At least I won't have to worry about you not eating properly.' She beamed at him and he opened his mouth to tell her about his weight loss, but she was already turning. 'Night, darling.'

'I lost five pounds.' He mouthed the words to her retreating back. She must have forgotten it was weigh-in day. He felt irrationally disappointed. Where had all the sparkly-eyed vroom feeling gone that he'd felt earlier? He reminded himself that he'd decided to do this for himself. He didn't need validation from Annabel. It would have been nice if she'd remembered, though.

Thanks to the black coffees, he was now wide awake. There was no way he was going to be able to sleep yet. He didn't want to lie beside Annabel tossing and turning, so he retired to the lounge and switched on the television.

After channel-hopping for a while, he remembered the WhatsApp group and he retrieved his phone from the kitchen. There were fourteen more messages since he'd last looked. Whoa! He scrolled through.

Admin had answered Ruby's question with a long screed of questions. Admin, who was clearly Cheryl now he looked properly, had numbered them.

1 Have you ever been on a diet and not lost weight in the the first week?
2 Have you ever been on a diet with unlimited deserts?
3 Have you ever been on a diet wich had ROAST CHICEN?
4 Have you ever been on a diet with assively huge portions?
5 Have you ever been on a diet with food like this?
No!!!!! Neither have we. If it looks to good to be true Then it probably is. And its discriminatory against dieters. We are tired of being the target of scams and conners.!

There were so many misspelt words and errors that Harry

assumed the typist must have been in a terrible hurry, or very cross, or perhaps, as he'd first thought, a bit tipsy.

Ruby's reply had been more considered.

I think we are jumping to conclusions. There is no evidence of a scammer or a saboteur as far as I can see.
Hear hear!

This was from Becky.

I lost weight. I am happy with the plan. Have you spoken to the hotel?

This question sparked off several more messages from both Cheryl and Iris now, pointing out that they were gathering evidence by setting up the WhatsApp group and they weren't going to be stopped.

There was one message from Dana, which said,

If you are concerned I suggest you raise it with the hotel directly.

Then she had voted with her feet and left the group.

Harry was tempted to do the same. This all felt like playground stuff. It was coming up to midnight and he had more important things to think about than imaginary saboteurs. He was also of the same mind as Dana. It was best sorted out with the hotel direct. Going on a witch-hunt wasn't the answer. He was a little surprised that Ruby had engaged as much as she had.

* * *

Ruby hadn't planned to get drawn in at all, but she had been so shocked when she'd seen Cheryl's opening message that she hadn't been able to hold back.

Saskia's words kept repeating in her head. 'I don't want to say too much, but I don't think it's you. Let me look into it.'

So did Saskia think there was foul play afoot too? She must think something was amiss to have said anything at all.

Ruby did not want to add fuel to the fire, so she decided not to say anything about this on the WhatsApp group, which seemed a bit petty and childish. But it had played on her mind.

Not least because it would be such a relief if it turned out that her weight gain wasn't, after all, her fault. That she hadn't done anything wrong and that the mistake had been in the meals. In some ways, that wouldn't have surprised her. She had always had a hunch that something was amiss. The meals had seemed too good to be true right from the start. What if someone really was sabotaging them?

But Harry had lost five pounds. That was indisputable. Becky had lost some too, although she'd said she'd starved herself for virtually twelve hours before the weigh-in. What if Harry had done that too? What if it was only the gold plan members who had religiously stuck to Mr B's meals (like herself) who hadn't done very well? That would be worth knowing. She was suddenly desperate to know whether Harry had stuck to the plan or if he'd done something different. And now she knew his number from the group she could message him and ask?

Or perhaps she should wait until the next time they met. But that wouldn't be for nearly a week. No way could she wait until then. A quick message couldn't hurt.

She started a new private WhatsApp message.

Hi Harry, I hope you don't mind me contacting you, but I'd like to pick your brains about something if I may? Is there a convenient time when we could have a chat?

She pressed send and waited a few moments. The message showed up as delivered but not read. He was probably asleep. After a few more moments, Ruby rolled over in bed herself and attempted to follow suit.

10

When Ruby got up the next morning and checked her phone, there was still no answer from Harry, although WhatsApp's blue ticks showed he had now read her message.

She felt slightly embarrassed. She saw when she looked back that he hadn't responded to the group chat at all. Not one single message and no acknowledgement. But when she checked, she could see he'd read hers at least, so he'd probably read them all. Maybe he had decided to sit on the fence. Or maybe he'd decided he didn't want to engage in what now seemed to Ruby to be quite a nasty smear campaign against Booty Busters. She didn't blame him.

A shout from Simon distracted her and she went and bent over his cot.

'Good morning, sleepyhead. I wondered when you were going to wake up. And how is my best boy feeling today? And what do you think of diets that are too good to be true?'

'Gah, gah, gah, gah, goo, ga,' responded Simon, giggling.

'I think you're probably right,' Ruby said, lifting him out for a hug and then putting him on his changing mat. 'It's a load of old gooh gah, isn't it? Your mummy is just a little tubby two legs who can't lose weight because she likes her food too much.'

Simon said something that sounded suspiciously like, 'yah.'

'Well, thank you very much for that vote of confidence, young man.'

On his back now, he kicked his legs and giggled again.

Oh God, she loved him so much. She changed him and picked him up for another cuddle and suddenly diets, whether they were failures or successes, didn't seem as important as they had last night. The only important thing in the world was that she could hug her baby, every last little delicious inch of him. She never got tired of how he smelled when he was clean and fresh and how he felt in her arms. A living, breathing external part of her. An amazing miracle, despite his unintended conception. How had she ever thought she would be able to part with him? It seemed impossible to believe now that he had ever not been in her life. And he had brought her family back together. They'd all celebrated his first Christmas and they'd all loved coming to his christening. Even in her family of workaholics, work had taken a back seat for once.

She chatted to him as she got his breakfast ready. 'You are very lucky you don't need to worry about diets. You are gorgeous just as you are.'

'Yah.'

Ruby reminded herself that Cheryl and Iris weren't the only ones who were suspicious of the diet plan. Saskia had her doubts too.

'I think I should probably steer clear of Mr B's meals until I get the all-clear from Saskia?' she told Simon. 'What say you?'

'Gah, yah, gah.'

Ruby giggled. 'That's good advice. Hey, at least now I could have breakfast. I could have a cinnamon swirl. I'm sure there are still a couple in the freezer.'

Her mouth watered as she went to check. But even as she opened the freezer door and felt its cold air waft into the kitchen, she knew that she couldn't have a cinnamon swirl. Whatever else happened, one thing was indisputable. She still needed to lose weight for Olivia's wedding. The prospect of being an overweight chief bridesmaid was too horrible to contemplate – no, it wasn't happening.

With a bit of luck, Saskia would phone soon, but in the meantime Ruby decided to revert back to Eco-Cow's organic fruit and veg range. Just to be on the safe side. Fresh not freezer – she remembered her mantra. She would make all her meals from scratch. She knew perfectly well what was healthy and what was fattening. She'd been on enough diets across the years. The problem she usually had was sticking to them, which made this diet all the more frustrating because she had stuck to it. Never mind. The one thing she was sure about was that she needed to lose weight. And the clock was ticking.

* * *

Olivia phoned her that evening. 'Hey, sis, how's it going? How was weigh day?'

Ruby told her and she heard her sister's indrawn breath.

'I'm really sorry. That doesn't sound right.'

'I didn't cheat, Liv. I honestly didn't.'

'I believe you.'

Ruby told her what Saskia had said. 'I'm not putting too much hope in that, but it is a bit odd, I think.' She paused. 'It couldn't be anything to do with Mr B and his prank-playing, could it? I know you said he has a track record. And we never did get to the bottom – if you'll excuse the pun – of the whoopee cushion. Could he have interfered with the food, do you think?'

'I wouldn't have thought so, no.' Ruby could hear her sister's quiet breathing as she paused to think. 'I can't imagine him ever messing around with food. He takes cooking really seriously. He considers himself one of the best chefs in the country. He's as arrogant as they come – I can't see him deliberately sabotaging anything connected to his kitchen and his ego. That's not his style at all.'

'There's that theory down the drain then.'

'It does sound as though something's amiss though. I'll ask Phil to put out a few feelers. He hasn't done much maître d'ing lately. But I'm sure he can find out what's going on.'

'Thanks. That's brilliant.'

They moved on to other conversations. The filming was going well. Olivia sounded as though she was in her element and Ruby was thrilled for her. It was about time things worked out well for her sister. No one deserved it more.

When they finally said their goodbyes and disconnected, Ruby saw that she had a new message. It was from Harry.

Happy to have a chat. When's good for you? I'm in all evening.

Ruby was about to type, 'Now?' But then decided it would be quicker to phone him. So she dialled his number.

It rang so many times, she thought it would go to voicemail, but then finally she heard his cheerful, faintly gravelly voice. 'Hello there, Ruby? How can I help?' His accent was more pronounced on the phone. Faintly Dorset but definitely not farmer.

He must have programmed her number in to know it was her. She felt a flash of pleasure. 'Hi, Harry. Thanks for responding. I won't keep you long.'

'Your timing is superb,' Harry said. 'On several levels as it happens.'

'Oh?'

'Yes, number one, I was just about to dig into a giant-sized bar of Galaxy, which is my favourite, and now that you've phoned and I've outed myself, I might not eat the whole thing in one go.'

'Don't do it,' she said immediately. 'You'll regret it. You're doing so well.'

'Thanks.' He sounded unsure of himself suddenly and not the confident man she knew him to be. 'That's nice of you.'

'I'm not being nice. It's true. You lost more weight than anyone in the group. You can't sabotage yourself now.'

'No. No, I hadn't looked at it like that.'

'Besides, why would you want to eat chocolate. Aren't Mr B's delicious desserts enough?'

'I haven't been eating them,' Harry admitted. 'Well, at least I haven't eaten many of them. Annabel, my wife, was convinced they couldn't be low-fat. We had a disagreement as soon as she clapped eyes on the chocolate profiteroles.' He cleared his throat. 'And while I don't really believe that we'd be supplied with meals that aren't what they seem, I decided to err on the side of caution and so I've been skipping them.'

'You've skipped all of the desserts?' Ruby asked.

'Pretty much. Yep.'

Well, that explained a lot. She let out a deep sigh, part relief, part worry. Then she told him that she had put on a pound after strictly sticking to the plan and her theory about why some people in the group had lost weight and some hadn't. And also, because, for some reason, she trusted him utterly, she told him what Saskia had said.

'Jeez, so that thing last night on WhatsApp might not be the total codswallop I suspected it was then!'

'No. But you're the only person I've mentioned this to,' Ruby said quickly. 'I'm with Dana on this one. I think that if anyone has a problem, they should report it direct to Booty Busters, not try to stir up a hornet's nest of bad feeling amongst the rest of the group.'

'My sentiments exactly. Don't worry. My lips are sealed.'

'Thank you. Saskia has promised to look into things, so I'm sure if there is a problem, she would let the whole group know. Not just me. I mean, obviously it would affect us all.' There was a little pause and she added curiously, 'So what are you going to do with that bar of Galaxy then? Where is it now?'

'It's right in front of me on the kitchen worktop. With the top row peeking out. Oh my God, it smells amazing.'

She heard him shift and then what sounded like the rustle of silver paper. Did Galaxy chocolate have silver paper, or was it brown? It was her favourite too and fleetingly her mouth watered.

'Harry, don't eat it. Stop it right now. You can't undo all your good work. Look, I have a plan.'

'You do?'

'Yes. Ask your wife to hide it?'

There was a pause. 'She's not here,' Harry said. 'She's away at a conference. Which is exactly why I bought it. When the cat's away, the mice will play.' It was his turn to sigh. 'No wonder she had to give me an ultimatum. But you're spot on. It would be mad to eat it. I'll get rid of it.'

'I'll hold on while you do it,' Ruby said. 'In case you get distracted.'

'In case I don't do it, you mean. Ha!' Some of the confidence had returned to his voice. 'Yeah, good plan. OK, I'm going now. I'm picking up the chocolate. I'll take the phone with me.'

'Fab.'

'And now I'm walking through the kitchen, and along my hall. I'm holding the chocolate at arm's length. Get thee behind me, Satan...' He gave her a running commentary as he went and Ruby wondered what his house was like. It must be quite big. She could hear his breathing as he walked along the hall. 'Now I'm at the front door. I'm unlocking it... I've still got the chocolate at arm's length.'

She heard the sound of a catch or something being turned.

'I'm outside.'

Now she could hear the sound of footsteps on gravel.

'And I'm walking across to the wheelie bin. God, I think this is the hardest thing I've ever done.'

'It's the only way,' Ruby said. 'Get rid of it. Put it right out of temptation's reach. Stick it down amongst something horrible. How about Mr B's gone-off desserts? Are they festering in there? Or are those in your food recycling bin?'

He chuckled. 'I didn't throw them away, I put them in the freezer for Annabel. In case she fancies a dessert.'

What a man, Ruby thought, trying to imagine loving someone enough to make such a sacrifice. She could probably do it for Simon. She wasn't sure if she could do it for a life partner.

'I've put it at the bottom of the bin itself,' Harry said. 'I can't reach it. I'd put my back out if I tried. This is the sound of the bin closing.' There was a bang. 'In case you don't believe me.'

'Congratulations.' Ruby tucked the phone beneath her ear and her shoulder and burst into spontaneous applause. 'I do believe you.'

'Ugh,' Harry added. 'I think I should probably wash my hands.'

A few moments later, Ruby heard the sound of running water and then Harry gave her his full attention again.

'Thank you,' he said. 'I really mean that. You just saved me from wrecking my diet.'

'I'm glad I called you then,' Ruby said, feeling a glow of pleasure. 'Saskia was obviously right. Being part of a group and ringing each other for moral support can really help.'

'Yeah. I can't argue with that. You talked me out of a moment of madness, for sure. OK, it's your turn. How have you been getting on? Have you been tempted to blow the diet? Or is your halo still shining brightly?'

She told him about the cinnamon swirl moment.

'But you didn't do it, did you?' he pointed out. 'And you didn't need to phone a friend, either. That sounds pretty amazing to me.'

'I've got to fit into my bridesmaid's dress,' she told him. 'That's what stopped me. Even so, it was quite a close thing. I was literally standing by the open freezer slavering. Luckily there's no one here to see me except my son and he's too young to know the difference between right and wrong.'

'I do get that,' Harry said. 'The being alone with temptation bit, I mean. Not the difference between right and wrong.' They both laughed in mutual understanding. 'I'd better go and make myself something healthy to eat,' he added. 'But thanks again and if ever you need anyone to talk you down, you can count on your diet buddy, Harry. I mean that. Phone any time and I will be right here, ready to talk you out of temptation.'

'Ditto,' Ruby said, as she finally disconnected.

She was amazed to see they'd been talking for almost an hour. Where had that gone? Harry was a lovely man. It was warming to know that lovely, happily married men existed.

11

The following day, just after lunch, Ruby got a message from Olivia.

There's definitely something going on at the Bluebell. Phil's spies said Mr B had a bust-up with Saskia. It's all kicking off and there are huge ructions with the nutritionist. I'll fill you in later when I get a break from filming. But I wanted to tell you I don't think it's your fault you didn't lose weight.

This was followed by a fingers crossed emoji.
Ruby texted back.

Wow, thank you.

She was itching with impatience to know what was going on, but as there was no chance of finding out until Olivia stopped filming, Ruby decided to pay a visit to Aunt Dawn and Mike's small-holding, which was about a half-hour drive from her through the gorgeous Dorset countryside.

Her aunt was what many people would have called eccentric.

Until recently, she'd had a vintage clothes shop on Weymouth Quay. She loved vintage clothes and her style was quirky – quirky if you were being polite. She tended to team vintage silk dresses with hobnail boots and denim jackets. A bit boho, Ruby conceded and then laughed at herself when she thought of the paint-spattered smocks and wide-fit M&S shoes she'd worn lately. Her post-baby wardrobe was a far cry from the designer frocks she'd worn to schmooze clients when she wanted to talk them into entrusting her with their art collections.

Her aunt also kept free-range hens, which she named after famous women. She had Greta, Emmeline and Clementine, to name but a few. Last year, she'd begun a relationship with her vet, Mike Turner, and everyone who knew them thought it was a match made in heaven. Mike Turner had a cockerel called Boris, two cats called Sherlock and Watson and an alpaca called Mrs Hudson.

The pair of them had fallen in love, sold their respective homes and bought a smallholding together on the outskirts of Weymouth. It was near a place called Osmington Mills, which was partway between where Olivia lived and Lulworth Cove. Osmington Mills itself was a picturesque coastal hamlet and Lulworth Cove was a very pretty horseshoe-shaped bay where the sea often looked turquoise as it lapped against a white pebble beach nestled on the Jurassic Coast path.

Aunt Dawn and Mike lived on the smallholding in blissful semi-retirement, although both of them were still pretty busy, as far as Ruby could see, Aunt Dawn with Amazing Cakes and Mike because he still worked part-time as a vet. Not to mention the menagerie of animals they owned between them and the market garden where they grew their own vegetables.

Ruby didn't bother to phone before she packed up the huge amount of gear that Simon seemed to need for even the simplest of trips. It was a lovely spring day – pink and white delphiniums were in full bloom in her garden – and she and Simon could both do with some fresh air. She decided that if they weren't in, which was highly unlikely, she'd carry on past their house and take her son to Lulworth Cove.

* * *

Both their cars were there, Ruby discovered once she'd parked her SUV by the wall outside the front of their house, although no one answered the doorbell. The magnolia tree to the left of the house was in full bloom, a gorgeous plume of rose pink that lifted Ruby's spirits. She loved magnolia. It seemed to hold all the hope of summer in its delicate pink and white petals and its scent, a mixture of sweet and citrus, drifted on the early afternoon. The air was full of birdsong.

Ruby put Simon into his baby papoose, strapped to her front, and wandered around the back of the house to investigate. Simon was getting a bit heavy to go in his papoose, but she consoled herself with the fact that lugging him about probably burnt loads of calories.

She found Mike first, digging a hole on the edge of the field closest to the house. He stopped when he saw her and put down his shovel. He was puffing and red in the face. Behind him, she saw that the fence was down and there was a broken fence post half in and half out of the ground.

'Hello, love. How's it going? Is this an impromptu visit or have I forgotten we were expecting you?'

'Impromptu,' she said reassuringly and he looked relieved.

He mopped his brow with a grey square that resembled an old rag but could have once been one of her aunt's vintage handkerchiefs. 'Your aunt's around somewhere.' He glanced vaguely about and Simon waved his hands and said, 'Gah.' He had just seen the fluffy brown alpaca behind Mike. 'Gah, gah, gah,' he chanted excitedly. He loved Mrs Hudson, the alpaca. Ruby had a feeling he was going to be an enthusiastic animal lover.

'She keeps escaping,' Mike remarked. 'So I'm making the fence more secure. Mrs Hudson, I mean – not your aunt.'

They both giggled and then Ruby saw Aunt Dawn in the distance on the other side of the field. She waved and began to stride towards them. She was in white welly boots and khaki hot pants and her hair, which was the same unruly brown as Olivia's, was swept out of her face by a bright red and white polka dot hairband.

'Hello, darling,' she called. 'I wasn't expecting you. Good timing. I was just going in for coffee and cake.'

'Bad timing,' Ruby said. 'I'm on a diet.'

'Just coffee then,' Aunt Dawn said. She wasn't like Mum. She wouldn't have argued that Ruby didn't need to diet. Not even to be polite. She was much more emotionally switched on, Ruby had often thought, despite her apparent eccentricity. Maybe that was why she and Olivia were so close. They were very alike in lots of ways. Ruby had never seen as much of her aunt as Olivia did, partly due to her own jet-setting lifestyle, but she had made up a bit for that since Simon had been born.

'I'll carry on with the fence, if that's OK with you two,' Mike said. 'Or you'll have Mrs Hudson in the kitchen with you, scrounging cake.'

* * *

A few minutes later, Ruby and Simon were installed in the gorgeous but incredibly old-fashioned kitchen of the smallholding. The whole place had stone floors which looked like they dated back to medieval times and pale cream cob walls and a vanilla-coloured

Aga that looked about a hundred years old. At least it had been converted from wood to gas, Aunt Dawn had told her when they'd first bought the place.

The kitchen, which was scented with basil and coriander from pots on the terracotta tiled windowsills, was immaculate. Ruby had half expected to see wisps of straw or a black rock hen strutting about. But then she remembered that this was where Aunt Dawn made cakes for the business. She must have got into the habit of keeping it scrubbed clean so she was ready to leap into cake-baking action.

'It's lovely to see you,' Aunt Dawn said, settling opposite her. While Ruby had been sorting out Simon on his Totter and Tumble play mat with some toys, Aunt Dawn had made a pot of coffee and now she put it on the oak table between them. 'I'm assuming coffee, or is it camomile these days?'

'Black coffee's great, thanks,' Ruby said as Simon gurgled happily.

Her aunt hadn't cut herself a slice of the fruit cake that was on a plate on the worktop either, Ruby noticed, and was touched by her thoughtfulness.

'Is this just a social visit then, Ruby? Or is there anything else I can help with?'

Ruby was about to say it was just a social visit, but then somehow she found herself telling her aunt about the diet and her first week's disastrous weigh-in.

'I couldn't understand it,' she continued quietly. 'Because, as far as I was concerned, I'd done everything right.'

She hadn't even told Olivia how devastated she'd felt when the digital display on those scales had shown a gain. She'd made light of it to everyone, even her sister, which was what she usually did when she was really upset about something, Ruby mused. It was a self-defence mechanism she'd perfected across the years. If you acted as though you were supremely confident, people assumed that you were. It had stood her in good stead in the art world.

'It hurts more when we think we've done the best we can,' Aunt Dawn said. 'I think it's because it feels unjust.' Her dark eyes met Ruby's and there was compassion in them.

'The weird thing is, I've since found out that it might not be my fault at all.' She let out the breath she'd been holding and told her aunt about Saskia's comments and Olivia's text this morning.

Her aunt listened without speaking and then said, 'It would be very reassuring if there's an explanation. I hope there is. But keep going anyway. "Whatever the struggle, continue the climb. You may be only one step to the summit."' She gestured towards the fridge and Ruby saw those very same words written in black italics on a fridge magnet in the shape of Mount Everest. Olivia sometimes joked that their aunt lived her life according to the maxims on her fridge magnets, but Ruby had never seen it in action before.

'I won't give up,' she said with passion in her voice. 'I don't like giving up on anything.'

'That's a very admirable trait, and one you've had since you were a little girl. I remember when you learned to walk. You were barely nine months old, but you wouldn't give up trying. Every time you fell over on your bottom, you pursed your lips and heaved yourself up again. I'm sure your mother has a video of it somewhere.'

'I think I'd better seek it out and destroy it,' Ruby said with feeling and then looked at her son, who was engrossed with his Tyrannosaurus Rex dinosaur. It was his favourite toy. 'I wonder if he'll walk early,' she mused. 'I doubt it somehow. He's much more laid-back than the other little ones his age at the mother and baby club.' Not that she'd been to that lately. She paused and then she added softly, 'I can't believe I nearly gave *him* up though. I shudder when I think about that now.'

Aunt Dawn leaned forward and touched her arm. 'The important thing is that you didn't give him up. You kept him. Even though you knew it would be hard.'

Ruby swallowed. She suddenly felt full up to the brim with emotion and in the mood to confide in someone. Aunt Dawn was such a good listener.

'The one thing I have given up on is men,' she said quietly. 'After what happened with his father, I don't think I could ever trust another one.'

She half expected Aunt Dawn to agree with her. Aunt Dawn had been single for years. She'd married her soulmate, Simon's namesake, young and she'd lost him young too. And for many years she hadn't wanted another man in her life. Then Mike had come along and they'd slowly got closer.

'I think you were very unlucky,' Aunt Dawn said, after a considered pause. 'Most people are pretty trustworthy. Men, as well as women. I know your mother thinks I'm cynical and possibly edging towards being anti-men, but I'm not really either of those things.' She smiled and a shaft of sunlight slanted through the small cottage windows and lit her face and Ruby thought, not for the first time, how beautiful her aunt was for a woman in her early sixties. It wasn't a manufactured beauty; she wore the bare minimum of make-up and she had laughter lines and older skin. The beauty came from the warmth and wisdom that shone out of her. 'The only reason I was single for so long was because I was happy as I was. I didn't need a relationship to make me whole. You don't either, darling. You and your sister, you've always been strong, independent women.'

Ruby felt the prick of tears again. Why was it that she so rarely cried over pain or hardship, but kindness brought the walls tumbling down? She glanced at her son. 'I wish he had...' she couldn't quite bring herself to say the word father, '... more male role models, I guess.'

'He has his grandad, and he has his Uncle Phil, and things will probably settle down after the wedding,' Aunt Dawn said, pre-empting Ruby's next words. Simon's grandad was away on a dig and Phil was away acting. But they would both be around more after the wedding. At least a bit more than they were now. 'And he has Mike,' Aunt Dawn added softly. 'You do know that you're welcome to come and see us any time you want to.'

Right on cue, Mike walked into the kitchen and they both looked at him.

'What?' he asked. 'Should my ears be burning? Were you talking about me?'

'No,' they chorused in unison. And after that, the conversation turned to more general subjects, such as wasn't it brilliant that Olivia was doing so well playing the lead part in *Nightingales* and how exciting it was seeing her up on their screens every week. Then they talked for a while about Amazing Cakes and how much Aunt Dawn was enjoying getting cake mix and icing on her hands again. Then Simon started to get restless, so the three adults took him on a tour of the smallholding and spent a happy half-hour saying hello and goodbye to all of the hens and the alpaca and the cats in person. Then, finally, Ruby gathered everything up to go home.

Which was slightly more than she'd arrived with as Dawn had pressed twelve free-range eggs on her and Mike had given her a spring cabbage and a bunch of rhubarb with earthy stalks, wrapped in newspaper.

'It's lovely stewed,' Aunt Dawn said. 'You could use honey instead of sugar, although, hang on a second...' She started rummaging in a cupboard and pulled out a bottle labelled Sweet Honey Skinny Alternative. 'This should work too – it's calorie-free.'

Ruby felt warmed as she drove back home. It was lovely seeing Aunt Dawn and Mike so happy, although she still felt a little unrav-elled and vulnerable. She had meant what she'd said about keeping

Simon. She loved the very bones of him and she couldn't imagine life without him, but her life had been very different before he'd arrived. She had been a very successful art dealer. She had known where she was going. She had dated like the happy-go-lucky girl about town – in the sense that she had never got serious with anyone. She had never been in love. And she certainly had never envied Olivia and Phil. But lately, on the odd occasion, she had felt the ache of loneliness. She knew she would never share the milestones of her son's life with his biological father because he'd made it crystal clear he wasn't interested. But it would have been amazing to share them with someone.

And not just for Simon, she thought as she drew into her driveway and unbuckled her son from his car seat and hugged him close. Today when she'd been at the smallholding, she had felt the love and the warmth between Aunt Dawn and Mike in a way she didn't often feel it, even with her own parents. It had been so tangible that it had coloured the whole afternoon with rose-tinted sunshine. They had a lightness and easiness between them that was wonderful, as well as inclusive to the people around them. It would be amazing to feel that way about someone.

Sighing, she went into the house. Olivia hadn't called back yet. Then eventually, when Simon was tucked up in his cot, she got a text from her sister.

Sorry. Rubes, filming's gone on a bit today. But nothing new to report from Booty Busters. Except maybe ease off on the calorie-counted meals. You might be right about a problem. I'll let you know as soon as I know more xx

Ruby texted back a thank you. She wondered how Harry was getting on. She was pleased she'd managed to talk him down from his gluttonous Galaxy moment and she hadn't heard from him again, so presumably he hadn't succumbed to temptation and bought any more chocolate.

Inspired by his willpower, she got the cinnamon swirl out of the freezer, liberated it from its plastic wrappings and put it in the food recycling bin. There was already a five-day-old banana in there, fermenting nicely, with a mush of leftover baby food which she had just started trying with Simon, so there was no chance she'd be retrieving it again. With a sigh of satisfaction, Ruby snapped the lid closed and went back into her house.

There were five more days until weigh-in and she had set herself a goal. This week, she was going to beat Harry's five-pound loss. She wasn't sure how, but she was feeling incredibly motivated. She wasn't touching Mr B's meals until she knew for sure if she should eat them. They were stacked up in the freezer. It was fresh not freezer all the way.

She decided to make a red pepper and mushroom omelette for tea. While she was at it, she decided she would stew some of the rhubarb that Aunt Dawn had given her. She chopped it up, put it in a pan and added some of the Sweet Honey Skinny Alternative. Very soon, the twin scents of deliciously simmering rhubarb and honey filled her kitchen and Ruby took a deep breath of satisfaction.

Nothing was going to stop her losing weight this week. She was on a mission.

12

Harry had found the second week of the diet harder than the first. This was partly because Annabel hadn't been around for the last couple of days to distract him. He missed her when she was away. Although, paradoxically it was also more peaceful being in the house by himself. There was less of the walking on eggshells feeling he'd had lately when she was around.

They had spoken each night though, which was nice, and she was back tonight anyway. He was looking forward to having a good catch-up. He'd decided to cook her a steak au poivre, which was one of her favourite things, and he'd messaged earlier to tell her. But at around five he got a text from her.

Hold the steak, Harry. We didn't want to drive out of London in the rush-hour traffic, so we'll be leaving the conference later. We'll grab something to eat on the way back.

The word 'we' twanged in his brain. She hadn't gone to the conference alone then. It was the first time she'd mentioned that.

His heart dipped a little as he readjusted his evening plans. But he supposed it didn't really matter. He could fry the steaks tomorrow, which was Saturday. They'd have plenty of time then. To be honest, that would be even better. They could have a nice meal, followed by a soak in the hot tub with Prosecco – bubbles and bubbles. He'd also got in her favourite ice cream. Some ridiculously expensive organic one they only made locally and sold in the farm shop. Then they could have an early night. That would be something to look forward to.

At eight thirty, Annabel texted again.

Don't forget to put the bins out, Harry.

Good point, he had forgotten.

He heaved himself off the sofa and went to do it. He was about to roll the black wheelie bin and the brown food recycling bin down the drive so they were on the right side of the electronic gates for the collection lorry when he remembered that the giant bar of Galaxy was in the wheelie bin and it wasn't in a sack.

The bin men weren't keen on rubbish not being in sacks. Especially if it was rubbish that wasn't supposed to be in there in the first place. He had a disturbing image of them putting the bin onto the mechanical lift and then it tilting into the refuse cart, but not tilting enough to dislodge the bar of chocolate. What if it stayed in the bin? Another even more disturbing image flicked into his head: what if Annabel decided to check the bins to see if he'd been sticking to his diet and discovered the bar of chocolate in there?

That was absurd. He couldn't imagine Annabel rummaging through a bin. But the thought persisted. What if she did? It would be simpler to dig out the chocolate and transfer it to the food refuse bin. It would only take him a moment. Feeling slightly ridiculous, he paused where he was in front of the house and lugged the black bin liners out of the bin and onto the drive. He wrinkled his nose.

These bins could do with a good clean, but probably not now. He tilted the wheelie bin towards him. The chocolate was in the bottom and it appeared to be stuck to the inside of the bin. It had been a warm couple of days, it must have melted. Good job he'd checked. With a sigh, and holding his breath, his face screwed up in distaste, Harry leaned in and freed it.

His heart pounded. This would be a very bad time for Annabel to rock up, he thought, glancing guiltily up the drive and then behind him for good measure. Fortunately, there was no sign of her. Feeling a wash of relief, he transferred the chocolate and then completed the task of taking both bins up to the top of the drive. Job done. He went back inside, washed his hands and then cut an apple into slices and settled back on the sofa to eat them. Not quite as satisfying as chocolate, but the ultimatum Annabel had given him, lose four stone or I'm leaving you, never quite left his head.

Things had gone very quiet on the Bluebell Booty Busters front, Ruby thought. The rest of the week progressed without any more news from either Saskia with anything official or Olivia with any insider gossip. Even the weekend had passed without so much as a ping from the WhatsApp group. Maybe Cheryl and Iris had abandoned the idea of a saboteur tampering with meals, or maybe they were plotting something between themselves. Or maybe the whole saboteur scenario had been hatched over a few drinks at the pub and had been forgotten as quickly as it had been created. They had certainly sounded pissed when they'd written the original messages.

It was now Tuesday again. Weigh Day. Ruby had high hopes for tonight. She hadn't eaten any of Mr B's meals. To her surprise, she'd enjoyed herself cooking meals from scratch once she'd got into the swing of it. It was hard work but immensely satisfying. Not one to do anything by halves, Ruby had found some low-calorie recipes online that she liked and then batch-cooked them and put them in the freezer.

Stacked in plastic containers alongside Mr B's gourmet meals were several portions of chilli, spaghetti bolognaise and chicken fricassee. The latter had been the hardest because she'd had to find a substitute for cream. She'd used fat-free fromage frais and she wasn't sure how it would freeze.

It didn't matter. She decided that trial and error was the key. She'd been eating fruit for desserts but had soon got bored of this and had discovered an Instagram page of healthy desserts that recommended freezing slices of fruit on a baking tray and experimenting. This had also been surprisingly successful. Frozen grapes and frozen bananas were her favourites. She was thinking of changing her mantra to freezer not fresh. Stewed rhubarb with the honey alternative which Aunt Dawn had provided was also a hit.

'We've got this,' she told Simon, as she gave into temptation and weighed herself on Tuesday morning. The scales had showed a loss of two and a half pounds. Not quite the big loss she'd aimed for, but it was a start.

She'd been comparing notes with Becky and she was tempted to follow the other mum's example and cut right back on food until after she'd stood on the scales tonight. That certainly couldn't hurt.

Ruby was just making Simon's lunch while her stomach rumbled madly when she had an unexpected phone call from the Bluebell Cliff, whose number was programmed in her phone. She snatched up her mobile, expecting to hear Saskia's smooth-as-velvet voice, but it was Clara, the manager.

'Good morning, Miss Lambert, I'm so sorry to bother you at home, but I'm afraid we owe you a huge apology.' There was the tiniest gap before Clara went on swiftly. 'It's about the Bluebell Cliff Booty Buster menus.'

'Oh,' Ruby said, stilled by the seriousness of Clara's voice.

'I'm afraid it has come to light that some of the meals you've been receiving under the gold plan aren't quite – er – what they should have been. An independent checker has found some errors in the calorie calculations.'

'Errors in the calorie calculations,' Ruby repeated cautiously. 'What does that mean?'

'It means that in some cases the calorie counts have exceeded the amounts stated on the menus. Not by huge amounts, but possibly by enough to make a difference.'

'Are you saying I haven't been eating the healthy low-calorie meals that I thought I was eating?' Ruby questioned, feeling immensely relieved that she hadn't been eating them this week anyway.

'That is correct in some cases. This applies mainly to the desserts, but also to one or two main courses. I am so sorry. You will, of course, be fully refunded if that is your preferred option.'

'What are the other options?' Ruby stared at the freezer and thought about all the amazing, albeit not as fat-free as she'd thought, gourmet meals in there. She could probably give those to Mum. She'd be thrilled.

'If you decided to give us another chance,' Clara went on, 'then we would, of course, deduct the cost of the two weeks' meals you've had so far. We would also refund you twenty-five per cent of the cost of the programme. In addition, we'd give you an extra week free, as a gesture of goodwill.'

She started to talk about how they would do this, but Ruby didn't pay too much attention. It was actually a huge relief to get confirmation that her lack of progress with Mr B's meals wasn't her fault. And that her metabolism hadn't come to an inexplicable halt.

The latter had occurred to her on that first sleepless night after the disastrous weigh-in when she'd been hunting for answers. There was a perfectly sensible, albeit unusual, rational explanation. The more she thought about that, the more relieved she felt.

'Would you like to stay with us?' Clara was asking now. 'We quite understand if you've lost confidence in the plan and feel you can't continue. Of course, it goes without saying that we will give you a full refund if you decide to cancel your membership.'

'No, it's fine. I'm happy to stay,' Ruby replied. 'I'm glad you've found an explanation. I was worried. Do you mind me asking what happened?'

'No, not at all. But I would prefer that this stayed between us for now.' Clara hesitated. 'It seems that there were disagreements and, er, miscommunications, between our chef and our nutritionist. I can also confirm that Mr B will be putting in an appearance at tonight's session so he can apologise to you all personally. I can also confirm that you will receive your replacement meals tomorrow – if you can bear with us.'

'I can,' Ruby said. 'Thank you for phoning.'

'Thank you for being so understanding.' Clara sounded relieved too and Ruby guessed that not everyone had been. She could picture oh-so well the conversation that Clara might have had with Cheryl and Iris.

* * *

As soon as she'd put the phone down, she called Olivia and her sister answered almost immediately.

'Good timing. We're on a break.'

When Ruby told her what Clara had said, Olivia blew out a low whistle.

'Clara is a master of understatement. I've just this second

spoken to Phil too and from what he's told me, it's been kicking off big time at the Bluebell. Mr B accused the nutritionist of being an incompetent morosoph and she said he was a devious pillock. Something definitely went awry in the calorie counting and they both blame each other. Apparently, they had the mother of all rows in the kitchen yesterday. She's Italian and quite fiery.'

'What on earth's a morosoph when it's at home?'

'A learned fool. It's one of Mr B's favourite words according to Phil. That and zounderkite. Phil says he doesn't do swearing in the traditional sense, but he has a habit of lapsing into unusual insults that no one else has ever heard of when he gets really rattled.'

'That explains a lot. Was it the nutritionist who made the mistake then?'

'From what I can gather, yes. Phil said she did come with great credentials, but she was hired in a huge hurry because Saskia's original lady pulled out at the last minute.' She paused for breath. 'Also, Phil thinks Mr B's too smart to slip up on something like a mathematical formula.'

'Is that how they work out calorie counts in food? A mathematical formula?'

'Phil thinks there's some kind of conversion table that's recommended by the Food Standards Agency. It is complicated but Phil just can't see Mr B mucking it up.'

'Isn't it regulated? I mean, I assume there's an independent checker?'

'Yes, but not for small outfits where the food goes direct from supplier to consumer. So Booty Busters is probably exempt.'

'Every day's a school day,' Ruby said thoughtfully.

'I'm really sorry that it had to impact on you though, Rubes.'

'It's hardly your fault.'

'I recommended it, didn't I?'

'Yes, but you weren't to know. Anyway, as it turns out I'm going to get a twenty-five per cent discount on the meals from now on, which can't be bad.' She paused. 'Also, in a weird kind of way, and probably for all the wrong reasons, it's made me a lot more careful about what I put in my mouth. I haven't been eating Mr B's meals for a few days anyway. After what Saskia and you had said last week, I was suspicious.'

'Yeah, I can see how that would work.' Olivia sounded pleased. 'I'm glad you're going to carry on, Rubes. I love your positivity. From what I've heard, not everyone has been so good about it.'

'I can imagine, but there is such a thing as personal account-ability, isn't there? I did think those menus looked too good to be true right from the start. A few of us did. We compared notes. There's a guy, Harry, who goes to Booty Busters and he was so suspicious that he made a decision not to eat any of the desserts, just in case.'

'Good call.'

'Tell me about it. He lost five pounds eating just the main cour-ses, despite some of them presumably being higher-calorie counts than they were supposed to be.'

'Blimey.'

Ruby chuckled. 'Yes. Men always lose more though, in my expe-rience. They use up more calories than us, lucky buggers, and he's quite big – height wise, I mean. Think Ben Affleck but carrying a few extra pounds.'

'Hey – this guy sounds hot. Is he single?'

'No, he's married.' Ruby felt a twang of lust. What was wrong with her? Married men came with a great big Do Not Touch, Beware, drawn in a circle all around them. They might as well have a No Entry luminous sign flashing over their heads as far as she was concerned. Even flirting with a married man was taboo in Ruby's book.

'His wife signed him up for Booty Busters, I think. He clearly adores her.' That should shut up the irritating inner voice that kept transporting Harry to the forefront of her mind.

'Shame,' Olivia said. 'Ah well, I'd better go. We're back on set in a minute. Thanks for phoning though.'

'My pleasure. Is it going well? Are you OK?'

'It is. And yes, all good my end. Let's catch up properly at the weekend. I'm coming back for a flying visit. I'm having a dress fitting. Do you fancy coming along?'

'Try stopping me. I can't wait to see you.'

It was only afterwards that Ruby thought she should probably have mentioned the WhatsApp group and its accusations to Olivia. Someone should probably warn Clara about that too. She contemplated sending Olivia a follow-up message so she could warn Phil – it might be better coming from Phil than from someone Clara didn't really know, but then she decided against it. Clara wouldn't have time to do anything about it at the moment anyway.

Besides, if Cheryl and Iris had been as vocal to the Bluebell as they'd been on the group, then Clara probably already knew about it. Ruby winced. No doubt she'd had her eardrums battered with complaints when she'd phoned them up to apologise. She certainly wouldn't want to be in Clara's shoes right now.

13

Harry was thinking something similar. Clara had left a message on his voicemail earlier and he'd been pretty shocked when he'd phoned her back and discovered what had happened. So Cheryl and Iris hadn't been so far off the mark by the sound of it. That was worrying.

He'd also been concerned for himself. He had tucked in happily to the gold plan meals all week. In fact, after last week's success, he'd relaxed a bit and he'd allowed himself the odd treat. The Saturday night steak had been the first of them. It had been worth every delicious bite, especially as Annabel had been in an inordinately good mood. Light and happy and looking very pleased to see him. She'd entertained him with stories of funny things that had happened at the conference and how pleased Nick was with her input to the meetings they'd had.

So they had gone to the conference together then. He'd felt a twang of jealousy. On the other hand, Harry couldn't remember seeing her so happy since the very beginning of their marriage. And her happiness made him happy too.

High on happiness, he'd forgone the ice cream. Just as he'd

forgone the Galaxy – OK, that had been more down to Ruby's help. Neither had he replaced it, but he had forgotten to take a Mr B meal into the office yesterday and had picked up a baguette from Maddie's deli for lunch.

'I don't suppose you've got any low-calorie ones, have you, Maddie?' He'd eyed the coronation chicken ones hopefully.

'I think ham salad and tomato's your best bet,' she'd said, wrapping one up before he could change his mind. 'Don't look at me with those puppy-dog eyes. It's for your own good.'

He'd succumbed to temptation and picked up a chocolate bar from the petrol station, too. The occasional treat couldn't hurt. Other than this, Harry hadn't deviated from the plan, but having had Clara tell him there were anomalies, he wasn't so confident that he was going to get away with it.

It was with some trepidation that he walked into the Bluebell Cliff that night.

* * *

Ruby was looking forward to Booty Busters. The weigh-in particularly, but she was also looking forward to the workout with Saskia. Thanks to all the extra workouts she did at home, she was definitely getting fitter. She did most of them first thing in her studio with Simon on his play mat. She occasionally had to stop midway through the burn to pick him up, but he loved the music and he waved his fists in time to the rhythm and laughed at her antics.

She no longer ached the morning after a session and she was beginning to feel a new strength in her muscles, especially her arms. That would be the exercise where you had to do a single arm plank. She hadn't been able to hold it for five seconds the first time she'd tried it – but she was up to fifteen seconds now.

The prospect of seeing Harry again had nothing to do with her lifted spirits, she told herself as she walked into the hotel with her sports bag in her hand. His car was in the car park so he must already be inside. Becky was coming tonight too – they'd had a brief exchange of texts earlier about the WhatsApp Group and the conversation that Clara had clearly had with all of them.

Ruby wondered if Iris and Cheryl would be here. That question was answered as soon as she walked into the foyer.

They were standing at the reception desk with their backs to her. Two curvy behinds in designer-cut black Lycra – they'd clearly come ready for the class – but right at this minute, Cheryl was berating the guy on reception, who didn't sound very impressed.

'As I've already said, madam, he's not here. I can't magic him up from nowhere.'

Ruby caught a glimpse of a grey beard. Zoe must be off. She'd had a lucky escape by the sound of it.

'Your manager said he would be here. I'm not going until I've seen him.' Cheryl actually stamped her trainer-clad foot at this point, like a toddler building up to a tantrum. It made a dull thud on the tiled floor.

'Me neither,' Iris agreed loudly, echoing the stamp by banging her fist on the reception desk.

Ruby wondered whether she should sneak past – she did not want to get drawn into this row, that was for certain.

'If Clara said he'd be here, then I'm sure he will be at some point. But I'd like to reiterate – he's not here yet.'

'I'm here now.' Mr B's voice came from behind them and Ruby halted guiltily with one foot on the first stair as both Iris and Cheryl turned towards him and she realised she was directly in their line of vision.

Not that that either of them seemed to register her presence. They were too focused on the chef.

Cheryl went hurrying towards Mr B, who was now halfway across the foyer, with Iris trailing behind. 'You have some serious explaining to do. What have you got to say for yourself?'

Mr B straightened his back. He was very tall and skinny and the dark suit he was wearing exaggerated both of these things. He held up his hands imperiously. Ruby was put in mind of Moses when he was commanding the Red Sea. Mr B would probably have had more chance with the Red Sea. She had no doubt it would be a lot more biddable than the designer twins. Unable to resist now, she stayed where she was to watch.

'All serious explaining will be done upstairs,' Mr B said.

'It will be done here.'

'It will not.' He didn't bother to raise his voice as he faced the two women.

For a moment, there was a stand-off in the spacious, vanilla-scented reception. Everyone was freeze-framed – Mr B was much taller than Iris or Cheryl and their anger was no match for the icy coolness that was coming off him in waves.

'Shall we?' Mr B gestured towards the foot of the stairs.

A woman who was just coming down greeted him politely and he inclined his head a fraction.

Ruby realised she was in the way and bounded up the first flight. A few moments later, she heard footsteps behind her. Cheryl and Iris were still grumbling, but more to themselves now than to the chef directly.

Ruby's fingers felt damp on the handle of her sports bag. She wasn't a fan of conflict, but she wasn't like Olivia, who would have done anything to avoid it. It looked as though it was going to be an interesting evening.

When she opened the door of their usual studio, Ruby realised that everyone else was already present. But instead of their usual mats, there were chairs. And there was a mic on a stand at the front.

They were obviously starting with a discussion. Dana was standing by the mic talking to Saskia, and Harry and Becky were sitting on the front row chatting.

There was a scattering of other people, Ruby recognised a few of them from the introductory talk. Had that only been two weeks ago? It seemed much longer. She guessed the silver plan members were here too. No one looked very happy.

Saskia waited until everyone was sitting down and then she pulled Mr B aside for a brief confab, which was too far out of earshot for anyone else to hear. Then finally she came back to the mic, tapped it to get their attention, and said, 'Good evening, ladies and gentleman.' She glanced at Harry. 'Apologies, but there will be a brief delay before tonight's workout begins. Please bear with us.'

There was silence. Even the designer twins stopped muttering.

Saskia looked towards Mr B and he stepped up to the microphone.

'Thank you for your patience. As you know, we have been made aware of some issues with your specially prepared menus. I'm aware that you are very anxious to find out what's going on. Believe me, we have been working tirelessly behind the scenes from the moment this came to light, in order to tell you.'

Cheryl waved her phone in the air. 'I'm recording this. It's going on social media.'

'Not without my consent, you are not,' Mr B said crisply. 'Switch it off.'

'No way.'

They glared at each other.

'It's illegal to post recordings on social media without the consent of the person you're recording. So if you have your device switched on now, you will also have my voice stating that it is expressly against my consent.'

Cheryl looked even more furious and red-faced – if that was

possible – than she had a few minutes before, Ruby observed, but she put her phone away.

Mr B clasped his hands in front of him and bowed slightly. 'I would like to extend my sincere apologies to you all,' he said. 'I can only imagine how frustrating it must have been to discover your weight losses on the first week weren't what they should have been.'

It seemed to Ruby that he was looking straight at her. She met his eyes. *Too right, Mr B.* She wasn't angry with him. But he definitely owed them all an apology.

And, to his credit, it seemed that this was it and it was no holds barred. Mr B might be – as Olivia had said – as arrogant as they came, but he certainly wasn't holding back on apologising now. Neither did he seem to be blaming anyone else. Which surprised her.

'I would like to apologise most unreservedly to you all.' If he said it once, he said it a dozen times over the next ten minutes and not once did he lay the blame at anyone else's door. Although he did say that there had been a miscommunication between himself and the nutritionist they'd employed to calorie-count the dishes. 'We had some disagreements on some of the specific ingredients that were used. As a result of these differences, some mistakes in nutritional values were made. Nevertheless, I am the chef who created these dishes. The buck stops with me. You should have been able to eat the meals provided to you with total impunity, but instead you have been, er hem, misled.'

'Conned you mean,' hissed Cheryl.

'And I will make it right.' Mr B flung his arms up in an all-encompassing gesture. He was obviously building up to a crescendo. 'I will put this right. I will personally ensure that each and every one of you has...'

But whatever he was planning to personally ensure was lost to them because at that moment the door burst open and a man who looked like a waiter rushed in. He was wearing dark trousers and a white shirt with the Bluebell logo emblazoned on the breast pocket and he hurried across to the mic where Saskia was standing and whispered something in her ear.

She nodded and her face seemed to visibly blanch. Mr B had clearly lost his thread now the focus wasn't on him and then the door, which had swung shut on its hinges, burst open again. This time it wasn't a member of staff but two guys, one with a camera and the other with a sound boom of the kind that television reporters carry about when they're filming on location. They, too, made a beeline for Saskia and the one with the boom spoke loudly enough for the whole room to hear.

'Ms York, I'm from BBC South, we understand that your new venture, the Bluebell Booty Busters, has been deliberately sabotaged by a rival club. Do you have any comment for our viewers?'

14

After that, it was chaos. Mr B, to his credit, stepped in front of Saskia with his arms out at his sides, in an effort to protect her. The Bluebell waiter tried, ineffectually, to shoo the TV crew back out of the room. Half a dozen people, including Harry, Cheryl and Iris had got up from their chairs, and they all headed towards the front.

Cheryl got there first. 'I have a comment for you,' she shouted. 'I'm the reason you're here. It was me who called the newsroom. We've all been duped. We all paid a fortune to lose weight. But Booty Busters is a con. We've all put on weight instead!'

'We think a rival slimming club has sabotaged the diet meals,' Iris added loudly.

'Is this true?' the reporter asked Saskia.

'It's not true, no.' She looked as though she was about to burst into tears and Ruby didn't blame her. Poor Saskia. She wished she had said something to Clara earlier. Warned her about the WhatsApp group. The Bluebell couldn't afford bad publicity like this. Neither could Saskia, who looked absolutely stricken.

'No one's been conned,' Mr B raised his voice. Even he was

looking slightly rattled at this turn of events. 'Our diet plan is fabulous. We simply have odontiasis problems.'

A few people looked bewildered.

'He means teething problems,' Becky said, turning round to speak to Ruby from the front row. 'My husband's a dentist. That's what he calls them.'

The reporter, who obviously also knew what odontiasis meant, turned to Mr B. 'Tell us about these teething problems. Has there been sabotage from another diet club?'

'Certainly not.' Mr B looked embarrassed and also very nervous. He clearly wasn't a fan of cameras. 'There were some anomalies in the calorie counts – that's all. Everything is under control. There is no third-party involvement.'

'It wouldn't be the first time the Bluebell Cliff has been the victim of a saboteur though, would it, Mr B? Isn't it true that the hotel faced ruin at the hands of a saboteur – when it was first opened for business?'

Mr B looked thunderstruck and began to back away and Ruby remembered an evening last Christmas when Phil had got tipsy and told them that when the Bluebell Cliff first opened they'd been the victim of a saboteur who'd tried to get them closed down. Fortunately, the hotel staff had worked as a team and had tracked down the perpetrators.

The reporter changed tack again. He moved towards the microphone and tapped it. 'How about we get some facts for our viewers.' He addressed the audience. 'How many people here have put on weight since they joined the Bluebell Booty Busters? Hands up anyone who has followed the diet plan to the letter and has subsequently put on weight instead of losing it?'

No one put up their hands. Ruby felt her face flame. She hated witch-hunts. She could see Cheryl scanning the audience, her hands on her plump hips, trying to find her. How did Cheryl know she'd put on weight?

Hang on a minute, now she was riffling through something – it looked as though she had a bunch of cards in her hands. The weight loss cards. How on earth had she got hold of them? Ruby was certain Saskia wouldn't have just handed them over. Cheryl must have slipped in and nicked them from the weigh-in booth, the cheeky mare.

Harry, who was now standing alongside the reporter, tapped him on the shoulder and then leaned into the microphone so everyone could hear him. 'I lost five pounds. The weight loss programme worked for me. I bet that applies to most of us.'

There were some murmurs of agreement. And also some shaking of heads.

'I did actually put on half a pound,' a woman at the back said, 'but I didn't totally stick to the plan.'

'Me too,' someone else called. 'I stayed the same. But I went to a party one night. I had a small slice of birthday cake. It could have been that.'

It was amazing, Ruby thought, how even though all the dieters here knew there were some issues with the plan, most of them were still happy to blame themselves for their own lack of willpower. Why was there so much guilt tied up with food and dieting?

'I stuck to the plan and I only lost a pound,' said a woman who sounded cross.

So much for that then, Ruby thought as there were a few murmurs of agreement. Oh dear, it looked as though the mood was swinging back in the direction of the designer twins again.

'The question is,' said the reporter into the microphone, 'has there been a Booty Busters boo-boo?'

'More of a weight loss wobble,' shouted someone else. 'That's a good headline. You're welcome to it.'

There was a smattering of laughter.

'Duped Dessert-ers Ditch Diet.' The girl who said this, drew out the word Dessert-ers and cackled at her wit and there were several groans from the audience.

The TV crew looked delighted. They were lapping it all up. Mr B seemed to have given up. He wasn't even in Ruby's eyeline any more.

Then suddenly Harry came to the rescue again. 'I don't think there's a story here,' he said. 'Well, not unless you want to use the headline, "Fast Food Beats Fasting". It's just an anomaly as we've been told tonight. The hotel has apologised and taken steps to redress the situation. It's no big deal. And...' he turned towards Saskia, 'Ms York is certainly above reproach. She couldn't have been more supportive.'

'Harry's right. It's no big deal.' Ruby raised her voice into the brief silence. 'Diets are not an exact science. Everyone knows that. I, for one, am confident that the Bluebell Booty Busters will be very successful. I'll send you my before and after pics if you like?'

'Hear, hear,' came a chorus of voices.

Saskia looked gratefully at them. She had recovered enough to go back up to the mic. 'I think you have your answer,' she said to the crew. 'There is no story here.'

After a bit more posturing, the film crew finally shut up and left.

Saskia linked her hands together and stood at the microphone once more, looking around at them all. Her face was very flushed. 'I very much appreciate your support. Now, we must prepare for tonight's workout. You are all more than welcome to participate – even if you don't usually.' This was addressed to the silver club members. 'Now, if Mr B has finished with you all.' She glanced at the chef, who was sitting down in a chair, looking shell-shocked, and he nodded. 'Perhaps we can all help to speed things up by swapping the chairs for the workout mats.'

Mr B didn't deign to help with this. He left the room, straight-backed, ushering the waiter who had tried to warn them about the TV crew towards the door.

A few other people left with them, including Cheryl and Iris, Ruby noticed. She wondered if they would ever come back. Or maybe they'd accepted Clara's offer of a full refund.

She hoped so. They had clearly been behind tonight's drama, which had been designed to cause the maximum amount of trou-ble, and Ruby was glad to see the back of them.

After the workout which Ruby enjoyed even more than usual because everyone threw themselves into it with such gusto, an anti-dote to the drama of the evening, the gold club members and a few of the silver club members who'd stayed for it queued up to be weighed.

Ruby went in first. To her delight, she had lost four pounds.

Saskia looked at her consideringly. 'That's amazing,' she said, 'but how? How did you do it?'

'After what you said last week, I decided to ditch Mr B's meals and I cooked everything from scratch,' Ruby told her. 'I do know what I should be eating. I just needed a kick up the backside to get motivated. So I'd like to thank you for saying something.'

'It's me who should be thanking you.' Saskia's blue eyes warmed. 'For your support tonight. I had worried you may have been on the Cheryl and Iris side of the fence. Not that I would have blamed you.'

'Well, I'm not. I certainly intend to keep going with the plan. Once the teething problems have been sorted out.'

'Thank you,' Saskia said again. 'I know Mr B has been working night and day on it since we discovered there might be an issue.'

'I bet he has.'

'And congratulations on your fabulous weight loss.'

'Thank you.' The two women exchanged glances of mutual respect.

As Ruby went out into the studio and walked back past the queue, Harry, who was standing just ahead of Becky, beckoned her over.

'I just wanted to say thanks for the other night,' he said.

Becky raised her eyebrows. 'Sounds interesting,' she said, her eyes sparkling. 'So what were you two up to the other night? It wasn't an extra workout, was it?'

'No it wasn't,' said Ruby, feeling her face flame.

'She saved me from myself,' Harry replied. 'Or, to be more precise, a giant bar of Galaxy.'

'I just phoned up at the right time,' Ruby said, still blushing.

'And I was very grateful.' He looked it. He looked happy, she thought, pressing down a little ache that she didn't want to think about. He and his wife were clearly blissfully happy and she was disappointed. How selfish was that.

'Good luck with the weigh-in,' she said to both of them, holding up crossed fingers before she left them to it.

* * *

Her mother was, if anything, even more thrilled than Ruby with the news that she'd lost four pounds. Although, including the one she'd put on the week before it was only three.

'That is such brilliant news, love,' she said, 'and in spite of there being all these issues too. Did they say what had happened?'

'From what I can gather, Mr B and the nutritionist didn't see eye to eye. To be honest, I think the chef is quite difficult to get along with. Especially when it comes to meal planning. He's not the type who'd appreciate being told what to do.'

'No, so I gather from Olivia. He does sound like an odd character.' Her mother tilted her head to one side in a question. 'More importantly, where do you go from here? Are you going to try it alone? Now you know you can?'

'No. I'm going to keep going with Booty Busters. They've given us a really good deal if we stay. The new, calorie-counted meals are being delivered tomorrow. Technically, we've lost two weeks of dieting, but the money's being refunded and we can keep the meals we've had. Which you are welcome to by the way.' She gestured towards the freezer. 'Always handy to have a standby for when you're in a hurry. And they are delicious.'

'Thank you, darling. Onwards and upwards then.' She raised her eyes up to the ceiling. 'His lordship has been very well behaved by the way. I only read him *Nick the Naughty Duck* twice and he was asleep. I haven't heard a peep from him since. He can almost say duck now, can't he?'

'I know.' They both glanced at the baby monitor which had a camera trained on the cot upstairs. Almost as if he was aware of their collective gaze, Simon stirred in his sleep, yawned and turned over. 'I'll tiptoe in and kiss him in a minute,' Ruby said. 'He seems to have a sixth sense for when I'm around. Thank you, Mum. Are you sure you don't mind babysitting when I go to the workout and weigh-in?'

'Don't be ridiculous. I love it. Although there may be times when I might ask you to bring him to me. He can always stay for a sleepover with his granny.' Her mother yawned too. It was catching. 'Are you looking forward to seeing your sister at the weekend? She said something about us all going along to Beautiful Brides?'

Her voice was deceptively casual and Ruby wondered if her

mother was trying to be tactful. She already knew that Ruby's own bridesmaid dress fitting was on hold for a few weeks.

'Is the Pope Catholic! Of course I am. I can't wait to see Olivia in her dress. It seems like ages since we all went to choose it. Are we meeting at the shop?'

'We are. Ten a.m. on Saturday. Your aunt is coming along too – it'll be a proper family outing. Well, the female side of the family anyway. Apart from Simon of course.'

On the doorstep, her mother loaded down with a carrier of Mr B's gourmet meals, they hugged once more.

'See you Saturday, then, Mum.'

'Toodle-pip, darling. Thanks so much for these.'

'I'll be relieved to see the back of them.'

They smiled at each other.

* * *

Harry was not smiling. His mood had plummeted the second he'd stepped onto the scales an hour earlier. He'd watched the figures flickering before finally settling on a number that was even worse than he'd feared. He'd put on a pound since last week.

He'd given Saskia a disconsolate look. 'I deserve that. I've cheated a bit this week.'

She'd shaken her head. 'You've still lost four pounds since you started,' she pointed out. 'And considering the meals you've been eating haven't been what they should have been, I'd say that's amazing.'

'Yeah. I guess that's one way of looking at it.'

'It's the only way of looking at it.' She'd hesitated and then said softly, 'Thanks for your support in there.'

'You're welcome.' He'd felt marginally better. And she was right. All was not lost. He could get back on track again. No one need ever know. It wasn't as though they had to announce their weight loss to anyone. Annabel was the only one who was remotely interested, and if last week was anything to go by, she wouldn't even ask how he'd got on.

Now, as he pulled in through the electronic gates of his house and parked behind her car, he found himself hoping that she wouldn't be in. With a bit of luck, she'd be out with Meg.

This hope was dashed as soon as he opened the front door and put his kitbag on the hall floor. He heard her voice calling out his name from the direction of the kitchen. 'Harry, is that you?'

'No, it's a burglar,' he called, falling back on one of their corny private jokes, and she appeared, smiling, at the end of the hall. At least she looked as though she was in a good mood.

'The question is – is it a thinner burglar than last week?'

Hell, straight for the jugular.

'Um. Well...' And then he remembered what Saskia said. He had lost weight and that was despite Mr B's dishes not being the wonderful diet meals they'd been sold as. He didn't need to lie. 'I am thinner, yes.'

She clapped her hands. 'By how much?'

'Four pounds.'

'That's fantastic. What did you lose last week?'

'Er, five pounds.'

'So you've lost nine altogether – in just two weeks. Oh my goodness. That's amazing. Well done.'

He was tempted to agree with her. It would be so much simpler, but his integrity wouldn't let him. 'Erm.'

'What?' Her face sobered.

He paused. 'That's not quite what I meant. I've lost four pounds altogether.'

Her brow crinkled up in a frown. 'I don't get it. I thought you said that you lost five last week.'

'I did. But this week I didn't do so well.'

She did the maths and caught up. 'So, what you're saying is that this week you put on weight. Is that right?'

'It is. Yes.' He would have given anything to wipe that disappointment from her face.

'I see. So you've been cheating. It was while I was away, wasn't it?'

'I haven't been cheating, no.' Now he was going to have to tell her there were issues with the meals and that was going to lead on to a whole new discussion about why he hadn't found this out earlier. After all, she'd been suspicious of them on the first day. And he'd promised he would speak to the hotel.

Harry was tired. The last thing he wanted was a 'full and frank' discussion about why he hadn't done what she had suggested and had a confrontation with the hotel in the first place. Even though he knew it was unlikely this would have made any difference. Especially as he'd have been on shaky ground, having lost so much weight the first week. The injustice of it all stung.

'I'm sorry,' he said, stepping forwards and putting his arms around her.

'I'm sorry too.' She stiffened and pulled out of his embrace. 'I really thought I could trust you, Harry.'

'You can,' he whispered, feeling cut to the core.

'It's quite clear that I can't,' she said and turned her back on him.

15

Beautiful Brides was on Weymouth Quay. It wasn't that far from where Aunt Dawn's shop, Vintage Views, was located. A stone's throw from where boats bobbed on their moorings on the viridian water which flowed lazily beneath the red and green lifting bridge. Not that Vintage Views belonged to Aunt Dawn, these days. Lydia Brooks who'd once worked for her aunt had bought the shop with her daughter and they were very happy, Ruby had heard. It had been handy when Aunt Dawn had owned the shop to park in one of her designated spaces at the back, but today Ruby had to find a car park that was empty. Always a challenge in nice weather. They were still a fortnight away from the end of May bank holiday, but it was a sunny day and it was busy.

As she pushed Simon in his buggy across the bridge, Ruby breathed in the scent of the water and the diesel of the boats and traffic and the smells of food drifting out from the nearby restaurants.

Simon spotted an enormous seagull standing on the bridge and waved his hands excitedly. 'Duck,' he cooed.

Wow, so they'd been right about duck being his first word. Ruby bent over the buggy in excitement. 'Yes, darling, duck,' she echoed eagerly, hoping he would say it again.

She didn't have the heart to tell him it was a seagull. 'Very good, darling. Duck.' She made a mental note to tell her family.

The seagull squawked loudly and took off from the bridge. That was an aerodynamic mystery if ever there was one. It was the size of a large cat.

Ruby liked Weymouth, but it was a while since she'd been here. Until last year Olivia had also lived a stone's throw from Weymouth Quay, but she'd sold her terraced cottage when she and Phil had decided to get married and they were currently renting while they looked for another property. Neither of them was in any hurry to buy. Olivia had said that filming and organising a wedding was taking up quite enough of her time. She and Phil certainly didn't need the stress of buying a house as well.

So many changes, Ruby thought. Most of them in the last year or so. At least their parents still lived in the same place. So there was some continuity. She hoped that Olivia and Phil wouldn't settle down too far away from Weymouth. They both still wanted to stay in Dorset, that was something.

By the time she reached Beautiful Brides, Ruby was feeling quite reflective. The perfect mood for seeing her sister in her wedding dress she thought as she swung open the door and manoeuvred the buggy through it. A young female assistant came across to help her.

'Thanks,' Ruby said. The shop smelled of bergamot and vanilla, which was a nice contrast from the slightly fishy smell out on the quay. She spotted a fat white candle burning in a holder on the counter, alongside a vase of fragrant pink blooms and a sign which said, *Appointments only – we offer a one-to-one bridal service.*

Along one wall hung a row of ivory dresses. A glass chandelier provided the lighting and a pink cushioned three-legged low stool sat in the centre of the polished wooden floor. Ruby couldn't work out whether this was for decoration or had a practical use. But whatever its purpose, the room was an oasis of romance.

'I'm meeting my sister, Olivia Lambert. She's having a fitting at ten.' Ruby glanced at her watch. It wasn't yet quarter to. 'I'm a little early.'

'Please have a seat.' The assistant gestured to an ordinary-looking chair by the window. But before Ruby had a chance to go and sit in it, the door opened again with a jangling chime and Olivia, their mother and their aunt swept in.

The women exchanged greetings and then the proprietor materialised, a petite immaculate woman with a posh voice who introduced herself as Bonnie McCloud. It was the kind of place where you were allotted a timed appointment to allow for the one-to-one personal service the shop prided itself on.

Olivia was swept away for her fitting to a room through a beaded curtain that separated the front of the venue from the back. It was a few minutes before Ms McCloud came back to where they were all waiting and said, 'If you'd like to follow me. We're now ready for you.'

The place was a lot bigger than it looked from outside, Ruby mused, as they followed her through into a corridor lined with mirrors until she paused and knocked softly on a door. 'Can we come in now?'

Olivia called out a yes and Bonnie opened the door and stepped back so they could go in ahead of her.

This room was also larger than seemed possible from the outward appearance of the building and it was also lined with mirrors and softly lit. Olivia stood in the middle of it smiling shyly. The full-length ivory dress she wore, with its simple scooped neck-line, floaty sheer lace sleeves and tiny pearls on the bodice was both understated and stunning. It set off the colour of her dark hair and slightly olive skin to perfection and was complemented by a pearl choker chain at her throat. She seemed to glow with beauty. As they watched, and as if by some prearranged signal from the proprietor, Olivia twirled slowly and the dress swished expensively, the silk and lace rustling, until she was facing them once more.

Their mother gave a little gasp. 'Oh, my darling, you look absolutely beautiful.' Her voice was croaky with emotion.

'Stunning,' Aunt Dawn echoed and wiped a tear from her eye. 'Totally stunning.'

'I'll second that,' Ruby said. 'There's no chance of anyone upstaging you at your wedding.'

Olivia giggled at this and the fairy princess mood became more down to earth. 'Anyone would look gorgeous in this dress,' she said. 'But I do love it. Do you want to see the veil?'

'I thought you weren't having a veil,' Aunt Dawn murmured, and Ruby blushed.

'I know. I changed my mind. It's quite a subtle one.'

Bonnie moved towards a bench which Ruby hadn't noticed before and picked up a frothy concoction of lace, which she arranged expertly with invisible fastenings on Olivia's head and then flicked its two tiered folds into place. Tiny pearls that glistened along its edges matched the ones in the bodice. As Olivia had said, it was subtle and quite short. Not much more than shoulder-length.

'It's beautiful,' Aunt Dawn said.

'You're beautiful,' their mother agreed, sniffing. She was dabbing at her face unashamedly now. 'It's so exciting. Less than three months to go.'

Ruby felt her stomach twist with anxiety. Two stone four pounds to go. Fortunately, Simon chose that moment to make his feelings known too and started to grizzle.

'I'll just take him outside for some fresh air,' she told her relatives and left them still chattering excitedly.

Outside on Weymouth Quay, it had clouded over a bit. Ruby pushed Simon up and down by the water, pointing out seagulls and boats to him until he settled down. As she walked, she wondered whether she would ever be trying on wedding dresses. It wasn't something she'd ever really considered before. It was one of the ways in which she and Olivia were different.

Olivia had always wanted marriage and a family. She'd always wanted a white wedding too. Ruby had fond memories of them dressing up when they were little. Mum had given them a box of old clothes to play with. One day, Olivia had suggested they play weddings. She'd pounced on a cream dress and fashioned an old net curtain into a veil over her dark hair and she'd told Ruby that she could be the bridegroom.

This had suited Ruby just fine. She remembered pushing her blonde hair up inside an old flat cap of their father's and donning a pair of dark trousers and white shirt that were too large. Then the two of them had paraded up and down the garden path while Olivia had sung, 'Here comes the Bride.'

'All fat and wide,' Ruby had echoed, which had earned her a glare from her sister.

'I will not be all fat and wide. I will be slim and beautiful,' Olivia had said haughtily.

Those words seemed strangely prophetic to Ruby now. But she had never guessed that she'd be the one who felt all fat and wide. She gripped the handle of Simon's buggy a little tighter and paused by a bench on the quayside. 'I will not be an overweight brides-maid. I will not be an overweight mum.' She had said those words so many times in the last few weeks. She just wished that she truly believed them.

She might have managed to come over all positive and moti-vated to Saskia and to her Aunt Dawn, but sometimes she didn't feel like that on the inside at all.

Her thoughts were interrupted by the voices of her family and footsteps behind her.

'Hey, sis. We're going for a coffee on the quay. Have you got time?'

'Of course I've got time.' Ruby snapped herself back into the here and now but not quite quickly enough to convince her sister she was fine. She caught Olivia's curious gaze and her mouthed words, 'You OK?'

Ruby nodded and put on her brightest smile. 'Simon said, duck,' she told them quickly and her son said it again obligingly.

'Duck, duck duck,' loving the attention.

There was much cooing over him and excitement before they walked along the quay to find a café.

* * *

Fifteen minutes later, they were settled in a quayside café, scented with percolating coffee and warm pastries, where they'd got a table by the window and had just ordered a cafetière, a pot of tea and some hot water for Simon's bottle.

'Can I get you any cake to go with your drinks?' the waitress asked them. 'We have a special deal.'

Ruby was aware that they all said no at once, as if by some prearranged signal, and even though she had no desire to deprive anyone of cake, she loved them for it. They had all been ultra-complimentary about her losing four pounds this week, despite the issues there had been with the meals. She knew she couldn't have had a more supportive family.

'I feel like a proper tourist,' Olivia said as the waitress came back with their drinks. She linked her hands in her lap and gazed out of the window at the people passing by on the quay.

Aunt Dawn laughed. 'I think we're both still fairly local – even if we don't live by the water. But I do know what you mean. It feels weird, doesn't it?'

'The winds of change,' Ruby said. 'I guess we never stand still, do we.'

They moved on to wedding talk. Olivia told them she was just about to schedule a hair and make-up test run.

'That involves all of us, so we'll need to compare diaries,' she said. 'Hannah said she can do virtually any Saturday in the next month or a Friday afternoon. If you can let me know as soon as you can, I'll fix the date with the salon.'

They all murmured their agreement. Aunt Dawn was the only one of them who was going to have some trouble. She also needed to check cake delivery dates. 'But we can work around that,' she said. 'I'll check when I get home.'

'Phil and I are seeing the celebrant next Friday,' Olivia told them. 'He's done Bluebell Cliff weddings before, so it's not too complicated. We're writing our own vows,' she added shyly. 'That's more difficult than I thought it would be. I guess we're more used to learning lines than writing them from scratch.'

'How romantic,' their mother said. She had gone all shiny-eyed again. 'What are you going to say?'

'You'll have to wait and see,' Olivia teased and then in an aside to the other two, 'I actually haven't got a clue at the moment.'

'What about a hen night?' Ruby asked her. 'Are you hankering after a weekend at a Scottish castle with twenty-five of your girl-friends? Or something a bit more understated?'

'Anything would be more understated than a Scottish castle,' Olivia said, laughing. 'And I don't have twenty-five girlfriends, although there are a few I'd like to come, and one or two ladies in Bristol. I'll give you a list.'

'Great,' Ruby said, thinking that she'd lost touch with most of her girlfriends since she'd had Simon. They were mostly in the art world and lived in London. None of them had kids. It surprised her how insular she'd got lately.

Later on, when they'd finished their drinks and both their mother and aunt had gone to the ladies', Olivia leaned across the table. 'I could really do with a proper catch-up. If you've got time? Are you around tomorrow lunchtime?'

'I certainly am.'

'I don't suppose you and Simon fancy a picnic on Pebble Beach?'

Ruby looked at her curiously. 'We would love that. Are you OK?'

Olivia nodded quickly, but her eyes told a different story. 'It's nothing really to worry about, but I don't want to say anything in front of Mum or Aunt Dawn.'

'OK.' Aware that their relatives were now both heading back towards the table, Ruby stopped speaking, but she felt a pang of concern. Olivia shared everything with Aunt Dawn, they had always been really close. What on earth did Olivia want to share with her that she couldn't share with their aunt?

16

Harry was not having a good Saturday. It had begun badly because he'd overslept. He knew this was partly because things had been strained between himself and Annabel and he hadn't been sleeping very well. After she'd accused him of cheating and he'd apologised, they'd settled back down into an uneasy truce. On the surface, things were OK again, but Harry was uncomfortable. He had hoped that him agreeing to do this health-kick thing that she was so keen on would please her. But so far it seemed to be making things worse between them, not better.

When he had woken up and had gone downstairs this morning, the kitchen had smelled of toast but Annabel had gone out. She'd left him a note on the breakfast island.

Meeting Meggie in town. See you later.

He was faintly surprised to realise he was relieved. At least they wouldn't be tiptoeing around each other all morning and going shopping usually put her in a good mood. So that boded well for later.

He made himself a black coffee. He'd stuck religiously to the new improved Mr B meals since they'd been delivered. Neither had he touched the desserts. He was aiming for a big loss this week. And nothing was going to distract him from getting one.

Another thing he felt more comfortable doing when Annabel was out was Saskia's online workouts. It still felt slightly ridiculous to be standing in front of a laptop following Saskia's movements on screen. He didn't need a witness, even though he was sure Annabel would have been supportive.

He had no doubt the workouts were good. But he still had to psyche himself up. So first a shot or two of caffeine. He sat at the breakfast island with his hands cupped around his favourite mug. Last night when he had finally managed to get to sleep, he'd dreamed about his father.

This had happened a few times lately. In the dreams, his father was looking at him with an expression that Harry could only describe as angst-ridden. He was also speaking – but there was no sound in the dream. So although Harry could see his mouth moving, he couldn't hear the words. In the dreams, his father was always in the office at work. Sometimes he was pacing up and down, sometimes he was sitting on the edge of the desk and occasionally he was sitting in his grandfather's office chair.

This last scenario was based on a real event. About a week after his grandfather's funeral, Harry and his father had gone into Gargantuul's office to sort out some paperwork. Grandpa George, who'd always been a larger-than-life character, had the kind of executive office chair and desk that had reflected his status as CEO. The desk was enormous, an expanse of polished mahogany that took up much of the office, in which the only modern thing present was a laptop. The chair was also bigger than your average chair. It was dark brown leather in a Chesterfield style with a deep padded button back and wings that Harry sometimes joked were for stopping his grandfather falling out of it if he fell asleep at meetings.

Both Harry and his father had always thought both chair and desk were OTT and rather intimidating. Grandpa George pooh-poohed this and said he needed a big desk so he could spread out on it and that the chair simply matched it. He also swore it was the most comfortable chair he'd ever sat in. He'd had it for donkey's years so maybe it was. No one but Grandpa George was ever allowed to sit in it, so this claim couldn't be put to the test.

On this particular day though, Stephen Small, Harry's father, had sat in the chair. He'd rested his arms along its arms and then rolled it forward across the office carpet. The chair was on wheels which squeaked as it moved and made Harry think it couldn't be as old as it looked. When had they started putting wheels on office chairs?

Stephen Small, who was neither as tall, nor as broad-shouldered as Grandpa George had been, didn't fill the Chesterfield-style chair. He looked out of place, like a child playing at being a grown-up in his father's office.

'I don't think I can do this,' he had told his son. 'I don't fit.' He had pressed his fists down in the space on either side of him into the chair to demonstrate, but Harry had known he didn't just mean in a physical sense. 'I feel like a round peg in a square hole,' he said quietly. But it wasn't his words so much that had struck Harry. It was the expression on his face. Pure angst. And it was this look of angst that Harry always saw in his dreams. He hated it.

Last night, he had woken up sweating, with his heart banging madly against his ribcage. And, as always, it had taken a few moments to realise that the dream was just a dream. He was safe in his bed. There was nothing he could do to help his father. Nothing he could do to take that look off his face. To make him smile again.

Harry still had his grandfather's chair and desk. He couldn't bear to part with them. Maybe he should. Maybe it would help him to forget the past. Although he had wondered once or twice, in the clear cold light of day, if it was guilt that had set off the dreams. Guilt that he hadn't done more to take some of the stress off his father's shoulders. Would that have prevented his heart attack? Harry certainly felt guilty that he hadn't done more.

This was despite the fact that he knew he wouldn't have been able to do much that was different even if it had been possible to turn back time. It wasn't as if he'd ever been a slacker – he'd always worked harder and put in more hours than anyone else in the sales team. He'd always felt that he needed to prove himself. Prove that he deserved the senior position he held and that there was no nepotism at play.

When Grandpa George had died and left Stephen Small holding the reins, Harry had worked even harder, doing his best to support his father. It hadn't helped. He had still died. And there had been no warning of the heart attack that had claimed his life. Harry's mother had booked a course of grief counselling sessions for herself a few months later and she'd suggested that Harry might like to do some too, but he hadn't taken her advice.

'I'd prefer to just get on with things,' he'd told her. 'Keep busy. I'll be OK.'

She had looked concerned, but she hadn't argued with him. They had both known he would be OK. Work had always been his saviour in times of trouble. And it hadn't been that much later that he'd met Annabel. He'd inherited Gargantuul four Septembers ago and he'd met Annabel at a wedding the following spring. She had been such a lovely diversion. They'd got married sixteen months later.

He wished he could recapture some of that loveliness now, Harry thought as he drained his mug and took it back to the sink. But he had no idea how to do it.

He glanced at his watch. Half the morning was gone. There was no putting it off any longer. He headed into the lounge. He'd recently invested in a 60-inch LED smart TV, which was connected to the internet. Doing one of Saskia's workouts on here was almost like having her in the room with him!

Half an hour later, he was done. The workout cleared the emotional hangover of the dream from his head and lifted his mood. Harry showered, changed into something more comfortable and decided to go into work. It was at times like this that he wished he played golf or something similar. Going into the office because he literally couldn't think of anything better to do struck him suddenly as rather sad. But it seemed pointless to waste the day. Before he left, he wrote a note to Annabel.

Needed to do a couple of things in the office. Should be back by four p.m.

He left it beside hers on the breakfast island. He also wished he had an elder brother or sister – or even a cousin. He'd have liked to ask someone if it was normal to communicate with your wife mostly via notes so early in your marriage. But there was no one. His father had been an only child, the same as him.

Deep down, Harry was pretty sure it wasn't normal. It certainly wasn't how he'd expected things to pan out when he'd paid for the glittering, celebrity-style wedding Annabel had wanted and the fortnight's honeymoon in Dominican Republic. He resolved to try harder. There must be a way of getting back to the sunny times he remembered from their dating days and the early months of their marriage.

* * *

When he got back from work about ten minutes before he'd said he would and parked beside Annabel's car, Harry had a plan. Annabel was a big fan of full and frank discussions so he would instigate a full and frank discussion with her about their marriage. Surely that would clear the air and he could find out what was bothering her and where the lovely bubbly girl he had married had gone.

He was feeling quite confident as he let himself into the house, but by the time he got to the kitchen and discovered Annabel sitting at the breakfast island with a scowl on her face and folded arms, some of his courage had flown.

'Hey, honey. Are you OK?' He put his briefcase on the floor by the kitchen door. 'How did shopping go?'

'Shopping was fine. Thank you. But no, I am not OK.' She left a dramatic pause.

'I see.' He resisted the temptation to ask why. She was obviously bursting to tell him. But that look on her face sent cold dread into his heart. It was the look she wore when he had upset her.

On the plus side, now was probably a good time to moot the full and frank discussion idea. It didn't look as though he had anything to lose.

'Annabel...'

'Harry.'

They spoke at the same time and he gestured for her to go first.

'I discovered something today. Something that grieves me greatly.'

'Oh?' She looked so sad that he felt the frost around his heart thaw a little. 'What was it? Are you OK?'

'I am. Yes.' She tutted. 'It's easier if I just show you.'

He followed her without arguing into the lounge, where he saw their smart TV was already switched on. Had he left it on earlier after the workout? That surely wasn't what had upset her.

The spare laptop was open too on the coffee table. He was sure he hadn't left that there. Annabel knelt on the floor in front of it and began tapping buttons and he saw what looked like CCTV footage come up on the TV screen. Where was that from?

'This is the footage from our security camera,' Annabel told him in clipped tones. 'I was checking it for something when I came across this. It was very... revealing.'

Before he had a chance to ask her what she was checking for, she pressed play and he saw a picture of himself on the screen. Large as life. He had just come out of the front door and had his back to the camera. There was nothing too incriminating about that. He frowned. Then, as they both watched, his image headed towards the wheelie bin and he opened the lid and began to lift out the bags inside.

With a sickening feeling of foreboding, Harry realised what was coming. He had a strange sense of déjà vu as his image tilted the black wheelie bin towards himself and in doing so moved it even closer to the camera. It must be the one they had over the front door. There were security cameras in a few places.

As he watched, the Harry on the screen looked over his shoulder at the camera and up the drive before leaning forward so his head and shoulders disappeared into the bin. When he re-emerged, he was holding something.

Annabel paused the image and then zoomed in on it frame by frame. It was a great-quality camera. It had been expensive Harry recalled. The dealer who'd sold it to him had said they'd have no trouble identifying anyone who broke into the house. Their facial features would be crystal clear.

As his were on the screen now. There could be no mistaking the expression on his face as he'd looked up and down the drive. Pure guilt. He remembered feeling it – he remembered wondering if he was going to get caught rooting around in the bin because Annabel had been on her way back.

Harry would have had no trouble identifying the oblong object in his hand, even if he hadn't already known what it was. A giant Galaxy bar with the inner foil peeled back so the top row of chocolate was revealed in all its naked glory.

'And there we have it,' Annabel said, in a voice colder than crushed ice. 'You – on camera – foraging for chocolate in a bin. It's not reasonable behaviour, is it, Harry? In fact, I don't think I've ever been so disgusted.' Her voice dripped contempt. 'Tell me, Harry. Would that have anything to do with you putting on weight this week? Or is there some perfectly rational explanation that I've missed?'

For the first time in his life, Harry knew the true meaning of fight or flight. From the heart not the head. From the deepest place inside himself. Fighting was not an option. He couldn't fight this and he didn't want to fight with her. He felt as if something had just died in him. That look of utter disgust on the face of the woman he loved.

Harry bowed his head. For a long moment, he was silent. Then he stood up and left the room. He had thought there were problems in his marriage. But he hadn't expected them to be insurmountable. He hadn't realised until this moment just quite how much his wife despised him and he had no idea where they went from here. This felt like rock bottom.

17

Pebble Beach was Ruby's childhood name for Chesil Beach. She hadn't been able to pronounce the word Chesil so had said Pebble instead and since then the name had stuck and become part of their family's own unique language.

Whether you called it Pebble or Chesil, this wild stretch of beach with its enormous bank of pebbles that sloped down to meet the English Channel beyond had been the backdrop to their entire family history. Or so it seemed to Ruby.

It had started before she and her sister had even been born – their parents were both archaeologists and they loved the Jurassic coastline of which Chesil Beach was so much a part – it was still possible to find fossils in pebbles and rocks tossed up by the eternally shifting sea that smashed down on this shore.

They had spent many a sunny – and not so sunny – day picnicking here when they were children. Olivia had liked it, even though Ruby had longed for sand and deckchairs and one of the tamer, more traditional beaches on the south coast, like Bournemouth or Mudeford or Sandbanks.

When Ruby had been pregnant with Simon, Olivia had accompanied her to her first scan. Then, afterwards, she and Olivia had come to Chesil Beach and trudged what seemed like miles along the ever-shifting pebbles and talked about the future. Would Ruby keep her unplanned baby and become a single parent or have him adopted? Not that she'd known she was even having a boy back then. But it was on Pebble Beach that she had made her decision. And it was here that Olivia had asked if she could be introduced to Ruby's unborn child and Ruby had stuck out her tummy as far as she could – she'd barely been showing – and Olivia had solemnly introduced herself.

Ruby had even painted a picture of this beach with herself and Olivia as stick women walking along it while the sun rose in a gloriously majestic backdrop. The picture was called 'Sunrise Over Pebble Beach' and it was now hung in pride of place in her studio. So many memories.

Ruby wondered what Olivia wanted to talk about as her sister drew up into the car park that abutted the beach at one end of Portland Bill. Olivia had picked her up twenty minutes ago, but she hadn't said much on the way over. She looked pale and a little strained and Ruby had decided to keep quiet and let her sister tell her in her own time about whatever was bothering her.

They got out of the car and Ruby's hair was immediately whipped away by the breeze as she went round to the hatchback to get Simon's buggy.

'Wow. Do you think the wind ever drops down below gale force here?' she quipped.

It wasn't quite gale force, but it was breezy. On the other side of the road looking out to the east of Portland, there were several kiteboarders, their bright blue and scarlet sails flying high against the blue. At least it was a lovely day.

'It will be more sheltered down by the water,' Olivia said. She glanced at Simon's buggy and frowned. 'I'm not thinking straight, am I? It'll be a nightmare pushing that over the pebbles. Shall we walk across the causeway instead?'

'Who said anything about walking? I thought we were going for a picnic?' Ruby glanced at her sister.

'We are having a picnic, but I thought we could do both. OK, let's just go down to the water. We can show Simon our favourite beach. I'm assuming you've never brought him here, have you?'

'Not since he's been born,' Ruby said lightly.

'It's good to see you, sis. Can you manage all his paraphernalia if I bring the picnic basket and blanket?'

'Picnic basket. Gosh, we are pushing the boat out – please note appropriate metaphor.'

'It's Phil's,' Olivia said as she lugged an old-fashioned wicker picnic basket out of the back of the car that had hitherto been covered by a throw so Ruby hadn't spotted it. 'It's heavy as hell, but I love it. It's very retro. It's got a red checked lining and these leather straps are where you put your wine glasses and plates.'

'Are we having wine then?'

'You are. I'm driving. I bought a bottle of fizz. It's nothing special. I've got orange juice for me.'

'No wonder it's heavy.'

'The wine's not even in there.' Olivia produced a bottle from the car.

'I'm happy with orange juice too,' Ruby said quickly. 'Let's not make the basket any heavier. What else is in it?'

'You'll have to wait and see.'

'I feel as though we've turned into our parents,' Ruby said a few minutes later as they crossed the wooden causeway that led across Fleet Lagoon and lugged the whole lot up the pebble bank and down the other side.

'Our parents wouldn't have brought a picnic basket. Mum would have refused to carry it and Dad would have put it down somewhere when he saw an interesting rock and forgotten all about it.'

'That's true. It would have been egg and cress sandwiches in a plastic carrier bag.'

'God, I hated egg and cress.'

'Me too. I'm sure we told them that.'

'We did, but they didn't listen.'

'Gah,' said Simon and waved his fists in the air.

'Even cheese tasted horrible when it had been sweating in a plastic bag.'

'Gah, gah, gah.'

'Yes, especially if it had tomato in it. Yuck. How did we ever survive?'

Simon started to yell.

'What, darling?' Ruby said, bending down by his buggy. 'Oh my goodness, you're right. I haven't been listening to you. You need changing, don't you? I really am turning into my mother.'

A few minutes later, they had found a spot on the seaward side of the bank of shingle, a little way from the sea, where it wasn't quite as windy. Simon was changed and comfortable again. Olivia had laid out the picnic blanket and opened up the basket and was now sitting beside it and getting things out. There wasn't a sandwich in sight, to Ruby's relief. There were instead mini quiches, strawberry shortbreads, hard-boiled eggs, dips and a selection of salads in little tubs. Olivia had been right about the picnic basket. It was retro and really cool with its red checked lining and leather straps that held everything in place.

'Wowsers,' Ruby said. 'Where did all this lot come from? It looks home-made.'

'It is, but I didn't make it. It's mostly courtesy of Mr B. He's a very handy person to know. I told him I was coming with you. The quiches are slimmer-friendly. They're crustless and there's no fat in them. But they are totally delicious. I tried one. He made them specially. Likewise the dips – he said the main ingredient is fat-free fromage frais.'

'That is so nice of him,' Ruby said touched. 'And you. Really thoughtful.'

Olivia looked pleased. Her eyes warmed.

'So would you like to talk first or eat?' Ruby asked her. 'Although we can probably do both, can't we? I think he's ready for some lunch. Today we have organic vegetables with rice and chicken.' She had Simon on her lap, his head supported in the crook of her arm and he was gazing up at her. His blue eyes fixed on hers. Her heart swelled with love for him. She felt so lucky to have him. She shifted into a more comfortable spot on the blanket, which was thick but which only softened the hardness of the pebbles beneath it a fraction. The sound of the waves swishing in over the pebbles and then hissing back in retreat was all around them. Somehow, being here in the place where she'd decided to keep Simon was extra poignant.

As she fed him, she became aware of Olivia's gaze and she glanced up, meeting her eyes. And just for a moment in the second before Olivia managed to hide it, she saw the ache of longing.

It was Olivia who spoke first. 'You know I told you I thought I was pregnant a couple of weeks ago when I was a few days late and then I got the period from hell. Well, I had a blood test done to check my hormone levels and I got the results back on Friday. I'm perimenopausal.'

'What does that mean exactly?' Ruby asked. Clearly it wasn't good. There was a bleakness in her sister's eyes she'd never seen.

'It's the stage before menopause. When your hormone levels

start to change. I mean, the doctor said that it's very early to be peri-menopausal and that this stage can last for years, but the important thing – at least as far as I'm concerned – is that it makes it more difficult to get pregnant.'

'But not impossible.'

Olivia sighed. 'Not impossible, no. But, as you know already, it's not just me. Phil's chances of conceiving are also pretty low.' She picked up a handful of tiny pebbles and let them clink back onto the beach one by one. 'His chances of being a father are around six per cent. My chances of being a mother are lowered and they're getting lower by the month. The odds are stacked against us, Rubes. It just feels like one more thing. One more punch in the gut. It feels so unfair.'

She stopped speaking and swallowed and Ruby could feel her pain. It was tangible in the salt air and across the eternal rhythm of the tide.

'That's because it is unfair,' Ruby said, wiping Simon's mouth. He always seemed to get more food on the outside of him than the inside. 'But there are things you can do – right? Are you still thinking of IVF?'

'We're still on the waiting list. But even with IVF, the odds are stacked against us. In the meantime, I've been given a fertility drug. It's just a pill you take that stimulates ovulation. We already do all the ovulation predictor stuff. We've been doing it ever since we decided to try for a family. Phil was quite keen at first, but I think it's getting to him, Rubes. It's quite a passion-killer – sex to order. Especially with the kind of work we do.' She sighed. 'We tie ourselves in knots trying to be in the same place when we know it's a good time. A couple of months, ago he drove from Buckingham where he was recording an audiobook for someone to Bristol where I was filming so he could get there in time for the four-hour window that we had

to make love.' She picked up another handful of pebbles and
dropped them again. 'The poor guy was absolutely shattered
because he had to leave again at five a.m. to get back to work in
time. Buckingham to Bristol for a bonk. Honestly, Rubes, you
couldn't make it up.'

Ruby shook her head, amazed. It put her dieting doldrums into
the shade. 'I had no idea,' she said softly.

'Why would you? It's not exactly dinner-party conversation, is
it? Or even close-friend conversation. I joined this fertility forum for
a while. It took me a week to work out all the acronyms to understand what they were talking about. Acronyms and fairy dust –
that's what it seemed to be. The acronyms being things like DPO –
days past ovulation – and BFP – big fat positive, as in pregnancy test
– and the term fairy dust, which just meant luck. It was good to be
talking to women in the same boat as me. But it was also difficult.
Especially when one of them got pregnant. Everyone on the forum
would wish them well and say how pleased they were and to be
sure to keep in touch to let us know how they went on, while at the
same time probably secretly hating them and feeling jealous as hell
because it hadn't happened to them. At least that's how I felt.
Maybe that just means I'm a horrible person.' She blinked away
tears and swallowed.

'You are not a horrible person, Liv. You are an amazing person.'

Olivia acknowledged this with her eyes and a moment later
she started speaking again. 'They never did keep in touch. The
women who got pregnant. I got to thinking that maybe they felt
too guilty to come back onto the forum. And I could see how that
would work. It would be like someone who's massively in debt on
a debtors' forum suddenly winning the lottery. They'd be unlikely
to come back either, would they? Unless they planned to share
their winnings with everyone else.' She paused. 'But you can't
share a baby. You can't help anyone else at all, apart from

empathising and wishing they find the same handful of flaming fairy dust that you did.' She broke off suddenly. 'I'm ranting, aren't I? I'm sorry.'

'Rant away,' Ruby said. 'I don't mind.'

'It's surprisingly cathartic, ranting. I guess that's because I don't often get the chance to do it.'

Simon spat out his last mouthful of organic chicken and vegetables and waved his arms. He'd spotted a seagull. 'Duck,' he yelled. 'Yah, gah, duck.'

'He agrees,' Ruby said. 'Mind you, he would. He's a seasoned ranter. Mostly at night.' She cuddled him and he was promptly sick down her front. 'Ew,' she said, grabbing a baby wipe and wiping his mouth and then herself before stuffing it into the rubbish bag she seemed to carry around everywhere. 'That's the not-so-fairy-dust side of having a baby. The puking and pooing. Do you want to hold him? He should be all fairy dust again now for a while.'

Olivia laughed. 'That's what I love about you. You always manage to ground me.' She held out her arms.

'Grounded is my middle name,' Ruby told her, handing Simon over to his aunt. 'Any time you want to rant or get grounded, I'm your woman.' She paused as Olivia settled him on her lap and then the two sisters looked at each other again. 'You do know, don't you, that if you want to go private, I am very happy to fund one or more goes at IVF. As many as it takes. As a gift I mean. Not a loan.'

Olivia didn't say anything for a few moments. Ruby could see she was struggling not to cry.

'You know I can afford it, Liv. And my motives are totally selfish. Simon needs at least one cousin.'

'Thanks,' Olivia managed eventually. 'That is amazingly generous of you. I don't know if Phil would accept. He's so proud.'

'He probably doesn't realise how well set up his sister-in-law-to-be is. Tell him that the commission I made last year on one Banksy would cover several goes of IVF. Seriously, Liv, tell him that if he argues. We could say it's a wedding present if that helps.'

'That's a good idea. I'll tell him it's a wedding present, Rubes. If you're really, really sure?'

'I am. I also think it's about time I got out some of this delicious-looking food,' Ruby said. 'Being the starving dieter that I am.' She busied herself with unwrapping things and putting them on plates while her sister and Simon had a conversation that mostly consisted of goos, gahs, dahs, ducks and buzzes. Buzzes being the latest sound he'd added to his vocabulary.

Then they ate, with Simon still sitting on Olivia's lap and her cross-legged on the blanket, but they didn't talk about IVF again. They talked a bit more about the wedding and Ruby said again how beautiful Olivia had looked in her dress.

By the time they'd finished eating and had packed away the remains of the picnic, the tide, which was on its way out, had retreated a little further away from them and the wind had dropped and Simon had started to grizzle.

'He's tired and irritable,' Ruby said. 'He needs his afternoon snooze. Don't you, darling? Maybe put him on the blanket for a second. He loves to move around. Then we could walk for a bit. But I think you're right – maybe up on the causeway would be good.'

Ruby readied the buggy while Simon shuffled along the blanket so he could grab pebbles.

'Maybe he's looking for fossils,' Olivia said, taking a pebble out of his hand before he put it in his mouth. 'It's bound to run in the family.' She turned it over in her hand. 'Oh blimey, I was joking about that. But I think he's found one.'

'No way.' Ruby glanced over her shoulder.

'Yes way. Look.' Olivia passed her the pebble in question. 'It could be swirly lines, but I think it's half an ammonite.'

'Good grief. You're right. We have to save that for Dad. He'll be thrilled. He already thinks his grandson has the hands of an archaeologist.'

They both laughed as Ruby put the pebble into a zipped compartment of her bag. Luck or genetics. Fairy dust or science. It didn't matter, Ruby thought. It was just so good to hear Olivia laugh again.

18

The truth was, Harry thought as he drove into work on Monday morning, there was a lot more wrong with his marriage than even he had imagined. This had become more and more apparent as the last dreadful weekend had progressed.

Black Saturday, as he'd already labelled it in his mind, had been just the beginning. He was still processing everything. But the truth was now clear to him. He'd been as much in denial about his marriage as he had been about his weight.

He wasn't sure which of the events had smashed his denial. It may have been the fact that Annabel had actually gone through their security-camera footage, presumably in the hope she'd find something incriminating. Or it may have been the expression on her face when she had showed him the clip of him reaching into the bin. That look of utter disgust and contempt that she'd directed at him.

Both things were burned on his brain. You didn't look for evidence to incriminate someone you loved. She had crossed a line there. Even so, he could possibly have forgiven her for that. Maybe he could even have forgotten it in time. Put it down to an overzealous concern about his well-being.

But he knew he wouldn't forget the way she'd looked at him. You didn't look at someone you loved like that. Not unless they had committed some terrible crime. And maybe not even then. Love didn't do that. At least the love he felt for her would never have done that.

But was it love? He'd started to ask himself that question. Maybe it had actually been closer to blind adoration? Harry was beginning to question his entire marriage.

It wasn't as though they hadn't talked either. They'd talked on Saturday evening and nearly all day Sunday. He'd had enough full and frank discussions to last him a lifetime. They had started with the wheelie bin chocolate and the issues with Mr B's calorie-controlled meals and the issues – at least as she saw them – with his weight. But they hadn't talked about that for long because it was quickly clear to Harry that the problems in their marriage had nothing to do with these things.

Now, as he pulled up in his space in the car park outside his office, he still felt shaky when he recalled the last conversation they'd had yesterday.

'The truth is I just don't fancy you any more,' she had said as they'd sat opposite each other at the breakfast island alongside the shiny range oven she'd insisted he buy but that she had barely used. There was a thin layer of dust across its surface, testament to how little it had been switched on. It was amazing how much irrelevant detail you noticed when you were in shock, Harry thought.

'I see,' he had said quietly. 'So when did you stop "fancying" me?' He'd mimed the quotation marks around the word 'fancying' with his hands. Even though on some level he knew the answer already.

She'd shrugged. 'I'm not sure. When you started putting on weight, I think.'

'I'm not obese, Annabel.'

'You are in NHS terms. Your BMI is too high.'

'Is it? How do you know? You don't even know what I weigh.'

'I do.' She'd flushed. 'Anyway, I don't need to know. It's obvious. You're fat.'

'My BMI is 27. I need to lose two and a half stone to get back into the healthy BMI range. But it isn't that, is it? You haven't wanted to sleep with me since soon after our honeymoon. And I was slimmer then.' He'd paused because another explanation had just occurred to him. 'Is there someone else?'

'No.' Her reply was too quick and she'd looked shocked. But her cheeks were now an even deeper pink and suddenly he knew he was right on target. Even though he hadn't ever suspected that she might be playing away. Not consciously at least.

'It's Nick, isn't it? Your boss, Nick.'

The expression on her face had told him he'd hit the bullseye. Not that she was going to admit it.

'Don't be so ridiculous, Harry. Nick is old enough to be my father.' She'd chewed the skin on the edge of her index finger. A sure sign that she was lying.

'Just tell me the truth, Annabel.'

He'd hardly recognised his own voice, it was so hard and cold. It wasn't a tone he used very often and it certainly wasn't one that Annabel had ever heard. He saw her tense on her stool at the break-fast island. She blinked fast several times before she had started to cry.

And usually tears would have done it – tears would have melted his heart and he'd have relented, given her anything she wanted – anything to stop the tears. He'd have capitulated to the spoilt child that he was beginning to see she was. But not today. Not now. He'd waited for her to stop, which she soon did, sniffing a few more times before dabbing at her cheeks.

'Are you having an affair with Nick?' he'd asked her the question again. 'I need to know. Have you slept with him?'

Finally, she'd nodded. Just one quick nod before folding her arms across her chest in a gesture of defiance, and some instinct had warned him that she was going to try to make this his fault. Even now.

'Was it when you were away at the conference?'

'What does it matter when?'

'Just tell me.'

'Yes. Yes it was.' Now she'd met his eyes. 'Probably at the exact same time you were foraging for chocolate in the bin.' Her lip had curled in distaste. 'Can you blame me?'

Harry hadn't deigned to answer this. It was so weird, he thought, how once the scales fell from your eyes about someone, they really fell. He had felt as if he was seeing Annabel for the very first time.

He'd remembered something that one of his mates had said when he'd first started dating her. 'Watch yourself, Harry. I'm not sure she's all she seems, that one. Are you sure she doesn't see you as a meal ticket?'

Harry had assumed that Clifford Brown, who he'd known for years, was jealous because Annabel was so stunning. Who wouldn't be jealous? Clifford had been single at the time, after a bad break-up with a woman who'd sucked him dry and then left him. He didn't trust women. For all Harry knew, he was still single. They'd hardly spoken since then. Partly because Harry had known, of course, that Annabel was different. She was a hotshot solicitor. She earned a lot. She didn't need to marry him for his money. Harry had always held on to that fact. Why she had actually married him was a mystery. At least it was now. Because it certainly hadn't been for love.

After that last conversation, Annabel had stormed out. Her parting shot had been, 'I can't live with your unreasonable behaviour, Harry. I'll be filing for divorce.'

He hadn't tried to stop her from going. He'd been relieved, even though he knew she would have to come back. It might be the end of their love, but it wouldn't be the end of their marriage. That would require solicitors and paperwork and money. Lots of money. He had no direct experience of divorce, but he had no doubt at all that it would be heartbreaking and expensive. Very expensive probably where Annabel was concerned. He didn't imagine she would want to walk away with nothing.

Harry came back to the present with a start. He realised that he was still sitting in his car outside his office. Still immersed in the weekend's conversations, which already felt vaguely surreal. As though they had happened to someone else.

His sore back was testament to the fact that it was all horribly real. He'd slept in the spare room for the last two nights. He couldn't bear to sleep in his own bed, with the empty Annabel-shaped space behind him serving as a reminder that she was gone. The hard mattress on their guest bed always made him ache.

Neither was slept a very apt description. He hadn't done much of that. Particularly not last night. He'd had vague nightmares about his father – the usual guilt ones – mixed up with images of Annabel, which varied between the sweet, loving girl he'd married and the contemptuous, cruel woman who had played him his own camera footage in which he had been the unwitting star. He still couldn't reconcile the two.

But neither could he sit outside his office all day. He got out wearily, locked up the Lexus and went inside.

Victoria, his PA, met him with a worried look on her face. 'There's a man waiting to see you, so there is. He's no appointment, but he insisted on waiting. I've put him in Liam's office for now. Will you see him? I thought I would check with you first?'

'That's fine,' Harry said. A persistent customer sounded like a good distraction from his personal life. 'If you wouldn't mind making me some coffee, then I'll see him. What's his name?'

'That's the oddest thing. He's not one of our customers. He said he needed to speak to you in connection with Mrs Small. Would you credit it?' She glanced at the business card in her hand. 'He's a solicitor. His name's Nick Lewison.'

Harry froze for a second. A lightning bolt of pain shot him in the gut. Wow. So not only did Annabel plan on divorcing him, it looked as though she was going to get her lover to instigate the proceedings.

Surely no one could be that blatant. Surely not. But he couldn't think of another reason the man was here. It seemed highly unlikely he'd called by to apologise.

'Slight change of plan,' Harry said. 'I'll have my coffee first. Perhaps you could bring it into my office. Tell Mr Lewison I'll see him in forty-five minutes. At 10.05 a.m.'

'I'll do that, I will.' Victoria looked reassured as she went to do his bidding.

Harry used the time to think. It was quite a smart move on Nick Lewison's part to come to his office. He might guess that his lover's husband's first instinct would be to want to flatten him. But he would also know he was unlikely to do this in front of witnesses and that if he were to show so much as a flicker of threatening behaviour, it would very much work in Annabel's favour.

Or he might have made the assumption that Harry would still

be too shocked to even think properly. That he wouldn't have gathered his defences. That he would still be hoping his wife would come back, apologising. That he would be vulnerable.

Harry considered the possibilities with detachment. It was the ability to be able to put himself in another person's shoes that had made him the brilliant salesmen he was. Empathy was one of the qualities that had rocketed him to the top of his game. Figuring out what a customer really wanted, even before he properly knew it himself was one of Harry's gifts.

The rational part of his brain had always stayed sharper under pressure. Stress made him think more clearly, not less. Another handy characteristic for a salesman. He already had a pretty good idea what Nick Lewison wanted, but he was smart enough not to make assumptions. He would listen carefully, find out exactly what the situation was and only then would he react.

* * *

At precisely 10.05, Harry went to collect Nick Lewison. He was sitting in Liam's office, where Victoria had put him, and he was fidgeting and looking at the clock. Harry's own solicitor charged £300 per hour, so Harry estimated that this impromptu visit was already costing the man money. He felt a flash of satisfaction. Small victories.

'Would you come this way, Mr Lewison?' he said pleasantly. 'Next time it might be advisable to make an appointment. I'm very busy. I can give you five minutes.'

The solicitor stood up. They'd met before very briefly at one of Annabel's work dos, but Harry wasn't sure he'd have recognised him if he'd passed him on the street. Today he was dressed in a hugely expensive suit, handmade, Harry judged. He was tall, but not as tall as Harry. Few men were. His neat dark hair was beginning to silver at the temples. Annabel hadn't been lying about him being older than her then. Harry would have put him in his early fifties, although he was wearing it well. He also looked stressed. There were beads of sweat on his forehead and the room wasn't hot.

Harry led him back through reception and into his own office, where he gestured towards a plastic backed chair. Harry had got the chair especially from the boardroom where it was used to prop the door open. No one had sat in it for years because it had a wonky leg. But Harry wasn't a fan of putting things into landfill, so the chair had stayed. It now also had a layer of dust on the seat.

After a moment's hesitation, the solicitor bent, brushed off the dust – Harry saw the flash of a wedding ring as he did so – and sat down. The chair wobbled, so he had to shift his position to compensate. Another small victory, Harry thought with satisfaction as he sat behind Grandpa George's enormous desk in the chair into which he'd always fitted perfectly and gave Nick Lewison his full attention.

'So, what can I do for you today?' he asked.

'I am acting on behalf of Annabel Small who has asked me to file a D8 – a divorce petition.'

'On what grounds?'

'Unreasonable behaviour.'

'And thereby lies a conundrum,' Harry said softly. 'The definition of unreasonable behaviour.' He leaned back in this chair and linked his hands behind his head. 'I'd think that most judges would agree that to sleep with a man's wife and then visit his office to serve him with a divorce petition would push the boundaries of reasonable behaviour.'

Nick Lewison looked startled. Maybe Annabel hadn't told him she'd already confessed to adultery. It didn't look like it. He was sweating freely now. He dabbed at his forehead with a handkerchief and his wedding ring glinted gold. 'I am merely acting under instructions.'

'Your instructions are noted.' Harry stood up and moved towards the door. 'Your five minutes are up.'

The solicitor had to practically brush past him to get to the door and he was visibly rattled. He'd expected to be in control of this situation – and he knew that he wasn't.

'I'll be in touch,' he muttered.

'I can't wait.'

The man shot out of Harry's office and through Gargantuul's reception as though he was being pursued by a platoon of soldiers.

Harry shut the door and leant against it breathing heavily. It had taken every ounce of his self-control not to fly at Nick Lewison, to punch him hard on the jaw, again and again. He had never felt like that about anyone in his life. But at least it was done. He didn't think the solicitor would be putting in another personal appearance any time soon.

The battle lines were drawn. If Annabel wanted a divorce, she could have one. But she was not going to get it all her own way. The time for that was over.

19

Ruby was looking forward to standing on Booty Busters' scales on Tuesday evening. That was a first. She knew she'd lost weight this week. The waistband of her favourite jeans was much looser. She was feeling great. She was – in diet club jargon – in the zone. She was looking forward to the workout too. She wouldn't say she was exactly hooked on them, which was how Becky had said she felt the other day, but she had to admit she always felt great afterwards. She even felt great after the ones at she did at home when she didn't push herself so hard.

It had been a night when her mother had asked if she could drop Simon off at hers – they were going to try their first sleepover, Simon with his granny – which Ruby had been both excited and nervous about. She'd been much more anxious than Simon, it had turned out, who'd barely given her a backward glance once she'd dropped him off with reams of baby paraphernalia and instructions.

This meant that Ruby was earlier than usual to Beauty Busters. As she drove along the winding coastal roads towards the Bluebell Cliff, her thoughts flicked back to the weekend.

It had been brilliant spending time with Olivia, both at Beautiful Brides but also at Pebble Beach, and she really hoped her sister would take her up on her offer to let her help them with some rounds of IVF. She hadn't been bragging or boasting when she'd said she made a lot of money. It was simply how it was. And although she liked the way it was, she never, ever took it for granted.

Ruby had not expected to make so much money from her passion. When she'd been at art college and got her degree in modern art, she'd fully expected to go on to be a struggling artist because that's what she'd been told would happen by all but one of her lecturers.

Ashley Rowling, the one who hadn't said it, was both a sculptor and lecturer and he had been – and still was being, as far as she knew – a fabulously inspiring guy. It was impossible to tell how old Ashley was. He had a white beard, a lesser amount of white hair on his head and cool blue eyes. As far as she could tell, he had never looked any different. She'd checked online, and despite the fact he had numerous mentions, there seemed to be only one photo of him in existence, no matter where you looked. In the photo, he wore the same as he did to teach – a Hawes & Curtis suit teamed with a pristine white shirt.

'The reason that artists struggle,' he'd told Ruby in a conversation that had changed her life, 'is because they do what they want to do, instead of what the market wants them to do.'

They'd been standing in a hall at the end of a lecture, where she happened to be the last one to leave.

'You mean they sell their soul,' she'd said flatly. 'Is that the only way out of the impasse?'

'They do not sell their soul, Ruby. They play it smart.' He'd raised his eyebrows and given her a cool look. 'It is perfectly possible to be a rich artist. But you must also play the game.' He sat on the edge of his desk and gestured her to a chair. 'Would you like to know how?'

'Is the Pope Catholic?' she'd replied, sitting down to listen.

He'd begun to count on his fingers. 'I am a sculptor. I am a marketing manager. I am a lecturer.'

'I have to be a lecturer?' she'd queried.

'No.'

'A marketing manager?'

He shook his head impatiently.

'But you're saying I have to be more than one thing.'

'Correct. And one of the things you decide to be will make you an income. The wisest thing an artist can do is to have more than one stream of income.'

Ruby had felt disappointed. She had heard this theory before. She leaped into the counterargument. 'But then you would be spreading yourself too thin. Diluting your passion. Surely an artist has to be totally single-minded and utterly focused to succeed.'

'You're not listening,' Ashley had said impatiently. 'We are all more than one thing, Ruby. None of us is just our work. As well as a sculptor and a lecturer, I am a brother, a son, a cousin, a hill walker, an avid reader of travel books and I'm not a bad chef. It is possible for all humans to be more than one thing. In fact, we cannot avoid being more than one thing. But the important thing is that we have a choice on where to put our focus. About five per cent of the artists who leave here with hopes, ambitions and dreams will make a lot of money.'

Ruby was caught up in the story now. Ashley was a good story-teller too, as well as all the other roles he'd mentioned.

'It is not entirely about talent either,' he'd said. 'I used to think it was when I was younger, but it's not.'

'Is it about luck?'

'Luck certainly plays a part. Yes. As well as those things I said I was just now, I am also clairvoyant. I can tell you with some authority what will happen when the students who are here right now have got their art degree.'

She was definitely hooked now. She had leaned forward.

'Some of them will abandon art altogether. They will decide that art is not for them and they will do something else entirely. Some will choose to be mothers or fathers and have a family and art will take a back seat for years and years, maybe to re-emerge one day when they are less busy. Some will see their vocation in the teaching profession, because that is indeed a vocation. One or two will be hugely successful artists. One or two – maybe the same one or two – will end up penniless, before or after their huge success.'

His eyes were both serious and bright with passion and his voice had dropped a little, so she had to listen hard to catch every word.

'My point is, Ruby, that we all have exactly the same amount of time. We all have twenty-four hours a day. Think of your hours as currency. Spend them wisely.' He'd paused for a couple of seconds to let that sink in. 'And to go back to the subject of money. What I am saying is that if you want to make money, you should choose carefully what you do. Because whatever you choose, there will always be sacrifices.'

Ruby had never forgotten this conversation. It was Ashely Rowling who had helped her to get a job with an art dealer in London when she left college. She had learned a great deal from her boss – a man who was well respected in the art world. She had learned how to read customers, how to tell the difference between browsers and buyers, when to offer help, when to simply engage them in conversation and when to say nothing at all. She supposed she had learned the art of schmoozing from the best in the business and she had learned a great deal about art in the process.

She had worked in the gallery for four years and then she'd had a nine-month stint in an even bigger one. Her salary went up and up as she began to make a name for herself and although she had been doing little in the way of grassroots art – she rarely had time to paint – she had enjoyed herself immensely.

It was because of Ashley that she had finally decided to go it alone. She credited him with much of her success. When she sold her first Banksy to a man in Dorset – not a million miles away from where she lived – she had sent her former lecturer a thank you. This took the form of a bronze carving which depicted the letters of the words thank you individually sculpted in bronze and entwined together on a plinth. 'The Thank You Dance' had been carved by an up-and-coming artist, who'd also once been a student of Ashley's so Ruby knew he would appreciate it even more.

He had responded with a card, which said, *The credit is all yours, Ruby. Star pupil.*

Ruby still had that card in a box where she kept precious things: a lock of Simon's hair from the day he was born, a twenty-first birthday card from her parents. She might be a hard-headed businesswoman, but deep down she was more of a sentimentalist than anyone would have guessed.

Occasionally across the years, Ruby had wondered if the sacrifice she had made for art had been not having any serious relationships. She had dated lots of guys, but she had never been in love. Not once. Usually she came to the conclusion that she was overthinking it and that she just hadn't met the right man yet, but since she had given birth to Simon, she'd begun to wonder if she'd actually missed the boat completely.

She'd certainly narrowed her options. She couldn't imagine

many men jumping at the chance to date an art-obsessed single mother. But despite his unplanned arrival, Simon was the best thing that had ever happened to her. She didn't need a romantic relationship to feel whole, that was for sure. Aunt Dawn had been right about that.

As she drew into the car park of the Bluebell Cliff, Ruby's thoughts turned back to Olivia. One of the best things about being wealthy was being able to share it with others. Hyperaware of coming over as too flashy, she had always been careful about how she did it. Buying expensive Christmas and birthday presents for her family tended to raise eyebrows and Ruby had no desire to make anyone uncomfortable. But now she felt as though she might really be able to make a difference. Giving her sister the chance to have what she wanted more than anything in the world, now that was truly exciting. It made Ruby feel simultaneously shivery and warm.

The first person Ruby saw when she got to the Booty Busters studio ready for the workout was Harry, getting the mats out of the store-room. He must have arrived early too. There was no sign of Saskia yet.

'Hey,' she said, heading across. 'Do you need a hand?'

'Cheers. Yeah.' He handed her a rolled-up mat, but his usual sparkle was missing and Ruby felt a surge of concern. He looked totally worn out.

Impulsively, she touched his arm and he blinked and shook his head as if he was seeing her for the first time.

'Are you OK?' she asked. 'Has something happened?'

He made a noise somewhere between a choke and a snort

before he recovered his composure again. 'Um. Lot going on at home.'

Before either of them could say anything else, Saskia bounded in with all the energy and grace of a beautiful gazelle. 'Good evening. You two are early. Harry, thank you. You are always on the case. It does not go unnoticed or unappreciated.'

She, too, did a double take, Ruby noticed, when she saw Harry's face and a frown wrinkled her pretty forehead, but she didn't comment.

The others began to trickle in and soon the room was busy with people. There was no sign of Cheryl and Iris. They must have decided to take the refund and run. Ruby wasn't too surprised. Even they might have found it hard to come back from getting the TV crew to come in on the strength of a fabricated story about sabotage. She had checked to see if the footage had ever been aired, but it hadn't looked as though it had.

At the beginning of the workout as they all stood by their mats, Saskia cleared her throat. 'Before we begin. I would just like to say a big thank you for sticking with the plan, despite the issues we had. Mr B and myself very much appreciate it. I am hoping that you have all had a good week, and that you have enjoyed the revised menus?'

'They're still pretty good,' Dana called out. 'Although I do miss the chocolate profiteroles, I have to say.'

'I heard a rumour that Mr B is working on a new recipe,' Saskia said. 'So watch this space.'

'Does it involve chocolate?' Ruby called. She glanced at Harry's face, expecting to see a smile, but instead she saw a flicker of pain, which concerned her even more. Whatever had happened had really got to him. It must be bad if not even chocolate could raise a smile.

'So what path are we on?' Saskia said to the group, punching the air. 'That's right. It is the easiest path.' She punched the air again for good measure. She was clearly on fire tonight.

* * *

The workout was up-tempo and energetic. By the end of it, Ruby was hot and breathless and her watch told her she'd been in the cardio zone for eleven minutes. Which wasn't bad out of the twenty-five-minute total.

She queued up for the weigh-ins and found herself in front of Harry. She wanted to talk to him but not in public. Something was obviously wrong and she didn't want to embarrass him. Maybe she should phone him. She was pretty sure he wouldn't mind that.

There was an air of jauntiness and excitement in the queue tonight and the occasional squeal of excitement from behind the sectioned-off makeshift weigh-in room. Clearly, there had been some great results, this week. Maybe Mr B was erring on the side of caution with his calorie counts after the disastrous start. She had noticed the meals had seemed a little smaller than before, but there had been no difference in the quality. This weekend's menus had included liver and bacon parfait and green beans, and baked salmon in parchment. Yum.

Ruby was still lost in thought when someone touched her arm. It was Harry.

'I think it's your turn,' he said.

She jumped, aware that he was right and stepped into the weigh-in booth.

Saskia beamed at her from behind the desk. 'So how do you think you have done this week?'

'I think I may have lost a pound or two,' Ruby said, discarding her gym shoes and stepping confidently up onto the scales, which immediately registered a stonking four-pound loss. Ruby caught her breath as Saskia clapped her hands excitedly.

'That is the understatement of the year. Congratulations, Ruby. That's our top loss of the evening so far. I am so thrilled for you.'

Ruby felt the warmth of success rising into her cheeks. It may be only numbers on a digital scale, but, wow, it meant a lot. 'I'm thrilled for me too.'

'You should be.' Saskia wrote the numbers on her card. 'That's more than half a stone already. It's fantastic. Keep going.'

'I intend to.'

Ruby floated out of the weigh-in booth, updated Becky, who squealed with excitement, and then headed back down slowly into the foyer of the Bluebell Cliff. She went through the automatic exit doors and then hesitated outside them.

Should she wait for Harry? She debated with herself. It wouldn't hurt. She was concerned about him. And if he told her to mind her own business, she would and she'd have lost nothing.

A few seconds later, the decision was taken out of her hands. The automatic doors swung open and he practically walked into her. His mind was clearly on other things.

'Sorry,' he murmured.

'It's OK. I was waiting for you. Harry, I don't want to intrude. But you seem really down. Are you OK? Do you want to talk about it? I've got time for a coffee if you like?' She hesitated. 'Or I could just mind my own business.'

He gave her the same blank look he had earlier and then he seemed to gather himself and make a decision. 'OK,' he said. 'A coffee would be good. Shall we have one here?'

She nodded. She texted her mum to see how Simon was settling down and received an instant reply in return.

He's absolutely fine. Go for a coffee with the girls, love, have some fun while you've got the chance.

Ruby thanked her and followed Harry through to the restaurant bar of the Bluebell. She wasn't sure fun was quite the right word in the circumstances. But she was concerned about Harry. He had always struck her as one of the good guys.

20

A few minutes later, they'd bagged a wooden picnic-style table on the Bluebell's outside terrace. It had been a nice day, hot for the third week of May, and there was still a breath of warmth in the evening air. They sat beside a terracotta pot overspilling with spring flowers. There were tea lights flickering in glass pots on every table, although Ruby realised when she looked closer that they were electronic, not real.

A waiter brought them the drinks they'd ordered from the bar. Camomile for her and black coffee for him and Harry stirred his thoughtfully but didn't say anything. Ruby was just wondering whether he was regretting agreeing to this when he finally put down the teaspoon and looked at her.

'Sorry,' he said. 'I don't know where to start really. I don't know whether I'm coming or going. I'm not even sure I'm going to continue with Booty Busters. I'm in two minds.'

'But it's working really well for you, isn't it? How did you do tonight?'

'I lost five pounds.'

'Harry, that's amazing.'

He palmed his forehead with a hand. 'Yeah, I guess. But I haven't eaten much the last couple of days. I don't eat when I'm stressed.'

'There's always a bright side,' she said, and then instantly regretted it. Someone might have died for all she knew and here she was making crass, stupid remarks. 'Sorry,' she added. 'Tact isn't one of my strong points.'

'No, you're right.' A smile flickered briefly in his eyes. 'That is a bright side. Although it's also pretty ironic in the circumstances. I think I told you, didn't I, that it was my wife who encouraged me to join Booty Busters in the first place... she signed me up.'

'Yes, you did.' Gosh, Harry's wife had certainly been on a mission. She wondered if she'd discussed it with him first.

'Well, yesterday she filed for divorce.'

'Oh my gosh.' Ruby felt a surge of compassion for him. She fished the camomile teabag out of her cup and put it in the saucer. 'I'm very sorry to hear that. I'm assuming you weren't expecting it?'

He paused for a long moment before looking at her again. 'My instincts are to say no, I wasn't expecting it – I thought we were very happy, but on some level I'm not sure that's true. I think my wife had been unhappy for a while. And I think I knew that. But I didn't know what to do about it.'

Ruby sipped her tea. 'How long have you been married, if you don't mind me asking?'

'It will – would have been – our second wedding anniversary in August,' he told her.

Ruby was shocked. She'd had him down as an old happily married, possibly to his childhood sweetheart. She wasn't sure where that had come from, except that he'd always had that air about him. The air of someone who was very settled and comfortable, despite the fact that judging from a couple of his throwaway comments in the past, Mrs Small wasn't the most supportive of partners.

'Do you have children?' she asked gently.

'No.' He shook his head. 'We were trying for a family.' Pain flickered in his eyes and again Ruby's heart went out to him.

'Maybe it's just as well you didn't succeed.'

'I think you're right.'

For a while, they sat in the not quite silence of the terrace. And considering that they were barely more than acquaintances and that this was also quite an awkward situation, Ruby felt surprisingly comfortable.

Eventually Harry started talking again. It was as though now he'd opened the door a crack to his emotions he couldn't stop. He told her how he'd met Annabel at a posh wedding that he'd gone to with a work colleague.

'I didn't even know the guy that well, to be honest. But he was desperate for a plus-one. It was his cousin's wedding. His girlfriend, who was the original plus-one, had just dumped him and so he asked me to be his stand-in. He didn't want to go on his own because he didn't know anyone. Also, he told me there would be lots of attractive single women there.' Harry's eyes brightened at the memory. 'And he was right. I met Annabel about ten minutes after we got there. It was just like it was in the movies. Our eyes met across a crowded room and bam.'

'Wow,' Ruby said. 'It sounds incredibly romantic.'

'It was.' Harry sighed. 'I knew she was out of my league really. She had that kind of head-turning quality that celebrities have. Do you know what I mean?'

'Yes,' Ruby said, trying not to feel jealous. She was slowly putting together all the pieces she knew about the unknown Mrs Small. She sounded pretty controlling, judging by the way she'd blackmailed Harry into coming to Booty Busters. The fact that she was a head-turner made it easier to see how she got away with behaving badly. In fact, the more Ruby heard about her, the less she liked her.

But maybe she was being unfair. After all, she'd never even met the woman. And there were always two sides to every story.

'She sounds like a stunning lady,' Ruby said diplomatically.

'She was. She is.' Harry stopped talking and looked at her. 'Sorry. Are you sure you don't mind me...? I mean, we barely know each other. You're married, aren't you? With a little one. Won't your husband mind you being here?'

'I'm not married,' Ruby told him. 'My baby's father was though. An important fact he neglected to mention when we were dating.'

Harry's jaw dropped. 'I'm sorry. I just assumed...' He broke off and looked at her with concern in his eyes. 'That must have been very difficult.'

'It was for a while. But I'm over it. Simon, he's my son, is amazing. And I have a very supportive family. Simon's on a sleepover with my mum tonight. His first one. She helps out a lot.' She showed him the photo of Simon that was the wallpaper on her phone and Harry's eyes lit up with interest.

'What a handsome chap.' He looked a lot less sad than he had when they'd sat down. But he didn't seem in any hurry to leave and Ruby decided this was because he had no place better to go.

'What do you do?' she asked him, deciding she'd better change the subject away from babies, in case it was too tactless, given his hopes for a family. 'Job wise, I mean?'

He told her about Gargantuul and after a few seconds she stopped him.

'I think I met your grandfather once. Is his name George?'

'That's right. Well, it was. He passed away six years ago. Were you a client of his?'

'He was a client of mine,' Ruby said. 'Briefly. He bought a piece of artwork from me once. I took it to his house. He had a big place on top of a cliff, not a million miles from here. It was a Banksy,' she added.

'You sold him the Banksy.' He looked at her in amazement. 'I have that artwork in my house.' He shook his head. 'It's a long story, but, wow. I have it in my front room. I inherited it.'

'Small world.'

'Isn't it?' He was still looking a bit dumbfounded. 'Ruby Lambert. I knew that was your name, but I didn't put two and two together. You're an art dealer.'

'Please don't hold it against me,' she said lightly, and for a second he looked mortified.

'I wasn't. I mean, you have a great reputation.' Then he laughed. 'You're teasing me.'

'I am. I'm sorry. I can't help myself. My sister, Olivia, says I'm too direct. I should edit my thoughts before I blurt them out.'

'Oh, please don't edit them on my account. I love direct.'

This was obviously true. It fascinated her how his feelings ran across his face. He was a strange mixture, she thought. Now she knew who he was, grandson of George Small, the founder of the huge software company, Gargantuul, she found it even more surprising that he wore his heart on his sleeve.

'Did you go straight into the family business? Or did you rebel and do something else?' she asked him.

'I'm not the rebellious kind,' Harry told her, and fleetingly he looked as though he regretted that. 'No, I've worked in the business since I left uni. I love it. I love people. I love the thrill of the chase, the adrenaline, the pressure, the buzz of closing a deal.'

Ruby saw in his eyes the same passion that she felt about the art world. The way he lit up when he talked about it, every bit of him engaged. That bright intelligence in his dark eyes and the small crinkles around them when he smiled. There was not an ounce of artifice about him. It was incredibly attractive.

She leaned forward and touched his arm. 'It's wonderful making a living at the work you would do for nothing, isn't it?'

'Yes it is.' Just for a second, they were totally connected. Locked into a bubble in which they were the only two people in the world. Ruby was totally aware of him, his dark eyes, his warmth, the charisma that people only had when they were completely themselves.

Wow, he's hot, said a little voice in her head.

He's married, she reminded herself. *Albeit, not very happily.*

He's still married. Down, girl.

They weren't the only two people in the world – or even on the Bluebell Cliffs terrace. There were a sprinkling of other people out here and the restaurant was still quite full. Occasionally there was the clink of knives and forks as a table was cleared or a burst of muted laughter from a group of people sitting near the walkway close to the lawns.

The air smelled of the sea and the scents of the flowers from the tub close to their table and Ruby realised the sky had got dark since they'd come out. Not that it was dark where they were. There were floodlights dotted about, sending pools of light across the outdoor space. The tea lights on every table flickered like little stars and, above their heads, the real stars flickered too, while the pale curved slice of a new silver moon sailed high in the sky.

The night air was getting cooler. Ruby glanced at her watch, aware that she was still wearing her workout gear. And she realised with a start that they'd been sitting talking for nearly two hours. How had that happened? She didn't want to move. She didn't want to break the moment, come back down into reality. She glanced at him.

'Sorry,' he said. 'I've kept you too long.' He shifted in his seat.

'But thank you. It's been lovely to talk with you.' He dropped his gaze. He had very long, dark eyelashes. 'It's really helped.'

'It's been lovely to talk with you too,' Ruby said, liking the way he said 'with' and not 'to', because although it was only a turn of phrase, it was how Harry was. He didn't talk to you or at you, he talked with you. A collaborative conversation. She had dated so many men across the years who'd thought it was perfectly accept- able behaviour to spout above themselves for hours and to fill every silence with chatter. Harry was comfortable with silences, as well as directness, it seemed.

He was getting up, reaching for his sports bag and Ruby got up too.

'Do you think you'll come to Booty Busters again or is this the last time we'll see you?' she asked him, trying to keep her voice light because suddenly the thought he might not come again filled her with an aching sadness.

'I'll be coming again.' He paused. 'It's weird actually, but although I started coming here for Annabel, I am also aware that it's been good for me. I did need to lose weight. I did need to get fitter and I'm enjoying doing both of those things.'

'You're now doing it for yourself, not for Annabel then?' Ruby queried.

He looked fleetingly surprised. 'Yeah. I guess I am.'

In the dark car park at the front of the Bluebell, he saw her safely to her vehicle and said goodbye once more before striding away towards his.

Ruby watched his tail lights drawing out of the car park, which now felt curiously empty. As though he had left behind a huge Harry-shaped hole.

Ruby felt stiff from sitting on the hard wooden picnic bench and she was suddenly aware that she hadn't even showered after the workout. Keen to get to the weigh-in session, she'd planned to do that when she got home. Her make-up never survived workouts so she would definitely not have been looking her best.

It was so strange. At face value, this evening had been a coffee between two diet buddies who'd agreed to help each other out with mutual support. And yet somehow, in some mysterious way that she couldn't begin to explain, sitting with Harry beside a tub of spring flowers, talking as the night air cooled around them, had been one of the most lovely and comfortable evenings of her life.

21

Harry had gone to Booty Busters for two reasons. The first one because he had no place better to go and he did not want to stay in an empty house. There had been no word from Annabel. The second one, as he'd told Ruby, was because he'd more or less made up his mind to tell Saskia that he was going to jack it in.

He'd been less inclined to do this after he'd done the workout, which had lifted his mood, as they usually did, and after he'd realised he'd lost another five pounds. Harry was aware that his clothes were looser. He'd needed to pull in the belt on his trousers a couple of holes.

Ruby was right, he mused, as he drew in through his electronic gates at the end of the evening. He may have started this whole health and fitness kick for his wife, but he was doing it for himself now.

As he let himself into the silent house, his thoughts flicked back to the evening he'd just spent with Ruby. When she'd asked him if he was OK, if he'd like to talk about it, he'd been tempted to say he was fine, just a tough day at work. But something in her face had stopped him. She'd looked so sweetly concerned and he knew from experience that Ruby was not a judgemental sort of girl. She was not like any woman he had met before. She was something of an enigma. She was confident without being aloof, and friendly without being flirty. These were the hallmarks of a woman who was comfortable with herself. And he'd assumed she was married. He guessed, mostly because he knew she had a young kiddie. Finding out she wasn't had been a surprise.

It had been even more of a surprise to find out that she was Ruby Lambert, the art dealer who'd sold his grandfather the Banksy. He remembered when Grandpa George had got that painting. He'd invited the whole family round, ostensibly to dinner, but in reality so he could show it off. Grandpa George wasn't a boastful sort of man. He wasn't flashy around his wealth, but he'd been really proud of his new acquisition.

'I never thought I'd own something as edgy and satirical,' he had told them all as they had stood in the dining room where the artwork was hung, and his chest had puffed out with pride. 'I like this boy's style. He's not afraid to speak out about what he believes in.' He had patted his son on the shoulder. 'This picture will be yours one day, son.'

Harry had watched his father nodding thoughtfully in that quiet way he had. He'd looked pleased. Harry had known that the painting would one day belong to him too, one of the other things his grandfather had said was that he wished it to be passed down to future generations of Smalls, but that day had seemed light years away. He'd never have guessed that less than a decade later it would be hanging on his own lounge wall.

When he'd first inherited it, he'd considered putting it in a vault. It had already increased in value hugely and there was a part of him that had wondered about the wisdom of keeping a painting that was worth several times more than his house on his lounge wall. But it was amazing how quickly he'd grown used to the idea and it was odd how quickly he'd forgotten that it had such monetary value and wasn't just another adornment.

It had impressed Annabel too. He remembered the way her hand had shot to her mouth when he'd showed it to her.

'You mean it's actually an original Banksy. Oh my God, Harry, that must be worth millions. Think of the house you could buy if you sold it.'

'I like this house,' he'd told her. 'Besides, I don't see it as mine. I see it as a gift for my future children. Grandpa George always wanted it to stay in the family. And that's what I want too.'

She had laughed lightly in that cute way she had that always lifted his spirits, then she'd stood up on her tiptoes and hugged him. 'Oh, Harry, you are so sweet and adorable.'

Harry came back to the present with a jolt. The echo of Annabel's silky laughter stayed in his mind like some ghostly taunt. The days when Annabel had thought him sweet and adorable were gone. If indeed they had ever been real at all.

He was beginning to realise deep down in a place he'd never thought he'd delve into that they hadn't been real. Annabel had never loved him. He must have been a means to an end, although he still wasn't quite sure why that was. Aside from the visit he'd had from her solicitor yesterday morning, there had been no word from Annabel. But doubtless he would be sent a list of her demands soon.

He supposed that the one saving grace, as Ruby had said, was that he and Annabel hadn't had children. That would have made the whole thing so much more unbearably painful.

* * *

A few days later, Harry was sitting in his office when Victoria asked if she could put through a call to him.

Victoria was the only one of his staff who knew what was happening at home. As far as the rest of them were concerned, it was business as usual. Harry trusted his PA utterly. She had worked for his family for so many years and she wasn't a gossip.

'Who is it?' he asked. 'It's not that smarmy solicitor again, is it?' The one thing he hadn't told her was that Nick Lewison was Annabel's lover as well as her solicitor. He couldn't bring himself to admit that to anyone. It was too damn painful.

'He says his name's Clifford Brown. Will I put him through, or will I tell him to call back?'

'Please put him through,' Harry said and a few seconds later he heard his old friend's voice. 'Hello,' he said cautiously. 'Long time no speak. I think that's probably my fault. Apologies. How are you?'

'I'm good, thanks, Harry.' Clifford sounded a little troubled. 'And no need to apologise. Is this a good time? Victoria said you were free.'

'It's as good a time as any. I just stopped for coffee.'

'I won't keep you long, but I heard on the grapevine...' He paused. 'Don't take this the wrong way. I heard that you and Annabel had decided to part.'

'News travels fast.' Jeez, it had only been a matter of days!

'My sister recently started working for Lewison's Solicitors,' Clifford went on without preamble. 'That's the only reason I know anything about it. I don't think it's common knowledge. Jess is training there as a legal sec – just like Annabel did.'

'I see.' Harry felt a tug of pain, despite himself. 'So did Jess tell you that Annabel has appointed her lover as her solicitor too.' He was amazed that his voice came out so calm and flat. Because that was not how he felt.

'She didn't mention that bit, no...' Clifford said, hesitating again. 'Just the bit about her appointing Nick. Not the rest. Jess said they were close but not...' He cleared his throat and sounded embarrassed. 'Look, I was phoning to warn you that Nick Lewison is not one to play it fair. Well, just that really. I was phoning to warn you. The man's a weasel. Watch your back.'

'Thanks, mate. I've already met him.' Something was clicking in his brain. 'When you said that Annabel trained there as a legal sec, that was a slip of the tongue, right?'

'Um, no. That's her job. Senior legal sec, right?' Clifford sounded surprised. 'Why?'

Harry sighed. 'She told me she was a solicitor,' he said quietly. 'I've always thought that was what she did.'

'You never checked?'

'No. Why would I? I took her at face value. I knew where she worked. I don't think I ever questioned anything she told me.'

When Harry put the phone down a few minutes later, his head was still reeling. He'd been a fool. A total and utter fool. He'd been blinded by Annabel's beauty from the moment they'd met. He'd been flattered that she'd been interested in him. This stunning woman who was also a hotshot solicitor. That was what she'd said. He'd seen no reason to question it or to check up on her. He had never once looked at the solicitor's website. He pulled it up now and scrolled along to 'Meet The Team'. He scanned the names.

Nick Lewison – Position: Managing director/solicitor.

There were several other names. Some of them were listed as chartered legal executives. But Annabel's name was not on the list.

He scrolled through to the bottom of the page and there she was.

Annabel Dickens – Position: Senior legal secretary.

Wow, so she wasn't even using her married name. Unless she had literally just changed it back.

Harry got up wearily and went through to Victoria's office. 'I need to go out for a bit. Can you hold all my calls, please? I'll give you an update later.'

'I'll do that.' She gave him a keen look, but asked no questions. Harry was grateful for that.

* * *

Harry drove the Lexus out of the car park with no real idea where he was going. He just wanted to gather his thoughts and he couldn't do that in his office. He needed to think. Or, to be more precise, he needed to piece together which bits of what he'd always thought to be true were actually true and which bits were nonsense. Fabrications from Annabel.

Driving helped him to think, but he had discovered lately that walking was even better. As he set off through the hot blue day, he found himself unconsciously heading for the coast.

It was a Friday and the roads were busy, but not as busy as they'd be later, so he avoided Swanage and kept driving out along the coast road. An hour later, he got to Durdle Door and he pulled into the big clifftop car park.

Durdle Door was one of Dorset's most dramatic coastal landmarks. It was a 200-foot-high arch hewn out of rock that jutted out from the coastline into the sea. One of nature's icons, Harry thought, and a demonstration of the sea's relentless power as it shaped the coastline to its will. It had always been one of Harry's favourite places. It had been the site of many a picnic spot when he'd been growing up. His parents had always been happy to lug a picnic down onto the sand below which was accessed by steps which always seemed a lot easier to go down than they were to come back up at the end of the day, even with the picnic box decimated.

Harry parked the Lexus and swapped his office shoes for the spare pair of trainers he'd kept in his car since he'd joined Booty Busters, just in case he wanted to get in an extra walk. It was surprising how quickly he'd started to enjoy the exercise. He headed towards the edge of the cliff, where he could see the waves smashing on the rocks far below and swirling through the arch in a froth of white spray. The tide was in, so there was barely any beach today. There were a lot of tourists here, despite it being so early in the season. Or at least there were a lot of cars. Their occupants must all be walking on the cliff path. Harry set off to join them.

It was good to walk. It was windy and he was buffeted by the salt breeze and the soundtrack of the sea in his ears. The endless roar of the waves crashing on the shore and the mournful cries of the gulls was soothing.

He passed hikers and the occasional dog walker, but no couples and for that he was glad. He had thought he would be with Annabel for the duration. He had dreamed they would marry, have children and bring them to places like this. They had talked about it in those very early days. Annabel wanted a little boy, she said, because the bond between a mother and her son was one of the strongest.

Harry hadn't minded what gender their children were. As long as they were healthy, it wouldn't have mattered to him. He'd fantasised though, in those heady early days about having a girl, who'd inherited Annabel's beauty, and a boy who would grow up with her integrity. It was odd how he'd always thought she'd had integrity. Part of that had come because she'd told him she'd wanted to be a solicitor ever since she was a little girl so she could help people. He had lapped it all up. Every single word. Only now did he wonder what other lies she had told him. She had said very early on in their relationship that her parents had died in a car crash when she was seventeen. She had told him this with a slight break in her voice and he had put his arms around her and held her tightly.

'Don't you have any other relatives? Any aunts, uncles, cousins?'

'No, Harry I don't.' Her huge blue eyes had brimmed with tears. 'There's just you.'

Had any of it ever been true?

Certainly no relatives had come to the wedding. Harry's mother had thought that very strange, but he had begged her not to raise it with his wife-to-be because he had been scared of upsetting her. His mother, who was not one to be easily fobbed off, had pressed him, saying, 'There must be someone, Harry. Surely?'

'What do you think I should do? Hire an investigator to check?'

'Of course I don't think that.'

'Then, leave it, Mum. Or we'll take off to some foreign beach and get married there.'

She had agreed, clearly exasperated, but knowing her only son well enough to realise he might actually carry out that threat.

He'd been so in love, Harry thought, that his strong matriarch of a mother had humoured him.

Now, as Harry walked with the scent of the sea in his nostrils and the well-worn path hard beneath the soles of his trainers, little stones occasionally skittering away from his feet, he felt the deep ache of betrayal. Not just for the future that Annabel had snatched away from him, but for the loss of the past. He had thought the past was incontrovertible. Watertight. No one could take happy memories from you. They were set in stone. But that wasn't true, was it? None of the past had been what he had thought.

Annabel hadn't been the hotshot solicitor he had believed her to be. She hadn't had independent means – he'd always relied on this a little heavily as proof that she must love him for himself. He'd insisted on paying for her car when she'd told him she'd put a deposit on it. He'd even covered the deposit, telling her to keep her money, he could afford it. Which, of course, he could. Not that it was about the money, it never had been. He would have happily bought her anything her heart desired. It was the lies and the deceit that had upended him so utterly and completely.

It seemed to him now that nothing of what she'd told him had been true. Annabel hadn't just wiped out his future hopes and dreams when she'd told him she wanted a divorce, she had destroyed all of the happy past memories too. None of it had ever been real.

22

Since Ruby's chat with Harry after Booty Busters last week, they had exchanged a few texts. Mostly of the 'keep your chin up' variety from her and the 'thanks, I'm good' from him.

They'd also had one brief phone call when Ruby had found herself fighting a major sugar craving one day after a night when Simon had kept her up because he'd had a tummy upset. His tummy had settled down by morning, thankfully, but she'd barely got any sleep and by the following afternoon all she had wanted was a sugar fix. This wouldn't have been so bad as she hadn't kept sweet temptations in the house since she'd been dieting. But then she had found a leftover Easter egg at the top of a kitchen cupboard she rarely opened.

It was a Smarties egg and quite small – the kind Dad might have got her as a joke because all of the family knew she loved Smarties. Doubtless, she'd been sidetracked by the posh eggs Aunt Dawn always bought and this one had been put to one side for later and then been stuffed in a cupboard and forgotten. Easter had been early this year and she hadn't been dieting back then, but even so, Easter eggs were one of her weaknesses.

As soon as Ruby had discovered the egg, her inner demons had begun to taunt her.

It's so small. It can't be that many calories.

You've been doing so well. You deserve that egg.

Ruby had gone backwards and forwards to the cupboard. Then she'd phoned Becky, planning to ask her slimming friend for some tips on how to resist. But Becky's phone had been constantly engaged.

In the end, Ruby had phoned Harry and he had talked her out of eating the egg with a mix of sternness laced with humour.

'Where exactly is the Easter egg now?' That was the first thing he'd asked.

'It's in front of me on the worktop. It's still in its box.'

She had reached out towards it, and as if he could somehow see her, he'd barked, 'Don't touch it.'

She snatched her fingers back.

'Step away from the Easter egg.'

'Yes, but, Harry, it's not very big. It can't have that many calories. What I was thinking was that maybe if I skipped one of Mr B's meals and had the egg instead, plus if I also did an extra workout, then maybe that would counteract it.'

'I like your thinking.'

'Then, you agree. You think it would be OK to do it?'

'I didn't say that. I said I liked your thinking. But that's probably because it's exactly like mine when I'm in denial about something and am trying to persuade myself that I'm not.'

'What are you in denial about?' she had asked him curiously.

'That's a long story, but trust me, I am a master at the art of denial.'

'So, what do you think I should do?'

'I think you already know that, Ruby. If you didn't already know exactly what to do with that egg, you'd never have phoned me.

You'd have already gobbled it up and hidden the wrapper at the bottom of the bin so as to keep the whole denial thing going.'

'I do not gobble,' she said, outraged. 'Nibble maybe. In a lady-like fashion.' Hell, was she flirting with him?

He laughed. 'OK. I admit it. I'm judging you by my own stan-dards. I'd have gobbled. But it's the same end result. Nibble, gobble, chew, consume, munch, chomp, whatever you do, the outcome is the same. The number on the scales goes up. The waistband gets tighter. Your goal of being a skinny bridesmaid falls by the wayside.'

'OK, OK, you've talked me out of it. Easter egg being trans-ported to the bin.'

'The outside bin.'

'Yes. All right, the outside bin.'

Ruby had thrown the Easter egg away and then stood beside the bin smiling. She had never thought she'd be able to do that, but she had.

She also loved that Harry understood exactly why the bin was the only place the egg could go. Someone who wasn't a foodie would have told her to just put it back in the cupboard and give it to someone else – her mother maybe. Or Olivia. They wouldn't have understood that if she'd done that it wouldn't have worked. The Easter egg would have called to her constantly, as persistent and relentless as a siren luring sailors onto rocks, until she'd succumbed. Only a foodie who struggled with their weight would ever understand this.

Now, on Tuesday evening, Ruby smiled at the memory. Thanks to sticking exactly to Mr B's plan once more, she'd had another good week. She was really looking forward to Booty Busters. She kept telling herself that this was because she'd lost another three pounds according to her scales. Which meant that she'd have lost ten pounds in total from her starting weight. Only another four pounds to go before she hit the stone landmark, which would be on week six if she repeated last week's success. That would be worth celebrating. Particularly in view of what had happened after their first week on the plan. In fact it was worth a major celebration.

The excited anticipation she was feeling as she left for Booty Busters had nothing to do with the fact that Ruby knew she'd see Harry there. Or so she kept telling herself. She had a horrible feeling that she may be in denial about this too.

The more she got to know him, the more she liked him. But she couldn't afford to fall for Harry Small. For a start, he was still married. He was about to embark on a messy, painful divorce by the sound of it. The last thing he'd want was another relationship. And even if he did, Ruby knew that rebound relationships never worked.

It was typical that, despite being slightly late for Booty Busters instead of early, Harry was the first person she saw. He usually arrived pretty promptly too. But tonight he pulled into the car park just in front of her.

They got out of their vehicles simultaneously.

'I thought I was late,' he said, his face friendly as he waited for her.

'Me too.'

They fell into step beside each other.

'I take it there have been no more huge temptations cropping up in Ruby's life?' he asked her.

Only you, she thought. 'No, none,' she told him. 'And thank you for talking me out of that one.'

'I was only doing what you did for me. So, I'd like to thank you again, too. How do you think you've done this week on the...' He patted his tum.

'I'm doing OK. Thanks in part to you. If Saskia's scales match mine at home, I think I'll have lost ten or eleven pounds, nearly a stone,' she said, as they reached the doors of the Bluebell Cliff.

'I'd say definitely. You can see it.' He gave her a swift appraising look and Ruby felt a tingle of longing. *Oh crap, if you can do that with your eyes alone.*

Stop that right there, she told herself a little breathlessly, only to find Harry looking puzzled.

'Sorry?'

Oh my God, had she said that last bit aloud? She felt her face flame red and distracted herself by rummaging in her sports bag. 'Just checking I've got my phone. Ah, I think I've left it in the car. I'll see you inside.' She ran back towards the car park and he nodded and went into the hotel.

Standing breathless by her SUV, Ruby realised that it was too late to deny the fact that she had fallen for Harry Small. Being anywhere near him set off a tingling awareness that she knew was the best kind of chemistry. He regularly dominated her thoughts. A couple of nights ago as she'd lain in bed, unguarded just before sleep, she imagined that he was lying next to her, and sleeping had been the last thing on her mind.

No doubt this fantasy had been sparked off by him confiding that his wife was divorcing him. But maybe it wasn't just that. Ruby knew she'd liked him for a while. He was a handsome, tummy-flipping, lovely, kind guy and the more she got to know him, the more she wanted to get to know him.

She shook her head to banish these unwelcome thoughts. Harry was vulnerable and he clearly saw her as a friend.

Certain now that he'd be in the studio, she went into the Bluebell Cliff.

'Welcome,' Saskia called to her as she headed into the studio. 'Right then, now we are all here. I want to run something past you.'

Oh heck. They must have been waiting for her. Ruby took up position on her usual mat.

'Before we begin,' Saskia continued, 'I wanted to let you know that Mr B is coming to touch base with us all next week. He's keen to get feedback on his meals. Which means that next week we're going to do things slightly differently. We will have the weigh-in first. In order to report back to Mr B.'

There were a few murmurs of assent. Although it seemed odd to make it a special announcement, Ruby thought.

'Now then,' Saskia continued, 'do any of you remember the first week we met when someone thought it would be a hugely hilarious joke to place the whoopee cushion beneath my workout mat?'

Everyone nodded. It wasn't the kind of thing they'd forget, Ruby thought.

Harry, who was standing alongside her, winked.

'It has taken me until now,' Saskia continued, looking around at them all, 'to track down the culprit. But I do now have some very good intelligence...' she tapped her nose, 'on who it might have been.'

'Mr B,' shouted Becky. 'How did you catch him? Did you find the whoopee cushion tucked inside a frying pan?'

'Something like that,' Saskia said. 'It wasn't in a frying pan. But it was hidden in something which did point, irrefutably, towards the Bluebell's esteemed chef. He thinks I've forgotten his little trick.' She leaned towards the microphone with a mischievous glint in her eyes. 'But I haven't. And I think it is payback time.'

'Definitely,' Ruby called. 'Do you by any chance need our help?'

'You've got mine,' Becky said. 'I'm always up for a bit of payback. As long as it's nothing too heinous.'

'I can assure you, it will not be heinous,' Saskia said. 'Just a little trick, that I think would be funny.'

'What do you need us to do?' Dana added.

'There's a great app you can get which makes it sound like someone is parping,' one of the younger women called out. 'My boyfriend put it on his boss's phone the other day. The whole office was in hysterics.'

'Appropriate as that might be, it could be difficult to implement,' Saskia said. 'Mr B guards his phone like a Rottweiler and it's password-protected with his fingerprint. I don't think we will be able to do anything that involves his phone.'

'Are we going to let his tyres down?' someone else called with a gleeful expression.

'No, nothing like that. We are not going to do anything that has lasting consequences.' Saskia leaned towards the microphone and her voice took on a conspiratorial tone as she said, 'Here's what I have in mind.' She outlined her plan and then at the end of it she said, 'Is everyone OK with that? If you'd rather not participate, please raise your hand. I totally understand.'

Ruby glanced around. It was crystal clear that there were no dissenters in the room. No one raised their hand.

'In that case,' Saskia said, 'we had better crack on.'

* * *

By 8.30 p.m., everyone had worked out and been weighed. It was another great week. Ruby saw Becky smiling and giving her the thumbs up as she came out and Ruby was more than happy with her three-pound loss. Harry seemed to have rushed off, so she couldn't ask him how he'd got on. She felt disappointed.

But then, when she reached the main entrance of the Bluebell, she saw that he was waiting for her.

'I've lost my first stone.' He sounded really pleased and he looked flushed from his achievement, although that could have been the workout. 'Do you – er – fancy a celebratory coffee on the terrace?'

Ruby hesitated. That was oh-so tempting. She could think of nothing she'd like more, but if she spent another evening in his company, she knew what would happen – she'd like him even more by the end of it. This was very dangerous territory.

'It's OK.' He pushed his hands into the pockets of his tracksuit. 'You're keen to get back to your little one. I totally get that.'

Ruby put on her cheeriest fake regretful voice. 'You're right. Another time, maybe?'

'Definitely.'

'That's brilliant news on your first stone. Congratulations.'

'Thanks.'

She hurried past him. She needed to get away before she changed her mind. It wouldn't take much.

'Ruby?' he called after her.

She pretended not to hear and speeded up. If she stopped, she knew that all would be lost. She would be suggesting they went for that celebratory coffee herself. She played out the next few scenes in her head. Coffee, then maybe a drink somewhere the following week, alcohol, and then dinner, low-calorie, of course, and the next thing she knew she'd have set herself up to be Harry's rebound relationship. Or even worse, she'd have fallen totally in love while he was still hankering after his wife. No way was that happening.

Harry stared after Ruby's retreating back. She was behaving as if she couldn't wait to get away from him. That was odd. He had thought they were becoming friends. He'd been planning to ask her how much she had lost this week.

Maybe she hadn't lost any. Despite resisting the Easter egg. Maybe she felt embarrassed, bless her. Especially as he'd been boasting about his stone. That had been tactless. He could have kicked himself. He would text her sometime over the next couple of days and see if he could put things right. The last thing he wanted to do was to upset Ruby. Right now, he needed all the friends he could get.

23

'Had you remembered that it's Mum and Dad's wedding anniversary on the fifth of June?' Olivia asked Ruby next time they spoke. 'Mum suggested we all go out for a meal to celebrate, but Aunt Dawn's had a better idea.'

'What is it?' Ruby asked, feeling her heart sink a little at the prospect of going out for a family meal. She could hardly take one of Mr B's meals with her and ask the chef to pop it in the microwave.

'She's invited us over to hers for a meal instead.'

'But isn't that going to be a lot of trouble for her? It would be better maybe if everyone came here.'

'No, it's fine. I have a cunning plan,' Olivia said happily. 'Obviously I don't want Aunt Dawn doing all the work, so my plan is that we have tapas and we all make a dish to take. That way we can all chip in. You can take one of Mr B's dishes, so you'll be set up, and Phil and I might also bring one of Mr B's dishes too, being as we'll have only finished filming the day before and it might be tricky to make something. But don't worry, I'll make sure they are diet-friendly.'

'You are lovely, Liv,' Ruby said. 'Thank you. Tapas is a brilliant idea. What shall we get them for a present? Do you know what anniversary it is?'

'Aunt Dawn seems to think it's their forty-second or forty-third. So it's flaming amazing.'

'What, that Dad's been able to put up with Mum all that time?' Ruby quipped.

'Yes. And vice versa. Seriously though, they're made for each other, aren't they? I hope Phil and I are going to be like that. I feel as though I've found him so late in life.'

'Everyone gets married later these days.' There was a pause during which Ruby tried to think of a tactful way of asking how her sister was getting on with the fertility drugs.

Olivia picked up on her hesitation, but misinterpreted it. 'I haven't said anything about your IVF suggestion yet. We haven't actually seen that much of each other lately.' There was a sigh in her voice. 'I will though.'

'Whenever you're ready, Liv.'

'Thanks. Thanks again. Anyway, back to the present for Mum and Dad. I was thinking maybe some kind of experience would be good for a change. You know, like one of those Virgin Experience Days. Or do you think we should get them something more solid. What did we do for their fortieth?'

'We got them that engraved fossil thing on a plaque, didn't we?'

'Oh God, yes, of course we did. They loved that.'

'Yes, but they've probably got enough rocks in that house. And they move them all into the summer house when they rent it out – to make sure no one nicks them. I'm surprised the wooden floor doesn't collapse under the weight of them.'

They both laughed. 'An experience day sounds great, Liv. What did you have in mind? A day at the races?' Ruby wasn't being entirely serious about this. She had her tongue firmly in her cheek.

The only experiences their parents were interested in were fossil related ones, or, more recently, grandchild-related ones, but Olivia didn't notice.

'Maybe not the races. Maybe some kind of cooking thing for both of them. Dad was saying the other day that he fancies learning to cook Italian.'

'Are you sure he didn't mean learn how to put a pizza in the oven? Mum's always complaining that he doesn't know how to switch it on.'

'He does a mean breakfast. But no, Mum said he actually fancies learning to cook properly. He's planning to tone things down a bit after the wedding, he says. As in, not go on so many digs.'

'I'll believe that when I see it. He said the same thing when Simon was born.' Ruby bit her lip. She'd been disappointed that all that had changed was that their father went away on his own on digs instead of with his wife.

'I think he misses Mum,' Olivia added.

'Well, here's hoping. I'd love to see more of Dad. But yes, OK, some kind of experience sounds great. I'll do some research if you like. I have a lot more time than you.'

'Are you sure? You've got Simon? How is he? And how's the diet going?'

'Simon is adorable and the diet is going very well. Fingers crossed, I'll have lost a stone by next Tuesday or the week after.'

'Wow, that's been so quick. That's amazing.'

'It's week six. It's not that quick.'

'Well, it sounds very quick to me. Well done.'

'I am thrilled,' Ruby conceded. 'Although it hasn't happened yet. Wish me luck. We're all doing pretty well actually.' She hesitated, wondering whether to tell her sister about the coffee she'd had with Harry.

There must have been some kind of telepathy at play because

Olivia said softly, 'How's the Ben Affleck lookalike getting on? Does he still go?'

'He does. He's getting divorced.' Why had she said that? It was completely irrelevant.

'Is he now? That's sad.'

'Isn't it?' Ruby said, crashing back down to earth. Because Olivia was right. It was sad. And it was nothing to do with her. She felt suddenly ashamed that she'd been flirting with Harry, however harmless it had seemed. She felt even more ashamed that she'd been fantasising about having a relationship with him. It was high time she grew up and accepted the fact that romance was off the table for her. At least it was until Simon was at least eighteen and heading off to university. Maybe she would think about it then.

'You've gone quiet,' Olivia said.

'Have I? I was just thinking about anniversary presents for the folks,' Ruby lied.

'Good,' said Olivia. 'I'd better go. Let me know if you see anything that strikes you as the perfect present.'

'Will do.'

They said their goodbyes and hung up and Ruby got on with the routines of her day, which revolved around her son. When he was asleep that afternoon, she logged in to her laptop and searched 'Experience Days'. There were one or two work emails she needed to look at too. The company might jog along pretty well without her actively doing any selling, but there were still clients who wanted her attention. And they usually wanted it immediately. Not when she got round to checking her emails.

* * *

Harry was also fielding emails, but they were emails of a much more intrusive nature. They were emails from Annabel's solicitor.

Or, rather, some minion at the company, sending them on her solicitor's behalf, he thought, annoyed, asking question after question about his financial situation. He still hadn't spoken to Annabel. She had either changed her number or blocked him on her phone. He wasn't sure which. His emails to her, asking if they could meet and discuss things instead of going through solicitors, had also bounced back to him with undeliverable address responses.

He had contemplated contacting her friend, Meg Price, but had decided against it. Meg was unlikely to tell him where she was. Meg would protect her friend and Harry guessed that Annabel didn't want to speak to him because then she would have to explain herself. Explain her lies. Explain her motivation for marrying him. Maybe she did have some pangs of conscience about that after all.

He hoped that she did. In his darker moments, he hoped that they kept her awake at night. In his more accepting moments, he realised that he didn't wish her any ill. The one thing he didn't hope for, though, was a reconciliation. That ship had sailed. Annabel could have crawled back to him begging for forgiveness, begging him to take her back and he'd have said no.

He might not wish her any ill, but he did wish he had never met her. He was done with relationships. No way would he ever allow himself to be that vulnerable again. His solicitor had advised him to change the locks on the house and the passcode on the electronic gates to prevent Annabel from going there without his consent and he had done both of these things immediately.

Interestingly, when he'd checked, he had realised that Annabel had already removed much of her stuff. Her huge collection of shoes, bags and clothes had been thinned out to the bare minimum and he remembered her saying a few weeks back that she'd decided on a wardrobe downsize so she could catch up with this season's styles. He just hadn't guessed what her motives were.

Annabel's approach to their divorce seemed to be to get her

solicitor to send as many emails as possible to his solicitor, which were then forwarded to him. Harry guessed this was designed to cost him the maximum amount of money. Presumably Annabel didn't have to pay her lover to send emails. He could fire them off from dawn until dusk without her incurring a penny.

Maybe she hoped to wear him down so he agreed to whatever settlement she had in mind. He didn't know what that was yet. But Clifford had been right about Lewison playing dirty. The grounds that Annabel had chosen to divorce him were 'unreasonable behaviour' and they had cited dozens of examples which made painful reading.

Harry realised belatedly why Annabel had used the word so often during their marriage. He was beginning to think she may have planned to divorce him from the beginning. That it had only ever been about fleecing him for money. It saddened him that he'd gone from 'gullible fool' to 'cynical sceptic' so swiftly.

Her words echoed back to him in the listings.

'Snoring is unreasonable behaviour.'

'Leaving your dirty washing (presumably she meant socks), lying around for me to clear up is unreasonable behaviour.'

'Eating biscuits in bed and leaving me to clear up the crumbs is unreasonable behaviour.' He racked his brains to remember if he'd ever done that more than once.

'Cheating and lying is unreasonable behaviour.'

'Poking around in the wheelie bin for food is unreasonable behaviour.'

He still felt shame when he remembered that video. Even though every rational, logical part of him knew that this was crazy. He hadn't been doing anything that warranted shame. But it didn't help. He felt it when he remembered the contempt on her face. And no amount of rationalising seemed to make any difference.

Adultery is unreasonable behaviour, his mother said, when they were talking about it one evening. His mother had been furious with Annabel when Harry had told her what had happened. He'd seen a flash of, 'I told you so' in her eyes but she had been too gracious to voice it. 'Maybe you should just counter-petition her with that?'

'I have no proof,' Harry said. 'She's going to deny it. I've already checked with the hotel where she and Lewison stayed when they went to the conference. They had separate rooms.'

'Of course they did,' Elise said with ice in her voice. 'I'm surprised she even told you about it.'

'I don't think she really planned to tell me.' He could still remember the painful things she had said when he'd asked her when she had slept with Nick. '*It was probably at the exact same time you were foraging for chocolate in the bin. Can you blame me?*'

No way could he share this with his mother.

'She's simply trying to wear you down, son,' Elise said with a hardness to her voice that he rarely heard. 'I know you want this over with. Heaven knows, I do too. But don't roll over and give her everything she wants. She is the guilty party, not you.'

'There's another factor that's going to determine how much money she can claim,' he added slowly. 'Do you remember that time, very early on in our marriage, when she introduced me to Leonard Stanley, he worked at SmithKline Beecham?'

'Vaguely, why? What's the relevance of that?'

'About six months later, we signed a big contract with SmithK-line and Annabel is claiming she's the reason we got the contract with them. She made the introduction.'

'But surely that doesn't entitle her to any money?'

'It may entitle her to an introductory fee. Like a finder's fee. Leonard Stanley wasn't the guy we ended up dealing with, but we certainly spoke to him.' He shrugged. 'Unless I can prove there was another reason we got that contract, i.e., we'd have got it anyway.'

His mother looked outraged and Harry frowned.

'I was warned that her solicitor would play dirty.'

'Warned by whom?'

'My old friend, Clifford Brown. You might remember him? His sister started working at Lewison's a few months ago. He phoned me to warn me.'

Elise gave him a long look. 'Yes, I do remember Clifford. Nice chap.' She paused. 'I am sorry, son. You don't deserve this.'

'I shouldn't have been so gullible, should I?'

'There's a saying isn't there.' She patted his shoulder which was the most demonstrative his mother ever got. 'Love makes fools of us all.'

The one silver lining on the clouds that seemed to be shadowing his life at the moment, Harry thought, was that the weight was dropping off him.

He was still on the Booty Busters regime, and he was glad of it because cooking was not something he fancied contemplating, but he hadn't been making it up when he'd told Ruby that stress stole his appetite. He could rarely finish Mr B's generously portioned meals at the moment.

He was walking a lot too. Walking helped to clear his head. Four out of five times when he left work, he drove out to the coast path instead of going home. Walking along the well-worn tracks with the scent of gorse and fresh air in his nostrils and the sounds of the tide and the endless seagulls calling gave Harry a peace it was difficult to find elsewhere.

It also saved him from having to go back to an empty house. Because, despite everything, it was still a major adjustment, the change from being one half of a married couple to living a solitary, bachelor lifestyle. Most of Annabel's stuff might be gone, but her ghosts were everywhere.

There was still half a tube of her expensive organic toothpaste in the bathroom, although her electric toothbrush had gone. There was a pack of her Moroccan mint infusion tea by the kettle. And, of course, there was the space beside him in the double bed. He had moved back into the marital bed – it was infinitely more comfortable than the guest room bed – but he had changed all the bedding. There would be no more rose-patterned Egyptian cotton bed linen. Harry had reverted to one of the sage green John Lewis sets that he'd used before he'd got married. He had about four of them in various forest shades.

In some ways, it had surprised him how easy it was to revert to the man he had been before, although he also knew that there was a part of him that would be for ever and irrevocably changed.

24

Ruby and Olivia decided on a couple's cookery lesson for their parents' anniversary present in the end. It was an Italian cookery lesson which they knew their parents would love. Italian being their favourite meal. Aunt Dawn had also greenlit this idea, Olivia told Ruby. It was interesting how many film-orientated phrases had crept into Olivia's vocabulary since she'd been starring in *Nightingales*, Ruby thought. She often said things like, learning her lines, or a project being greenlit, when the context was something entirely different from filming. Ruby had got used to her sister appearing as the troubled Lucinda Fox on the hospital drama each week now, but it was still quite mind-blowing, knowing that Olivia Lambert was a household name. At least she was in households that watched popular soaps, which was a huge percentage of the country.

Ruby was really looking forward to the tapas anniversary celebrations at the smallholding. They hadn't had many family get-togethers lately – the larger their family got, the trickier it was to get them all in one place at the same time and this had been complicated even more by Olivia and Phil's filming schedules. It would be great to meet up.

But before the anniversary meal, she was hoping to lose her first stone and to bask in the warmth of Saskia's congratulations. She was also looking forward, with some gleeful anticipation she had to confess, to the tricking of Mr B, which would also be happening this Tuesday.

By some synchronicity, just as she and Harry had both turned up a little late last week, this week they both turned up a little early. Once again, Ruby found herself following his silver Lexus into the car park. At this rate, he'd think she was stalking him, waiting up the road somewhere, parked behind a hedge, so she could follow him in.

No, he wouldn't. That was just her overactive imagination kicking off again. Besides, there weren't many hedges you could hide behind as you approached the Bluebell.

Once again, he waited for her to get out of her SUV.

'This feels like déjà vu,' he said, his eyes meeting hers.

'I was just thinking the same thing.' He still looked pretty stressed. Bless him. 'How's it all going?' she asked as they walked side by side towards the Bluebell. 'Are you still having a divorce?'

Crap, that had come out wrong and he looked taken aback. She wanted to clap her hand over her mouth. Like it was any of her business.

'Sorry, Harry. I should have edited that.'

'No, you shouldn't. It's fine. And yes, sadly I am. And it's not getting any less stressful.'

'No, I don't suppose it is.' She shot him a sympathetic glance. 'How's the diet going?'

'Nice recovery,' he acknowledged lightly. 'I'm pleased to report that's one part of my life that's going swimmingly.' He paused. 'How about you? I must admit I was concerned when you dashed off so quickly last week. I thought maybe you'd had a bad week. I planned to text you. But I've been so wrapped up with everything that's going on in my life that I forgot. Apologies.'

'You definitely do not need to apologise,' she said, reddening when she remembered what had happened. She had run away because she didn't trust herself to spend the evening with him without it going any further. What planet had she even been on? It was crystal clear to her now that Harry was desperately sad about his divorce. It was written around his eyes in tiredness lines. He was probably still hoping for a reconciliation with his head-turner of a wife.

They'd reached the front doors which swished open automatically and he gestured her ahead of him.

'It will be interesting to see how Mr B reacts to Saskia's payback plan,' he said quietly as they went into the foyer. 'That's assuming she still plans to go ahead with what we agreed.'

'I guess we're about to find out,' Ruby acknowledged. 'I'll see you in the weigh-in queue.'

Ruby usually got changed into her workout kit before she arrived, but tonight she hadn't. She'd also brought a change of clothes so she could shower at the Bluebell. Her mum had asked if she could keep Simon for the night again and Ruby had thought she might ask Becky if she fancied a quick walk along the cliffs after the workout – or if not a walk, she might be able to persuade her to have a celebration coffee in the bar. Presuming she'd lost the stone she was hoping for, that was, and had something to celebrate.

She had, she discovered, less than ten minutes later. Saskia had rocketed through the weigh-in queue tonight.

'Congratulations, Ruby,' she'd said, sounding almost as

delighted as Ruby felt. 'That is really great work. You're nearly halfway to your target, aren't you?'

'I know. And I can really feel the difference. Thank you so much.'

'None of it is down to me. It is your own hard work and the effort you have put in. Congratulations. So what path are you on?'

'The easiest path,' Ruby said, without a trace of self-consciousness because she was so high on the success of achievement.

'Correct. Now, I think you are the last one in the queue, so it is time to play a trick on Mr B.'

* * *

There was an air of expectation in the group tonight as Saskia welcomed them all and reminded them that Mr B would be dropping in for his catch-up on their progress at seven-thirty sharp.

He was nothing if not punctual. At seven twenty-nine precisely, Mr B appeared.

'Good evening, everyone.' He was clearly in a good mood as he stepped up to the microphone. 'I trust you are all well.' There were mutters of assent. 'And I trust the meals are to your satisfaction.' He rubbed his hands together. 'I understand from Saskia that we – or rather you...' he encompassed them with an outstretched-arms gesture that he must have copied from the fitness guru, '...are well and truly back on track. But I did just want to swing by and hear it from the horse's mouth – directly as it were.' He gave them a microsecond to react and then, when no one spoke, followed this up with the words, 'Fabulous. All going well by the sound of it. Does anyone have any questions about the meals? I'm assuming there are no quality issues.'

He said this with an air of smugness, as if he were perfectly sure there could be no quality issues. Ruby had sometimes doubted

Olivia's claims that Mr B was one of the most arrogant men she had ever met, but looking at him now, she didn't doubt it at all.

Mr B was just in the process of handing the walk-around mic back to Saskia when Dana's hand shot up. 'This isn't a question exactly, Mr B. It's, er, more of a concern.'

'Oh?' Mr B looked at her keenly. 'What kind of concern? Nothing that arises from my menus, I hope.'

'I'm afraid there's a strong possibility that it does.' Dana cleared her throat. 'I've stuck to the diet rigidly, but this week I've put on half a pound.'

'That is discouraging. But half a pound doesn't sound too terrible. Maybe it was just an off week.'

'I've put on weight too, Mr B.' That was one of the younger girls. She sniffed and looked as though she was about to burst into tears. 'I've put on three quarters of a pound. I'm really disappointed.'

'That is very unfortunate.' Mr B blinked. 'However, I'm quite sure that...'

Before he could finish, Ruby cleared her throat and called, 'I'm afraid I've put on weight too.'

He was starting to look rattled.

Ruby swallowed. It was hard not to laugh and give the game away.

'Yeah, same here,' Harry said. 'Two pounds in my case. Something's amiss.'

'That's not possible.' Mr B's voice grew more clipped with each sentence. 'The meals have been prepared to my exact specifications. No one can possibly have gained an ounce. The meals are totally foolproof – a fopdoodle couldn't go wrong.' He glanced around as if expecting to see a fopdoodle lurking in their midst. Not that anyone except him probably even knew what a fopdoodle was, Ruby guessed, remembering what Olivia had said about his tendency to use whacky insults when he was stressed. Mr B folded his arms.

'You cannot possibly have gained an ounce. Not one of you. Not if you've been sticking to the plan.'

'I've put on four pounds,' called one of the younger women. The same one who had suggested the week before that they let Mr B's tyres down. She clearly had a cruel streak in there somewhere. 'It's disgusting. I'm complaining to the management. I can't believe this is happening again.'

'It isn't. It can't be.' Mr B shot a desperate look at Saskia, who had grown more and more serious as these revelations had been unfolding. She was now poker-faced. 'I don't understand it,' he yelped. 'It's impossible. Unless...' He flung up his hands in horror. 'The only explanation is that someone has been tampering with my meals. I will kill them. I will personally throttle them. The pediculous, flagitious scumbags. I will make them wish they'd never been born.' He paused, his mobile face changing suddenly as he if another thought had just struck him. He shook his head. 'No. No, it can't be.'

'What can't be?' Saskia asked in her most angelically innocent voice.

'It's the new nutritionist. I've had my suspicions for a while. She's as bad as the last one. What's wrong with these alleged food experts. Can't they do anything right? Clearly not,' he said, answering his own question. 'Morosophs the lot of them.' He looked around at them all. 'Fear not. I'll fire her. I'll do it now.' He strode towards the door and seconds later it slammed behind him.

The room exploded with laughter. Saskia was bent double with it.

Then suddenly everyone was talking at once.

'Did you see his face? Oh my word, that was priceless.'

'Hook, line and sinker.'

'I'm amazed no one laughed.'

'I'm amazed he believed us. That was classic.'

'What's a fopdoodle?'

'What's a flagitious scumbag?'

'I don't think they're compliments,' Harry said dryly and everyone laughed some more.

At least he didn't look quite as strained and sad as he had when she'd first seen him tonight, Ruby thought, glancing at his face and then back towards the front of the room.

Saskia was standing up again and wiping her eyes. 'Oh my goodness, thank you. That was perfect. I think I should go after him and tell him we were just playing a joke – before he really does go and fire anyone. Don't worry. He is full of hot air. I will be back in two minutes.'

She disappeared and the chatter continued. 'What do you think he'll say when she tells him he's been had?' Becky asked. 'Is he the kind that can take a joke when the tables are turned on him?'

'Fingers crossed,' Harry said.

'I think he probably is,' Ruby added.

Dana shook her head and gave another little chuckle. 'It can't be the first time someone has pranked the prankster, that's for sure.'

Saskia didn't come back and, after a few minutes more, Harry said, 'Maybe I'll just go and check she's OK.'

'I'll come with you,' Ruby said.

When they got downstairs to the reception desk, they saw that Keith was on the phone to someone and there was no sign of Saskia.

'I'll do that, sir, leave it with me,' Keith said and put the phone down. 'If you're looking for Saskia – she went that way.' He cocked a thumb in the direction of the main doors. 'She's trying to catch up with Mr B. He stormed out about five minutes ago. Something about firing the nutritionist and handing in his notice to Clara. Beats me!' He shook his head nonplussed. 'I'm sure it's a storm in a teacup. It usually is with those two.'

Harry and Ruby exchanged anxious glances. They hurried through the restaurant and reached the car park, where they were met by the sight of Saskia knocking on the closed driver's window of Mr B's car, which was parked in the middle of the car park while he revved the engine. She must have only just caught up with him in time.

'Please will you just let me explain,' she was shouting. 'Open this window.' As they reached her, she turned. 'Oh my goodness. He's being so stubborn. I should never have started this. I think he's involved Clara already. He was on his car phone just now shouting at someone.'

Saskia was the one who looked hot and bothered now, not to mention very worried. Ruby really felt for her.

'It wasn't just you who wound him up. It was all of us.'

Mr B finally deigned to lower the window. He looked furious. A pulse was beating in his cheek.

'No one has put on any weight,' Saskia said. 'It was a joke. We were teasing you.'

'I see.' He glared at her. 'So there is nothing wrong with my menus.'

'No.'

'And no one at all has put on any weight.'

Saskia shook her head.

'That's right,' Ruby said quickly. 'I've just lost my first stone.'

'And you?' he asked, looking at Harry.

'I've not put any on either.'

'No one has,' Saskia said. 'It was just a joke.'

'Your meals are brilliant,' Ruby said diplomatically.

'First-class,' Harry backed her up.

'Superb,' Saskia said in hasty agreement. 'They are faultless.'

'You are preaching to the converted,' Mr B said, looking pleased. In fact, it was hard to tell now that he'd ever been cross.

'And the nutritionist is obviously the right one,' Saskia said. 'She hasn't made any mistakes.'

'I know that too.'

Was that a little smile playing around his mouth? Ruby stared at him suspiciously. 'You knew all along that we were winding you up, didn't you?'

He rolled his eyes. Then he tipped back his head and began to laugh.

'How did you know?' Saskia demanded. 'Did someone tell you?' She looked astounded and then relieved.

Mr B was laughing properly now, his shoulders shaking. He reversed the car back into the reserved chef's space behind him and got out and came towards them, still laughing. 'You'll have to try harder than that,' he said, catching his breath and looking at them all with amusement. 'Much harder. You can't kid a kidder. Particularly not one who is as practised in the art of wind-up, as myself.'

25

Ruby was saving the story of the joke that backfired to tell her family when they all met up for the anniversary dinner at Aunt Dawn's and Mike's.

It was finally here. It was now Saturday afternoon and she'd arrived at the smallholding just under half an hour earlier. They'd just finished doing presents and congratulations. Marie and James had loved the Italian cooking lesson from their daughters. They'd also loved the gorgeous engraved 'his and hers' silver rings that Aunt Dawn and Mike had got them and the handy, five-in-one archaeological tool pen and novelty mug that Phil had gifted. But the star present had been, without a doubt, the half ammonite fossil that Simon had found on Chesil beach.

Ruby swore that her father had tears in his eyes when she'd presented it to him from his grandson.

'I knew it,' he'd said, blinking rapidly. 'He's a Lambert through and through. He has fossils in his DNA.'

'You're the only old fossil round here,' Marie had quipped, but she'd been thrilled to bits too.

The Lambert women, which meant Ruby, Olivia, their mother

and Aunt Dawn, were now doing a complete tour of the animals of the smallholding for Simon. They were currently standing by the paddock in the summer sweet air, where Mike had fixed the fence so that Simon could get reacquainted with Mrs Hudson the alpaca. He loved alpacas so much that Ruby had brought him a jumpsuit dotted with blue alpacas and he was wearing that now with a little straw sun hat. He looked adorable and was loving being the centre of everyone's attention.

'Pa, ppp, paca,' he shouted. 'Pa, pa, paca.'

'Duck was his first word and I wouldn't be a bit surprised if alpaca was his second,' Ruby remarked, keeping a close eye on her son as he stroked Mrs Hudson's woolly neck. Not that she was too worried as Mrs Hudson blinked sleepily in the sunshine. She seemed to love being the centre of attention almost as much as the youngster did.

'He's very bright,' her mother said proudly. 'He's got good genes. He's bound to be.'

They all laughed because Marie was for ever saying things like this and, of course, no one ever contradicted her.

'We've decided to get Mrs Hudson a companion,' Aunt Dawn said. 'We think she's escaping because she's lonely. Mike and I are going to see a male alpaca that needs a home next week.'

'Brilliant idea,' they chorused.

'How are the chooks getting on?' Olivia asked Aunt Dawn as they strolled back towards the house. 'Are they out and about?'

There had been a fox incident at the place Aunt Dawn had lived before and everyone was aware how protective she was of her hens.

'Funnily enough, we don't see as many foxes in the countryside as we used to see in the town,' she told them. 'But I do still take precautions. Come with me, I'll show you.'

They all followed her back on a path towards the house's large garden, past rose bushes that fragranced the air with their gorgeous scent and other flowers scattered around that Ruby didn't recognise but that smelled divine. As they got closer, Ruby saw that some of the main garden had now been sectioned off with a red-brick wall.

'I've always wanted a proper walled garden,' Dawn said, as she unclicked the latch of a wrought-iron gate and let them through. 'So, with that in mind, we've just had this done.'

Several chickens, recognising the bringer of treats, half ran and half fluttered to greet them, and Dawn scattered a handful of what looked like corn and seed across the bare earth. There were patches of grass and some shrubs and the remains of a couple of old tree trunks and by one wall there was an old summer house that must have been there before with a small wooden decking frontage.

'It's a work in progress, as you can see,' Dawn said. 'But there will be a flower bed along that wall, where we'll plant some perennial shrubs when we get a moment. Right now, it's a safe playground for my chooks.'

'And Boris,' their mother remarked, as they all watched the big black and golden cockerel with his bright red comb and shiny black tail feathers strutting proudly around his women.

'I don't know how you get time for it all,' Olivia said wonderingly. 'How do you ever find time to make my cakes?'

'Superwoman genes also run in our family,' Aunt Dawn said, looking at her with affection. Aunt Dawn wore a blue silk shirt over denim jeans, very conservative for her, and looked tanned and happy. She might be busy but semi-retirement clearly suited her and Aunt Dawn had never been one to enjoy being idle.

* * *

They finally got back to the house, where Phil was helping Mike and Dad put out the tapas dishes, which they'd been heating in the oven. The scents of garlic, olives, cinnamon and spices filled the old farmhouse kitchen.

Ruby saw the tender look that Phil gave her sister when they arrived and she felt warmed. One day she hoped that someone would look at her like that.

Phil was perfect for Olivia. He had dark brooding looks and was frankly drop-dead gorgeous. He had that kind of head-turning presence that made both women and guys give him a second look when he walked into a room, but he only had eyes for Olivia. When Ruby had first met him, she'd also thought he might be a bit sulky because he didn't smile much, but he was a really good bloke and she'd heard enough about the pranks he and Mr B had played on each other across the years to know that his sense of humour was very much alive and kicking.

Over the first courses of tapas dishes, which were tortilla, Spanish potatoes, piquillo peppers and garlic mushrooms, plus, of course, Ruby's especially prepared dishes from Mr B, Ruby told them all about the winding up of Mr B and how it had backfired.

She was feeling slightly guilty because he'd been so happy to do the tapas dishes for her, despite the fact he must have known she was part of the prank they'd played on him. He had even done some extra ones that Olivia had brought along. Mr B had a very kind heart behind his mischief-making and his posturing.

Phil was now smiling across the table at her. 'I wouldn't worry too much,' he said, having guffawed loudly when Ruby had got to the part about Mr B revving up his car in the car park. 'That is absolutely classic Mr B. I don't know how he does it, but he is absolutely brilliant at sliding out of trouble or sniffing out a wind-up when he's the victim. No matter how carefully you think you've planned a wheeze, he's very good at getting the last laugh. He must have known what you were going to do.'

'I'm not sure how he found out,' Ruby said. 'We were all sworn to secrecy. How could he have known?'

'Are you sure none of you discussed it anywhere at the Bluebell?' Phil's black eyes danced with amusement.

'I guess that's possible.' Ruby remembered that she and Harry had been talking about it when they'd come into the foyer of the Bluebell. Surely he couldn't have overheard them.

'Oh, he definitely could,' Phil said when she mentioned this. 'He has spies everywhere. Someone else may have done the same thing. It sounds like far too many people were in on the joke. No, the only way to really keep something secret from Mr B is to plot the whole thing single-handedly and not tell a soul. Like the little wheeze we have planned for our wedding.' He glanced at Olivia and she rolled her eyes.

'Which I assume you can't tell us,' Ruby pressed.

'We could, but then we'd have to kill you,' Olivia said.

'He's very good at finding out what's going on,' Phil added. 'He makes it his business to know – like every good paranoid conspiracy theorist should.'

'It's why he's known only as Mr B,' Olivia put in when their father looked at her curiously. 'He's scared of having his identity stolen.'

'Ah, yes that does ring a bell,' Ruby said. 'I think we've had this discussion before.'

Their parents were now both nodding. Their father was usually so immersed in archaeology and the past that he often missed what was going on in the present. 'Weren't you telling us about some of his shenanigans once before?' their mum asked. 'I have a memory of green rice pudding.'

'That's right,' Phil replied. 'That was a classic case of Mr B turning a trick to his advantage. I put green food colouring in the milk and he made green rice pudding, which all the kids loved and earned himself a bonus from Clara. I know it's juvenile,' he added, 'but it's the kind of thing that goes on in hotel kitchens. It helps to alleviate the stress. It can get pretty hectic working with the general public all the time.'

'Does the same kind of thing happen on set?' Mike wanted to know. 'Pranks, I mean?'

'Not so much,' Phil said.

'It probably depends a bit on the director,' Olivia added. 'But there tends to be a lot of money involved so you don't get pranks played on set very much. When you're not actually filming, it's open house though.'

For a while they talked about what went on behind the scenes on a set, which was fascinating for most of the family to hear but probably a bit of a busman's holiday for Phil and Olivia.

'Not that I'm expecting to ever get tired of talking about it,' Olivia confessed when Mike made the busman's holiday remark. 'It took me so long to get to where I am now.'

'Me too,' Phil agreed. It had taken him just as long to get the role of his dreams as it had taken Olivia. 'I can't imagine ever taking it for granted.'

Ruby watched their animated faces and felt thrilled for them once more. The only thing missing from their lives was the baby they both longed for, although having a baby would certainly make their lives a lot more complicated. She wondered if Olivia had said anything about her IVF wedding present yet. Maybe if they had a quiet moment today some time, she would ask her.

The talk moved on inevitably to the wedding plans.

'You wouldn't believe how complicated the seating plans are,' Olivia said. 'We're not even having that many people for the sit-down meal.' She turned to Ruby. 'Are you bringing a plus-one by the way? Should I be reserving one seat or two at the top table? Aside from young Simon, obviously?'

'Oh definitely one seat,' Ruby said, even though an image of Harry Small had just popped into her head. What was wrong with her? She'd already decided that Harry was banned from her thoughts. However nice he was, however much they'd seemed to click. She was just not going there – not even in fantasy land.

'I'll ask you nearer the time,' Olivia said breezily. 'We've got another two months to decide.'

'Let's talk about your hen night,' Ruby said, changing the subject pointedly. 'Would you like small and intimate or big and rowdy?'

'Small and intimate, definitely. Maybe just close family and Hannah and a couple of other friends for a meal and drinks somewhere.' She got out her phone and shared some contacts. 'I'd love these women to come if they're free.'

'Consider it done,' Ruby said.

'Could we book a bridesmaid dress fitting?' Olivia asked.

'Nope. I'm not ready yet. I'd like at least another two months of Tuesdays before I do that. Don't worry. I'm on target to slip straight into that size-twelve dress. And if anything happens to stop that, you will be the first to know.'

'I can see that,' Olivia said. 'You look amazing.'

'I've got another stone and a half to go,' Ruby said stubbornly.

'OK. Another two months of Tuesdays it is,' Olivia said. 'I'm really proud of you. You do know that, don't you? I know it hasn't been easy.'

'Nothing that's worth having in life is easy,' Ruby said. 'I'm really proud of you too.'

The sisters smiled at each other, locked in a moment of closeness. Beside Ruby, Simon was chattering contentedly in his highchair. Recently he'd started stringing vowels together like bah bah bah and bee bee bee or ta te te and de da deh.

'Mm mm ma,' he said now.

'Did you hear that?' Olivia breathed. 'I think he just said, "Mama".'

The whole table shushed from talking and they all listened.

'Say it again, Simon,' Ruby prompted. 'Say mum mah.'

'Mm, mmm mmmm,' said Simon, smiling and happy because he knew he was the centre of attention. 'Mum mah, mum mmm mah.'

'He did, he said it.' Everyone was clapping and Ruby felt her throat close with emotion. She had never dreamed she would feel like this. The love she felt for her son was so overwhelming it was almost painful. The power of it stole her breath. She blinked a couple of times and glanced at Olivia. Her sister was clapping the hardest of them all. But Ruby knew she was covering an ache of desperate longing behind that smile and her heart went out to her.

26

Maybe Simon saying 'Mama' had been just a happy accident, Ruby thought, because despite all their further prompting, they hadn't managed to get him to say it again and neither did he say it over the next few weeks which whizzed past.

But several other things did happen. Her weight loss slowed down so that she was only losing a pound or two each week and on one terrible Tuesday, four weeks after her parents' anniversary meal, she actually put on half a pound.

'Try not to worry,' Saskia said, her eyes kind. 'It's quite common for weight loss to plateau when you've been dieting a while. I'm sure if you ask around, you'll find others have had the same experience.'

Saskia was brilliantly discreet, she never disclosed whether anyone else had had good or bad weeks – it was always left up to the individual whether or not they wanted to share that information.

But when Ruby did ask around, she discovered that both Becky and Dana had had the same thing happen. So had Harry, who'd clearly overheard her conversation with Becky and Dana in the studio and had wandered across.

'I didn't lose any last week,' he said. 'I thought it was maybe because I'd started eating normally again.'

'Is that because things are easier at home?' Ruby questioned.

'I'm getting there, yes.' His dark eyes warmed a fraction. 'Thanks for asking.'

She hadn't spoken to him alone for a while. She hadn't been avoiding him exactly. She'd just made sure they hadn't been alone and they hadn't met by chance in the car park either. Maybe he was avoiding her too. She didn't know, but it had helped. He hadn't popped into her thoughts so much, although she did really look forward to seeing him at Booty Busters.

It was crazy. On very many levels. She didn't think she'd ever had a guy take up so much of her headspace. Especially in view of the fact that other than Booty Busters and that one evening she'd spent in his company she'd spent less than a day with him, ever.

* * *

Harry had been thinking about Ruby too, but for a different reason. Over the last few weeks, he'd been bombarded with correspondence from Annabel's solicitor, but at least he now knew exactly what she wanted.

It was a ridiculous amount of money. And not one he would be able to raise without selling some assets.

The last time Harry had gone up to London to meet with his own solicitor, he had put his hands up mid-conversation and said, 'OK. What's my best route out of this legal trap?' He couldn't even bring himself to call it a marriage. 'And what's the worst-case scenario? Just tell me exactly what you think and we can plan an exit strategy.' The words 'exit strategy' had a terribly hollow ring to them. He'd never imagined himself saying them about his marriage, but it was where they were. There was no denial left inside him.

'OK, Harry. I'll be frank. Lewison's aren't going to let this go. Their strategy to date, as I think we've already discussed, is to cost you the maximum amount of money possible. In a bid to persuade you it would be cheaper in the long run to pay what she wants.'

Harry had sighed. 'Because I'm going to end up paying it one way or another anyway. Either in your fees or in her settlement.'

'Precisely that. Yes.'

'So your advice would be to come to an agreement, even though it's unjust.'

'I'm afraid so.'

'And we can't play the adultery card because we have no proof that my wife slept with Nick Lewison.'

'Correct. We could try, but that would simply prolong matters, particularly if she was to deny that adultery had taken place, which I think we're in agreeance that she will. Correct?'

'Yep. And it doesn't matter that she has no proof either of the unreasonable behaviour I've been accused of? Apart from the CCTV footage, of course.' That had been a bitter pill to swallow. The fact that Annabel intended to use his own CCTV footage against him if she needed to. She had a copy of the digital file and she had told him it wouldn't be returned until they had come to an amicable financial agreement. Not quite blackmail but borderline. Harry would have hated it to have been made public. Gargantuul had a superb reputation, which had been started by his grandfather and built upon by him. Their reputation, and indeed their entire branding, was built on words like trust, quality and reliability.

Gargantuul offers gargantuan solutions to gigantic problems.

Harry could just imagine the heading on the clip of him rummaging in the bin if it ever got onto Twitter.

Gargantuul boss reaches gigantic size after eating ginormous choco-late bar.

Or something similarly damaging.

That would not do the company's reputation any good at all. It would destroy his grandfather's great reputation. It would destroy his. And while he could weather the storm of shame on a personal level, he couldn't bear to bring Gargantuul's name down with him.

'Can we get a court order to stop her publicising that footage?'

'A gagging order. Yes. Maybe. But we cannot stop leaks.' His solicitor had cleared his throat delicately. 'There is also the SmithK-line Beecham introduction which your wife claims to have initiated and without which your company would never have gained such a lucrative contract. That is the case, isn't it?'

Harry had nodded.

Annabel had never let him forget the fact that she had intro-duced him to the right person at SmithKline Beecham. Without her help, Gargantuul wouldn't have called them at exactly the right time. This was debatable, but it couldn't be denied that she had instigated the initial introduction.

He'd sighed as his solicitor continued, 'The judge would certainly take that into account in his or her basis for justification of recompense. However, we will negotiate down on this figure.' He had written a slightly smaller figure on the notepad and pushed it across. 'But I don't think we'll get it much below that.'

Harry had taken a deep breath of the dry air that seemed to characterise the legal firm's London office and then let it out again in another sigh.

'OK,' he had finally said. 'I'll see about selling some assets.' His mind was on the Banksy. It was the obvious thing to sell. He'd made a decision to ask Ruby to come and value it next time he saw her. Then he remembered that he had her phone number and decided to give her a ring instead.

* * *

Ruby was driving back from her mother's where she'd just dropped Simon because they were having a grandma/grandson bonding afternoon when she saw Harry's number flash up on her mobile.

Perhaps he was having another moment of temptation, although she doubted it, after their recent conversations. He may not be quite as stressed as he'd been in the beginning, but he was still in the throes of a divorce that she imagined was pretty painful. Also he was very near his target. Why would he have a relapse now?

She answered it hands-free and then pulled into a lay-by along-side a five-bar gate.

'Diet Buddy Helpline at your service. How may I be of assistance?'

'I do need your help,' Harry said. 'But it has nothing to do with diets. This time it's in a professional capacity. I'd like you to sell some artwork for me.'

He paused to let her take that in and Ruby had to admit it was the last thing she'd been expecting.

'That's assuming you're not on a complete sabbatical. In which case maybe you'd be good enough to recommend someone else?'

'I'm not on sabbatical. I'm happy to help. I'd need to make an appointment to come and have a look. Where is the artwork? It's not the Banksy, is it?'

'That is one of the pieces – yes. I'm in Brancombe and I'd like to do it as soon as possible if I may? I know you have your little one, but you'd be very welcome to bring him along.'

'Thanks.' She hesitated. 'I could come by this afternoon if you like? I'm child-free as it happens. I've just dropped Simon at my mum's.'

'That would be perfect. Thank you. If it's not too far out of your way?' He gave her the address.

Less than five minutes later, Ruby was turning her SUV around and heading back towards Brancombe.

Harry had sounded very formal on the phone. She guessed he wasn't the type of person who mixed business with pleasure. She caught herself there – business with pleasure – who was she kidding?

He lived quite near to the Bluebell Cliff she realised when she drew up at the postcode he'd given her and found herself at the top of a long drive signposted with the house name Studland Views. The drive led up to a pair of twelve-foot-high electronic gates. She was about to get out and press a button she could see on one of the gateposts when they swung silently open. He must be aware of her arrival then.

Ruby was used to seeing posh houses, particularly among her London clients, but it was hard not to be impressed with Harry's property. The driveway that had led up to the gates was lined on either side by tall poplar trees and the gates had opened on to a gravel frontage twice the size of Ruby's own. There was parking enough for seven or eight cars.

A few moments later, she was parking her SUV alongside his Lexus and heading for the front door. Her heart was thudding hard and not just because she might have the opportunity to sell the Banksy for him, she realised, but at the prospect of unexpectedly seeing him again. Traitorous heart.

The front door opened before she reached it and he was standing there, smiling. 'Thanks for coming over so quickly. I really appreciate it.'

'My pleasure.' She held out her hand, aware suddenly of the need to keep this visit on a formal footing and, after a moment's hesitation, he shook it.

That had been a mistake. Shockwaves of chemistry bounced

through her at his touch. Her head might think it was formal. Her body had other ideas.

'Please, come in.' Harry's voice was solemn. 'Are you in a hurry? Can I offer you a coffee?'

'A camomile tea would be lovely, if you have one? Thank you.'

'I'll check the cupboards.'

She followed him curiously into the kitchen. 'Wow, this is gorgeous,' she said as they went into a huge room with a skylight above so that light flooded down on everything. There was a gigantic oak breakfast island, a black range oven, a double sink and oak cupboard doors everywhere.

'I fell in love with this house the moment I saw it.' He turned from his search of the cupboards, smiling. He wasn't so formal now they were face to face. 'Sorry, I don't think I do have any camomile.'

'Coffee's great. Black, no sugar, please.'

He arched an eyebrow. 'Of course. Did you always have it like that? Or have you just got used to it?'

'I've got used to it,' she confessed. 'Before Booty Busters, I was a caramel latte girl. Although I do like camomile too, I must admit. How about you?'

'I dream of caramel lattes. I guess that once we are at our target weight we could have one to celebrate, couldn't we?'

'It's a deal. A large caramel latte with chocolate sprinkles to celebrate. Bring it on. You must be nearly there now?'

'It wouldn't hurt me to lose another few pounds. But I'm in the correct BMI now apparently.'

'Oh, Harry, that's fantastic. Really brilliant. Why didn't you tell me?'

'I just did. You're virtually there too, aren't you? You look great to me.' He gave her a quick glance of approval and the same thing happened that had happened last time he'd done that. She melted. If she wasn't careful, she would end up in a pool of lust at his feet.

So much for getting him out of her fantasies, he'd just retaken the starring role in them.

She shook her head to clear it. 'I've got half a stone to go and it seems to be the hardest half stone. I'm having real trouble shifting it. I'm not quite so motivated as I was at the beginning. Is that bad?'

'I have a strategy for keeping motivated,' he told her.

'What? Other than phoning me?' she quipped. It was so easy to slip into banter with him. Banter was better – it helped distract her from the raging chemistry she felt every time he came within ten paces.

'Indeed.' His voice was light, but then his face sobered. 'I play back a sequence of events that involves me going to the wheelie bin to find the chocolate and retrieving it.'

'Why did you do that? Did you have second thoughts?' She laughed. 'I wouldn't blame you if you did. Do you remember when you saved me from eating that Easter egg? I nearly got that back out of the bin. It was only because I'd put it in amongst some rotting food that I didn't. The power of chocolate. What are we like!'

'Yes, the power of chocolate. But no, it's not just a memory in my case. I have photographic evidence of my misdemeanour. Well, I did have evidence. My wife has it now.' He told her what had happened and for a few moments Ruby couldn't quite believe her ears.

'She was just messing about though, right?' she asked.

'No, I'm afraid she wasn't. She has CCTV footage of me going to our wheelie bin and rummaging around for that bar of Galaxy. The irony of it is that I wasn't getting it out because I wanted to eat it. I was worried she might check the bins and find it and realise that I'd bought it in the first place. That wouldn't have gone down very well. So I was moving it to the food bin. Naturally, that bit isn't on tape. There's just footage of me holding a huge bar of Galaxy that I've just got out of the bin. It's now part of my wife's evidence of my unreasonable behaviour. She's said I can have the footage back... once I've paid her a huge settlement and the divorce is final.'

He'd relayed all this in a matter-of-fact voice as though he was telling her something that had happened to someone else. But just for a moment there when he'd said the words 'unreasonable behaviour', he had looked absolutely stricken and Ruby found herself breathless with disbelief.

'Harry, that is awful. Utterly wrong. It's blackmail, surely? Is that why you're thinking of selling the Banksy? Oh my God!' She hesitated before adding quickly, 'I'm so sorry. That's none of my business.'

'I wouldn't have told you if I didn't trust you.' He met her eyes. 'The only other person who knows is my solicitor.'

She nodded slowly. There was so much she wanted to say about his wife. But none of it was complimentary. She wanted to rage about injustice and manipulation and downright deviousness. How could you do that kind of thing to someone you'd once professed to love? But that was not why he'd asked her to come here. He needed her help, not her sympathy.

Ruby struggled to get her professional head back on. 'Thank you for trusting me. Shall we go and look at the picture now?'

'Follow me,' he said.

27

It was odd how Harry instinctively trusted Ruby, but he did. He had trusted her since that very first time they had met, he realised, as he gestured her ahead of him into the lounge. That had been the first thing he'd known about her. He hadn't really noticed how pretty she was until later on. Then, when he had noticed, he'd put it out of his head because he was married to Annabel, and other women, however pretty they were, were out of bounds. He had taken his vows very seriously.

It was odd though, whereas Annabel's manufactured beauty had slowly faded in his mind across the time he had known her, Ruby's had increased. And now, suddenly, as they stood beside each other in his lounge, he knew why. Ruby was lovely from the inside out. She was very much au naturel – today, she was wearing the minimum of make-up, but she didn't need it with that flawless skin and that wavy blonde hair that put him in mind of Scarlett Johansson. She wore jeans and a light grey figure-hugging T-shirt which had a splodge of something that could have been baby food on the shoulder.

If Annabel had been delicately painted bone china, Ruby was

all gorgeously wholesome earth mother. Ruby had never struck him as overweight either – just deliciously curvy – whereas his wife had always been stick-insect thin. Annabel had worried about her weight, beating herself up if she put on so much as a pound and taking herself off for a run or a sauna to sweat it off again. At least that's what Harry had assumed she was doing. Maybe she had always just been running away from him.

Women seemed to labour under the misapprehension that men didn't like curves, but this wasn't true. Or at least it wasn't true in Harry's case. He'd tried to tell Annabel this, but she'd never believed him.

Ruby, on the other hand, wasn't like any woman he'd ever met. He had thought, back in the beginning when they'd first met, that he'd have liked someone similar to Ruby as a sister. *Similar*, being the operative word, because his feelings towards Ruby right now weren't in the slightest bit brotherly. Aware suddenly that he was staring at her, Harry dragged his gaze away.

'Erm,' he said, feeling blindsided suddenly. Where had all that come from? 'It's... there, the, er...'

Not that he needed to tell her where the Banksy was – it hung over the fireplace and she was already quite close to it.

She glanced at him and Harry felt his face flaming. Fortunately, the light wasn't so good in here, this room had blinds and they were only partially open, so hopefully Ruby hadn't noticed his discomfort. She'd shown no sign of it. She took a few steps forward and was now studying the picture.

Harry forced his head back onto business. He strode across to open the blinds fully, which let the afternoon sunlight into the room, and then joined Ruby by the fireplace.

'I never get tired of looking at masterpieces,' she said.

'Me neither,' he replied, but he wasn't talking about the painting. She was a hair's breadth away from him now and he could smell her scent, something soft and floral. His head spun for a moment and he wanted to sit down.

Hell, no he didn't. He wanted to hold her. He had a strong, strong urge to draw her into his arms and breathe her in and do... He struggled to switch off his thoughts. He wanted to do a great deal more than hold her. It seemed that now he'd acknowledged how he was feeling, the feelings just kept on coming. This was totally crazy. This wasn't why he'd asked her here. He reminded himself he needed her professional opinion. He stepped deliberately away from Ruby and stood by one of the Chesterfields in the room. Putting a Chesterfield between the pair of them suddenly seemed very wise.

Ruby hadn't shown any sign that she was aware of his thoughts. Thank God. She'd probably run a mile if she knew what he was thinking. But now she turned. 'Are you OK, Harry? You seem... preoccupied. Is it the thought of selling this? Is there perhaps another way? Do you have any other paintings that might be valuable?'

He rubbed his forehead distractedly. 'There is another picture that Grandpa George always said he paid a fair whack for. I could show you?'

Hell, no he couldn't. He'd just remembered where it was. It was in his bedroom, hung over the bed. If he took Ruby in his bedroom, he'd never get her out of it again – metaphorically at least. He'd be lying there every night visualising her there, reimagining that soft floral scent, remembering how he felt right now. Wondering what it would be like to undress her. None of which was going to help his insomnia one bit.

'I'll leave you to have a look at it,' he said, while I make us some more coffee. 'It's down there, last door at the end.'

She went off in the right direction, and he escaped gratefully to the kitchen, relieved that, thanks to Annabel's tidiness obsession, he always made the bed when he got out of it and didn't leave any clothes lying about. He just had time to get himself back together and splash cold water onto his overheated face – a freezing cold shower would have been better – before she came back again.

'You could be onto something there. Damien Hirst is another very sought-after artist, especially now. The price of his work has gone up lately. Mind you, the same is true of Banksy's work. Your grandfather was very financially astute.'

'I know,' Harry said. 'He loved his art. I'm not massively keen on selling any of his collection, but I'd rather sell that one than the Banksy. How much do you think it might be worth?'

'I'll make some enquiries for you. I've taken photos of them both. Is that OK?' She held up her phone to show him. 'It's the easiest way to show buyers the condition.'

'It's fine. Thank you. Thank you for coming over.'

'My pleasure.'

He pushed the mug of coffee towards her and she glanced at her Apple watch.

'Actually, Harry, I think I might skip the coffee if that's OK? I probably should get back. And the sooner I do, the sooner I can find out about valuations for your paintings.' She tapped the phone.

'Of course. I really appreciate it.'

'See you at Booty Busters,' she said, as he stepped forward to open the front door for her.

'I'll look forward to it.'

'I'll try to get in touch as soon as I have some information for you. Is that OK?'

'Great.'

'Take care of yourself, Harry.' She hesitated and then she reached up and kissed him lightly on the cheek. She was slightly shorter than Annabel – he guessed five seven or eight – and she was wearing flat shoes and had to stand on tiptoe. 'Not all women are like your ex, I promise.'

He couldn't speak for her closeness and when he could, his voice came out in a mixture of throaty and gruff and he could hear his Dorset accent, which only surfaced when he felt stressed, strongly. 'I know they aren't. Thank you.'

Ruby had to stop herself running for her SUV. Good grief, what had she been thinking? Why had she kissed him? She knew she'd wanted to offer him some comfort, but the poor man had looked terrified.

It hadn't done her any good either. Now her heart was thumping madly and every one of her nerve endings was jangling. Thank God you didn't use an ignition key in the SUV. She'd never have managed it – her fingers were shaking so much. She had thought she had felt chemistry with a man before, but she hadn't. Nothing like this. Oh my God. She had to get out of here.

The electronic gates were already swinging open as she turned. Obviously Harry was keen to see the back of her too. They closed again almost as soon as she'd exited. She saw them in her rear-view mirror, locking her out.

Her hands felt damp on the leather steering wheel. Her whole body felt overheated. Shaking her head, Ruby switched on the A/C, enjoying the instant drop in temperature as the cold air swirled around the interior. It was a hot day. That was what this was.

No it wasn't! Who was she trying to kid?

A few miles up the road, she decided to stop and gather herself. She wasn't far from Corfe Castle. Perched high up on the hillside, the great grey monolith was magnificent even in ruins, as it was now, ten centuries after it had been built by William the Conqueror.

Making an impulsive decision, Ruby parked in the car park opposite the hill on which the castle stood and phoned her sister.

'Liv, have you got a minute? Something totally mad just happened.'

'Of course I have. That sounds intriguing. Does it involve a man?'

'How did you know that?'

'It's in your voice.'

'Give me a sec. I'm just transferring you to my phone. I might lose the signal. I'm in a dip. If I do, I'll phone you back.'

She got out of the SUV into the afternoon sun with her phone's earbuds in place. It was a hot July day. The car park was busy, she'd been lucky to find a space. The sun bounced off the bonnets of cars which weren't in the shelter of the trees. Some people had left makeshift sunshields in their windscreens, but Ruby knew the weather wasn't the only cause of her overheated state.

'Liv, are you still there?'

There was no answer. Ruby wasn't entirely surprised. Her phone was flicking between one bar and zero. She needed to get out of the shelter of these hills and the only way was up. Slinging her handbag over her shoulder and feeling like a tourist, she headed out of the car park and up towards the castle via its ticket booth. It was years since she'd been here. It was odd how you rarely visited the tourist attractions in your own home county. When she'd been at art college, she'd come here more. She'd once painted the castle, loving the challenge of getting the stones the right shade of grey. Somewhere at home there were some charcoal sketches that she'd been quite pleased with too. She must look them out.

Ruby was about halfway up the path which sloped steeply up to the castle ruins when she had the strong feeling that she'd forgotten something important. Then she realised with a little shock that it was Simon. Pushing his buggy had become second nature. Although, she was relieved she wasn't pushing it up here. It was hard enough work without it.

Pausing to catch her breath, she glanced at her phone and saw that she had a signal now. She phoned Olivia back.

'Thank goodness,' Olivia said. 'The suspense was killing me. Where are you?'

'I'm at Corfe Castle. Literally. I've just done something really touristy and bought a ticket. It wasn't cheap.'

Olivia laughed. 'That is touristy. I wondered why you were out of breath. The view's good from the top, though.'

'All I can see at the moment are sheep and sightseers.'

'Never mind sheep, tell me about this man. It's the Ben Affleck lookalike, isn't it? The one who was getting divorced.'

'It is, yes.' Ruby stopped, surprised that Olivia seemed to have pre-empted her. 'He asked me to go to his house to value some paintings. Oddly enough, I sold one of them to his grandfather a few years back.'

'Wow. Small world. So what happened? Did he entice you into his bedroom for a private viewing?'

'No, of course he didn't. Although, actually, I did go into his bedroom. But that was on my own. Look. Let me start at the beginning.'

'Sorry. I'll stop interrupting.'

'Interrupting's good. It gives me a chance to catch my breath. I thought I was fitter than I am, what with all those workouts. Anyway, I'm almost at the top.' She paused. 'I'll just find a quiet spot and sit down. It's pretty busy up here. Tourist city. Right, that's it. We're alone,' Ruby added a few seconds later. 'I've got my own patch of grass. The crazy thing is that nothing at all happened. But the chemistry was mind-blowing. It might all be in my head, of course. But there was a moment – just a moment – when I caught him looking at me and there was an expression in his eyes. It was literally just a moment when we were in his lounge.'

'Did he say anything?'

'No. He looked hot. I don't mean hot in the "wow he's fit" sense, although actually he is. But it's not that. I mean hot, temperature wise. I think he'd been staring at me. I had my back to him, but I felt his eyes. You know how you do.'

'I know exactly. Yes.'

'Well, then I turned round and he looked a bit dazed and he stopped looking at me and got all brusque and efficient again, but I'm sure I didn't imagine it, Liv. Oh God, I don't know. Maybe I did. What I do know is that I've never in my life felt like that before. It was as though there was this blazing chemistry going on, even though neither of us said a word.' Ruby ran her hands over the cool grass where she was sitting. 'How did you know with Phil? Was it the same?'

'Yes and no. It was more of a slow burn with Phil. We were doing *Hamlet*, weren't we? And he was superb. So I'd noticed him, sure, it was hard not to. But we didn't start dating straight away. I was still getting over my ex.'

'I remember.' Ruby paused. 'He's been in my head for a while. Harry, I mean, not your ex. I've been trying to get him out, to be honest. I mean, obviously I do see him. I see him at Booty Busters every week and we've spoken on the phone a couple of times. As friends. Nothing more. But today...' She tailed off. 'Am I making any sense?'

'Perfect sense. Did you say you went into his bedroom?'

'Yes. It was just after we'd been in the lounge. I'd asked him if he had any more paintings he'd like me to look at and he said yes, he did. But then he didn't come with me. He literally ran out of the lounge and said, could I look at it on my own, while he made coffee?'

'Perhaps he was scared he wouldn't be able to trust himself if you were both in his bedroom?' Olivia suggested.

'Do you know, there was a part of me that thought exactly that. It was something about the way that he said it and then shot off to the kitchen. But then I thought I must be imagining it. I was pretty flustered and I think he was too. But he was pretending not to be. So was I. Oh my God, I have so little experience of this.'

'You dated plenty of guys before Simon came along,' Olivia reminded her. 'There was chemistry then, surely?'

'Yes, of course there was. Or Simon wouldn't be here. But it's just – I don't know, this feels different.'

She stared out over the hillside back towards the village of Corfe, where she could see a church spire rising up from the Purbeck grey rooftops of the houses and green fields beyond with misty blue skies arching above it all.

For a moment, the memory of being in Harry's bedroom overrode the view. His bedroom had been tidy, but not excessively so. The forest green duvet cover had looked rumpled as though the bed had been hastily made and there had been the jacket of a suit over the back of a chair in one corner. The room had smelled of the citrus cologne he always wore, mixed with the faintly indefinable scent that she recognised as being Harry's. There was a big built-in mirrored wardrobe that took up most of one wall and, on the bedside table, a hardback book with a Kindle balanced on top. Ruby couldn't see the cover and she'd longed to know what he was reading, so she'd shifted it to look. John Grisham's latest by the look of it. Then, feeling slightly guilty for nosing, she'd turned her attention to the Damien Hirst.

'What are you thinking?' Olivia's voice prompted her gently

back to the present and Ruby felt a soft breeze drift across the hill-side and touch her face. It was cooler up here but not much.

'I'm thinking that I've fallen for this guy. I'm not sure how he feels about me, but I think there may be a spark.' She felt a wash of sadness. 'It's not going to go anywhere, though, Liv. It can't.'

'Why can't it? I thought you said he was getting divorced?'

'Yes, he is, but it's definitely messy. He told me a bit about it – not in a hurling blame kind of way, not at all, but just reading between the lines of some of the things he said, I think his wife is a real piece of work.'

'Then maybe he deserves to meet someone nice?'

'I don't want to be his rebound relationship, Liv. I can't risk that. There's not just me to consider. There's Simon.'

'Does he know about Simon?'

'Yes.'

'Then he'd be going in with his eyes open, wouldn't he?'

'I suppose so.'

'Anyway, rebound relationships can work out. I was on the rebound when I met Phil. I'd only been separated from Tom a month and I know we weren't married, but we might as well have been. We'd been living together for years.'

Ruby sighed. 'That's true. I'm sorry, Liv. I've been bending your ear for ages and I haven't even asked how you are.'

'I'm very good,' Olivia said. 'And as you're asking, I do have some news. Phil's agreed to your IVF wedding present.'

'Oh my God, that's brilliant news.' Ruby didn't realise she'd spoken so loudly until a little girl in a scarlet dress, who must belong to a passing family, turned to stare at her curiously. Ruby waved at her and the little girl stuck her thumb in her mouth and hurried to catch up with her parents. 'I'll transfer the money now if you like. When are you going to get started?'

'Straight after the wedding. There's no rush. Anyway, it's a wedding present. You can't give it to us in advance.'

'Of course I can. I'm so pleased. I thought he may say no.'

'So did I. I had to pick my moment.'

For a while they talked about the wedding, which was now less than a month away, and the hen night, which was in three weeks' time, and then Olivia brought the conversation back to Ruby.

'Don't worry about having a rebound relationship, Rubes. Just do what feels right. Let things unfold, hey?'

'You're very wise sometimes.'

'Only sometimes?' Olivia teased. 'I thought elder sisters were supposed to be wise all the time.'

They said their goodbyes and disconnected. Ruby's legs felt stiff as she uncurled them and got up from her position on the grass. She stared past the imposing stone walls and watched the shadow of a cloud drift across the adjoining fields. Somewhere overhead a small plane droned and she could hear the distant thrum of traffic on the roads below and the sound of the steam train's whistle – the steam railway was close by. It carried journeying tourists through the Purbeck hills and gorgeous countryside.

Closer by were the sounds of birdsong and the squeals of children as they chased around within the stone walls and the smells of the fresh country air, mingling with an underlay of the distant sea.

Ruby resumed her tour of the castle, looking up at the ancient stone remnants that rose steeply above her head and trying to imagine it whole. She wondered how many love stories had been played out within these walls in the ten centuries it had been standing. The place was steeped in history. She visualised long-ago kings and queens, even William the Conqueror himself striding along the ramparts. Maybe she was completely mad imagining her own love story might be starting here too. Or maybe Olivia was right and the seeds of it had already been sown. Maybe her own love story had already begun.

28

Harry couldn't get Ruby out of his head. Even though he tried quite hard. He had enough to focus on already. He did not need the complication of another woman and he certainly did not need to give Annabel any further ammunition. He was half regretting asking Ruby to come and value his paintings because she was now in his house. She was in every room. So much for not seeing her in his bedroom. The knowledge that she'd been in there was enough. He had to keep their relationship on a business footing. He reminded himself that it *was* on a business footing – apart from in his head.

She didn't keep him waiting long for an answer about the paintings either. She called him back within a couple of days and he'd programmed her name into his phone so he was able to prepare himself and get his best casual voice on.

'Ruby, hi, good to hear from you.'

'Hi, Harry. I won't keep you. I just wanted to let you know that I'll need to make a few more enquiries, so it's not a done deal, but I have a lot of interest in your Banksy.'

'Not the Damien Hirst?' He heard the wistful note in his voice.

'Not yet. But these things take time. Are you in a huge hurry?'

'No,' he said.

Yes, he thought, and he was pretty sure she heard his thoughts, not his voice, because she added quickly, 'Silly question. I'm sure you just want to get things settled, don't you?'

'I do,' he said quietly, and if it meant that he had to say goodbye to a part of his heritage, then so be it. Maybe there were some parts of the past you had to let go of in order to embrace the future.

* * *

It was at the penultimate Booty Busters on 27 July that Ruby reached her target weight.

Ruby was pretty sure her squeal could have been heard downstairs in reception when the numbers on the digital scales flickered up and down and then finally settled on her target weight. Oh my God, she had dreamed about this moment. She had visualised it over and over to ward off the sugar cravings, which didn't come as often these days, but still came. It was hard to believe it was finally here.

'Am I really at my target?' She covered her eyes with her hands. 'Am I really there?' she asked Saskia. 'Or am I dreaming? Quick, pinch me and prove I'm not dreaming.'

'You're not dreaming,' Saskia said. 'But I am not pinching you. Congratulations. No one deserves it more.'

'I bet you say that to everyone?'

'Some people.' Saskia's beautiful eyes warmed. 'Worth a celebration – yes?'

'Oh yes. Definitely.'

'I think others are close too.'

Five minutes later, it became clear that Dana had reached her target too and so had Harry. Becky was still a pound away.

'You'll be there next week,' Ruby reassured her friend. 'We can all celebrate together then.'

'I know I will be. I'm doubly determined now. But I don't think we should wait. I think we should all celebrate now with a coffee at the Bluebell. Black, obviously. Have you got time?'

'I've got time for a quick one.' Ruby looked at Dana and Harry. 'Have you guys got time?'

They nodded enthusiastically and a few minutes later the four dieters and their workout guru were sitting on the terrace outside the Bluebell in the same place that Ruby and Harry had sat on that evening that seemed ages ago now.

Ruby didn't order the caramel latte with chocolate sprinkles she had promised herself. It didn't seem fair on Becky. She ordered black coffee. So did Harry and for a moment as the waitress took their orders, their glances caught and held in mutual understanding. She really liked that about him. His kindness, his sensitivity.

Men like Harry didn't come along very often. They should be treasured and valued, not used and abused. Again, her thoughts flicked back to Annabel Small. She would have liked to have got hold of her and shaken her – preferably by the neck. She blinked away the thoughts, reminding herself she didn't know the full story. Perhaps Annabel had contributed hugely to the marriage. Perhaps that was why Harry was now having to sell his art to free himself of her. But if that was the case, then surely she wouldn't need to blackmail him with incriminating camera footage.

Ruby dragged herself back to the present. The others were chatting and smiling, but suddenly Ruby became aware that Harry was staring at something through the open door that led back into the hotel. He was sitting beside her but at a slightly different angle and he looked shocked.

Ruby shifted slightly to see what was holding his attention and she caught a glimpse of the rear view of a couple. She had a snapshot image of a petite blonde, holding the hand of a well-dressed older man.

She touched Harry's arm and said in a voice only loud enough for him to hear, 'Harry, what is it? You look like you've seen a ghost.'

'Not a ghost. I've just seen my ex with her solicitor.' His voice was icy.

'They looked, er... very friendly.' She glanced at his face, which showed a mix of shock and resignation.

'I believe they are. But I've never been able to prove it.'

Ruby shook her head. 'Tell me you're joking.'

He seemed to be frozen, but then he was suddenly galvanised into standing.

Ruby stood up too. 'Are you planning to confront them? Will that help your case?'

He wavered. 'No. No, it won't help. She'll say they're just having a business meeting over dinner. He's her employer as well as her legal representative... As well as her lover.'

'I see.' Ruby felt the adrenaline coursing through her. 'So right now, you have the advantage because they don't know you've seen them.'

'Yes. You're right. I guess I do.' He seemed to relax a little. The frozen shock on his face had gone, but he still looked dazed.

Saskia, aware of their movements and intense conversation, glanced in their direction. 'Everything OK?' she mouthed.

'Everything's fine,' Harry said, as both he and Ruby sat back down again.

Harry's Adam's apple bobbed, and Ruby knew he was trying to gather himself, rein in his emotions, get his happy-go-lucky 'I've just got to my target weight and everything's wonderful' face back on. It was weird how quickly she had learned to read the nuances of his face.

'If they were staying here and you could prove they were staying together, would that help?' Ruby asked him quietly.

'I don't know. Um. Yes.' He sighed. 'Yes, it probably would.'

'I'm sure we could discreetly find out.'

'They might just be having a meal in the restaurant,' he murmured.

'They were heading towards the stairs,' she pointed out.

'That's true.' There was resolve in his eyes now and it was strengthening by the second. Harry wasn't used to having someone fighting his corner, Ruby guessed. He was looking at her with something close to hope. 'Do you mean I should ask Saskia? I don't want to put her in a compromising position.'

'You won't have to. My sister's fiancé works here. He's the Bluebell Cliff's part-time maître d' – I think he might be working this week. But even if he's not, I'm sure he'd be happy to take a look at the guest book.'

'They'll probably have signed in under a different name.' He looked downcast.

'It wouldn't hurt to check though, would it?' Ruby was on a roll. 'I know this is none of my business, Harry, but if I can help, then I will. Just say the word.'

'Thank you,' he said. 'OK. Yes, that would be helpful.'

'I won't be long.' She got up again at the same time as the waitress came back with their drinks. 'Excuse me,' she said to the table in general and she strolled into the foyer.

There was no sign of the couple. It was gone eight thirty, presumably they'd just finished their dinner and had retired for the night. God, that was brazen. Poor Harry. Knowing that his wife was sleeping with her legal representative whilst also taking him to the cleaners.

Ruby could feel her heart thudding with outrage on his behalf as she slipped into the restaurant. Almost immediately, she caught sight of Phil's familiar outline on the other side of the room. He had his back to her; he was standing at a table. She headed towards him.

He finished and turned just as she reached him. 'Ruby, hey, I didn't know you were in tonight. Are you eating?'

'No. Just celebrating getting to my target weight. With black coffee,' she added quickly, 'so I'll still be on target for your wedding.'

He smiled at her. 'You always look great to me. What can I do for you? Or were you just saying hello?'

'This is a little bit delicate actually. I don't suppose you've got a few minutes, have you?'

'Sure, just let me put this order in and I'm all yours.'

Five minutes later, in a quiet corner of the dining room, she had told him what she wanted, as well as a very brief outline of why she wanted it, and Phil was nodding gravely.

'If pretty much anyone else had asked me to do this, I'd have said, no. It breaks every rule in the book.' His eyes were very serious. 'But in the circumstances, I think I could have a look at our booking system. I think I know the couple you mean – the blonde and the older guy in the smart suit?'

Ruby nodded.

'This isn't going to backfire on the Bluebell, is it?'

'No.'

'Who's on reception?'

'No one when I passed.'

'Then, maybe if you were to look over my shoulder while I check our online booking system for something, would that do?'

'That would do perfectly.' She followed him back through to reception where the desk was still unmanned. Then Ruby readied the camera on her phone while Phil tapped some keys on a keyboard.

'It looks like they're leaving tomorrow. They booked a double room on Saturday under the names Mr and Mrs Lewison for four nights,' Phil said quietly and stood to one side so Ruby could see the details on screen. 'Is that good enough?'

'It would be even better if I could get a photo of them eating their breakfast tomorrow morning,' Ruby said. 'I'm sure it would be fine if they were just in the background, you know, of someone else's photograph.'

'Remind me never to get on the wrong side of you,' Phil said, glancing at her with a raised eyebrow. 'But yes, I'm sure an impromptu photography session of the dining room could be arranged tomorrow morning if they come down for breakfast.'

'Thanks. I owe you big time.'

'Happy to help,' he said and closed the registration system down.

Ruby slipped back out onto the terrace. The others were still where she'd left them, sipping their drinks.

'Hey, you,' Becky called. 'We thought you'd sneaked off to get cake.'

'As if.' Ruby patted her stomach. 'Nope. This tummy is staying flat, at least until after my sister's wedding.'

'When is it?'

'In eleven days' time. And I have my final bridesmaid dress fitting on Saturday. Just before the hen night.'

Her only bridesmaid dress fitting since she'd lost weight, she thought, as she slid back into the bench seat beside Harry. Fingers crossed, it fitted.

'And talking of flat tummies,' Saskia said, picking up her mug of coffee, 'now we are all here, I would like to propose a toast. Congratulations, ladies and gentleman, on reaching your target weights. Do you realise that on this table alone we have lost a grand total of eight and a half stone so far. That includes yours, Becky. That's enough to make up a whole extra person. Where did they go?'

Becky glanced around as if she was expecting to see someone slipping away across the terrace.

'That's an incredible achievement,' Saskia continued, 'in just – what? Fourteen weeks? So I'd like you to join me in a toast. If we could all raise our mugs, please. Here's to high achievers.'

'To high achievers,' they all said, lifting their mugs in unison.

Ruby and Harry exchanged a glance and she gave him a little nod. She had acted entirely on impulse and she was starting to wonder if she should have got Phil involved. She was already feeling guilty about that. On the other hand, there were some situations where the end definitely justified the means. She couldn't just stand by and watch Harry get conned into selling his family paintings – not when she could help do something about it.

Shortly after the toast, the little group disbanded. Harry and Ruby walked round to the car park together and she hesitated in the shadow of the Bluebell's wall before they went their separate ways.

'Mission accomplished,' she said to him. 'They booked a double room on Saturday for four nights in the name of Mr and Mrs Lewison. As soon as I get home, I'll forward you a photo I took earlier of the booking system. Hopefully it will help your case.' She decided not to tell him about the other photo she'd arranged, in case Phil couldn't do it.

'Thank you. I don't really know what to say.' He swallowed. 'Ruby, you do realise that you might be doing yourself out of a commission, don't you? If I can prove that Annabel and Nick are a couple, I may not have to sell my artwork.'

'I very much hope that's the case, Harry. But I will await your further instructions. Good luck.' She paused and, still high on adrenaline from the events of the evening, she added wickedly, 'I'd shake your hand or kiss you or something, but you never know who's watching, do you? So I'll resist the temptation.'

He glanced at her and in that moment she caught it again, that flash of agreement in his eyes. She wasn't imagining the chemistry. He might be denying it as much as she was. But he definitely felt it too.

'Good night, Harry.'

'Good night, lovely Ruby,' he said softly. 'Will I see you again?'

'I'm planning to be at next week's workout session, subject to Mum having Simon one more time. Just because I'm at target, I'm not planning to miss the last session.'

'I'll look forward to that then.'

Ruby was already looking forward to it too. Very much.

29

Ruby had called Olivia on Wednesday morning both to tell her how thrilled she was that she'd reached her target weight but also to apologise. 'I'm sorry if I put Phil in an awkward position last night,' she told her sister. 'Not to mention this morning. I hope he didn't mind.'

Phil had just sent her a very clear, and very compromising, photo of Annabel Small and Nick Lewison holding hands over a toast rack and gazing into each other's eyes. They were sitting behind some planters in the Bluebell's restaurant-cum-breakfast room but their faces were very visible, as was the fact that their relationship was neither platonic nor professional.

'Phil was happy to help,' Olivia told her. 'He said Clara's been asking him to sort out an overhaul of the planters in the restaurant for a while, so what could be more natural than taking some shots of the existing ones. And if he happened to catch the odd guest or two in the background of the shots, well, that was a bonus, wasn't it?'

'I'm really grateful,' Ruby said. 'Tell him I'll buy him a drink when I see him next.'

'Totally unnecessary. He was pleased to help. He said he's got an audition coming up for the role of a PD and it was good to get into character.'

'PD?'

'Private detective.'

They both giggled.

'The things we do for love,' Olivia added. 'Seriously, Rubes. We can't ever repay you for your wedding present.' Her voice husked slightly over the words. 'But just to say it again. Thank you.'

'It is my absolute pleasure, Liv. You know that.' Ruby glanced at her son, who was at that moment lying in his travel cot, blowing bubbles and looking totally angelic.

'I know. Look, I've got to go. But you can give me an update on the whole Harry situation on Saturday morning. I'll see you at Beautiful Brides.'

'Looking forward to it,' Ruby said, crossing her fingers behind her back. Thanks to her stubbornness about not going for a dress fitting until the last moment, there was precious little time left to make any alterations. Which meant she was actually slightly worried about Saturday morning.

* * *

And now the moment of truth was finally here. She was in a fitting room, which was luckily large enough to accommodate Simon's buggy, and Bonnie McCloud had just unwrapped her gorgeous, dusky rose-pink bridesmaid dress from its cellophane and left them alone with the words, 'I'll give you a minute to put it on.'

As Ruby slipped the smooth satin creation over her head and wriggled it down over her hips, she held her breath. Despite the fact she knew she'd lost two and a half stone and that she could now fit easily back into her size-twelve jeans, she had still worried this dress wouldn't fit.

She risked a glance in the mirror. Wow. Not bad – if she did say so herself. She was a little curvy in the hips, but the dress seemed to accommodate that OK. She turned side on, not exactly a super flat tummy either but nothing a bit of Spanx couldn't sort out.

'What do you think?' she asked Simon. 'Does Mummy look pretty?'

'Duck,' he said giggling.

'Yeah, thanks for that.' She blew out a sigh of relief and peeked through the curtain. 'I've got it on.'

Bonnie McCloud came back into the fitting room, tape measure in hand.

'Perfect,' she said, circling her slowly and then fiddling with the zip before smoothing down the satin back with her hands.

'Does the zip do up?' Ruby asked.

'The zip is done up. It's a perfect fit. Fortunately.' Bonnie's voice was dry. It clearly wasn't just Ruby who'd been worrying about the last-minute dress fitting.

'So, shall we see how Hannah is doing? Then I will call your sister to come in.'

Hannah had got her dress on too and the two young women stepped out of their respective changing rooms to show Olivia their dresses.

'Oh my goodness, you two look stunning.' There were tears in Olivia's eyes. 'Give me a twirl.'

They twirled in unison, the cool satin rustling on the wooden floor as they moved. 'I feel like a princess,' Hannah said. 'These dresses are gorgeous.'

'I feel like a grown-up,' Ruby said. 'It had to happen some time. We won't let you down,' she added. 'We will be model bridesmaids, won't we, Hannah?'

'We'll look the part. That's all I'm promising,' Hannah said with a cheeky grin.

'You look amazing, both of you.' Olivia blinked a few times. 'In a week I'll be Mrs Olivia Grimshaw. It's all starting to feel very real. Group hug?'

The three women hugged.

'Right then, ladies,' Bonnie turned back into her bustling efficient self, 'let's get these dresses back into their cellophane. We don't want to mark them before the big day, do we?'

Outside, once more on Weymouth Quay, back in their jeans and T-shirts again, the three women and Simon in his buggy stood in the fresh, briny air and chattered about the hen night that evening. This was taking place a few hundred metres away in Olivia's favourite seafood restaurant on the quay. It was just family and a few close friends, so very intimate as Olivia had requested. Then Hannah went off to get what she said was some last-minute shopping for later.

As soon as she'd gone, Olivia turned to Ruby. 'So come on then? What's the latest with Harry. Any news? I'm desperate for an update.' Her eyes sparkled with curiosity. 'Did the incriminating evidence help?'

'Yes it did. Although nothing's ever simple, is it? Harry told me on the phone that he may still have to pay his conniving ex a hefty settlement because apparently she can prove that she contributed significantly to his company landing a major client just after they were married and is therefore entitled to recompense.'

'Unbelievable,' Olivia said, shaking her head. 'So even though she's committed adultery, he's the one who has to do the paying out.'

'Very possibly. And they've been married just under two years. No kids. It's really unfair.'

They were standing close to the quayside, the smell of bait from a nearby fishing boat that had just moored up was in the air and opportunist seagulls squawked and circled hopefully. Ruby glanced at the water that sparkled greeny-blue in the morning sunshine and shook her head. It was still hard to keep Harry out of her mind, even though she hadn't seen him since Tuesday.

'But the million-dollar question is,' Olivia continued, 'are you and he...?'

'Any further forward than we were a few weeks ago,' Ruby finished. 'No, I'm afraid not. I'm trying really hard not to muddy the waters, Liv. He's got so much on his plate already.'

'So you're not bringing him to my wedding as your plus-one then?'

'Not unless a miracle happens,' Ruby said ruefully. 'No.'

'Here's hoping for a miracle then,' Olivia said.

'Duck, duck,' shouted Simon, which proved to be a timely remark as seagull poop spattered the ground nearby.

'It's supposed to be lucky if it hits you,' Olivia said.

'I've always thought it's much luckier if it doesn't,' Ruby giggled at her son. 'His all-in-one suit arrived yesterday. The bow tie is adorable. He looks amazing in it. It's a good job I waited until the last minute to get it, though. He's growing so much.'

'I can't wait to see it.'

'One week to go.'

* * *

Ruby wasn't feeling downhearted about going to the wedding on her own, she realised as she drove home. This was not because she didn't still feel hugely attracted to Harry either. The feelings, if anything, kept getting stronger. But for the first time in her life she wasn't in a hurry to push things. Maybe that was because she had Simon to think about now. Maybe she was getting all responsible in her old age. She'd only been half joking when she said she felt grown up in her bridesmaid dress earlier.

She wasn't sure why but whatever the reason was, she felt good, knowing that she wasn't putting any more pressure on Harry than he was already under. He had her number. They were good enough friends for him to know he could call her any time. If he did feel the same way as she did – if he ever felt it – then he knew how to get in touch with her, didn't he?

* * *

Harry was in his office catching up on some paperwork. He hadn't been at work enough lately. He'd taken his eye off the ball, because of the divorce negotiations that were taking up so much of his headspace.

It had been a shock seeing Annabel and Nick, albeit at a distance, last week. He had known he was bound to see Annabel again. It was inevitable, given that there was still two years of her possessions in his house, packed into boxes by him, waiting for her to collect – but he hadn't expected to see her out with Nick. He had never expected her to be so blatant. Was she so sure of herself that she could swan around openly with her lover, not caring that she might bump into the husband she was divorcing for 'unreasonable behaviour'? Maybe she hadn't expected him to be at the Bluebell. Most likely she hadn't. She probably thought he'd only ever gone there because she'd asked him to – there was some truth in that – and had knocked Booty Busters on the head as soon as she'd left him.

Harry was relieved he hadn't reacted on his instincts and challenged the couple. He knew he had Ruby to thank for that. She'd been right to stop him charging out and confronting them. That would have achieved nothing and might even have made things worse.

As things stood now, he had a much stronger case, which he was hoping to make even stronger. Ruby hadn't just stopped him from making a mistake, she had also inspired him. He didn't need to sit back and let Annabel walk all over him. Paying her off just to save him money, as his solicitor had suggested, no longer seemed so appealing. He had spent too much of his life not acting and later regretting it. He had decided to fight.

Last night amidst bouts of insomnia, he'd dreamed about his father again. As usual, his father had been staring at him with that angst-ridden expression that was so familiar. As usual, he'd been mouthing words that Harry couldn't quite hear. It was as if he was trying to tell him something important, but someone had switched off the volume and Harry couldn't hear what it was.

Then the dream had taken an unusual turn and the volume had reappeared and suddenly he could hear what his father was saying. It was the word, Pritchard, over and over again. 'Pritchard, Pritchard, Pritchard.' Then Harry realised there was a second word. 'Alms. Pritchard Alms.'

Harry had jolted awake in the four a.m. darkness with his father's face still clearly in his mind and the words Pritchard Alms, circling in his head. Not that he was any the wiser. Pritchard Alms meant nothing to him.

Feeling dehydrated and thirsty, Harry had rolled over in bed, reaching for the glass of water on his bedside table. He'd sat up to drink it. Then before he could forget the name that his subconscious so clearly wanted him to remember he'd made a note on his phone, rolled back over and finally got back to sleep again. He didn't wake up again until the eight a.m. sunshine was streaming in at his window.

He'd showered away the restless night and had gone into work. Something was niggling in the back of his head. A memory that was not yet fully formed. Pritchard Alms sounded as though it might be a pub. The Pritchard Arms. Could that be it? It seemed unlikely that Gargantuul had ever had a single pub as a client. A brewery chain possibly. But he couldn't think of one.

In an attempt to jog his memory, he embarked on a search through some old accounts. They had a very up-to-date electronic filing system, but Grandpa George, who'd been meticulous when it came to filing, had also kept some old paper records that went back to the early years of Gargantuul.

Harry had wanted to throw them out when Grandpa George had passed away – on the grounds that anything important had already been transferred to the computerised system, but his father had stopped him.

'Humour me,' he'd said. 'We don't always know what things might be important. They're not taking up much room.'

Harry had agreed and his father had sorted through some of the old correspondence and then filed it neatly in an old box file which he'd labelled 'Archived Correspondence'. It was now on a shelf, covered in dust. It hadn't been moved since the day his father had filed it.

Harry got it down and put it on the enormous desk. Then, feeling as though he might very well be wasting his time, he began to flick through the documents, taking each one out and scanning it as he went.

He had no idea what he was looking for, but he hoped he'd know it when he found it. And he was right. He'd been searching for half an hour when he came across a letter that had been sent to his grandfather. It was dated a decade ago, but the illegible signa-

ture, or more pertinently the printed name below it, made Harry sit
up straight in his chair.

Not a pub called the Pritchard Arms, but a man's name, Richard
Arms. That had to be it. It was so similar. Harry glanced at the
address at the top of the letter and the hair stood up on the back of
his neck. It was an enquiry that had been sent to his grandfather
from SmithKline Beecham to arrange initial talks about installing a
new software system.

It predated Annabel's introduction to the company by several
years. Could it help? He had a feeling that it could. He opened the
online filing system and went to the SmithKline Beecham account.
There was so much correspondence, but all he needed was a link.

And then he found one. Richard Arms had never left the
company. He had always been a senior buyer. There had been
several letters and emails back and forth since that first letter. There
had been some emails with Leonard Stanley too, but Richard Arms,
who was the main man, had already known about Gargantuul. This
letter was the proof Harry realised that his company hadn't needed
Annabel's introduction. They had already been in discussion with
the client. This was what his father had been trying to tell him.

Harry rested his arms on the arms of the big office chair into
which he'd always fitted so much more comfortably than his father.
'Thanks, Dad,' he whispered.

30

The hen night was fabulous. Apart from the fact that all the women except Olivia wore pink glitter hats that pronounced 'hen night' and Olivia wore an exotic silver one that said 'bride-to-be' (the hats had been what Hannah had rushed off to collect after the dress fittings), you'd have been hard-pressed to tell it was a hen night.

'Which is exactly what I wanted,' Olivia said, leaning across the table at the end of the evening. A lovely quiet meal out in my favourite restaurant with the women I love best in the world. 'I have quite enough drama in my day job.' She hesitated. 'I know it sounds mad, but after years of doing my utmost to get firmly into the limelight, now I've got it, all I seem to do is try my best to stay out of it.'

They all laughed. Olivia hated being recognised when she was out and about. But for some reason this didn't seem to happen so much in her home town. Lucinda Fox, the character she played in *Nightingales*, was characterised by her incredibly heavy eye make-up and scarlet lipstick and the fact that she dressed in smart suits and always wore her hair in a French plait. It was a distinctive look and Olivia didn't look much like her character in real life.

'Are you youngsters going on anywhere else?' Aunt Dawn asked.

She'd insisted on picking up the bill for the evening and they were now all sitting around their coffees and mints, their empty plates having been long cleared. 'Or will you all be going to bed relatively sober?'

'I need to get back for Simon,' Ruby said, yawning. She glanced at their mother. 'Not that I'm too worried about him. It's great that he's got the chance for some proper bonding time with his grandad.'

'And I haven't heard a peep from Grandad James,' their mother said with a grin. 'He's obviously mastered the art of nappy changing.'

'Or he's waiting for you to get back and do it,' Hannah said with a wink. 'That happened to a friend of mine once when she asked her dad to babysit.'

'Ew, no. Really?' Ruby screwed up her nose in disgust. 'Maybe I'd better go now?'

'I promise you he'll manage the nappy, Ruby. He's not a total beginner, contrary to what you girls might think.'

They all laughed again.

'Is Dad back until the wedding now?' Ruby asked.

'He is, darling, yes.'

'As are Phil and I,' Olivia said. 'Neither of us are filming again until the end of August. Which is partly why we booked our wedding for the first week.'

'And Amazing Cakes has no commissions,' Aunt Dawn said. 'Apart from yours, Olivia, of course, which is in my store cupboard, awaiting collection. By the way, did I tell you we got another alpaca to keep Mrs Hudson company. We've decided to call him Mr Holmes.'

They all smiled. 'What else could he be called?' Ruby said, thinking of Sherlock and Watson, Mike's two black cats.

'Neither of them have escaped either,' Aunt Dawn added.

'Everyone needs company,' Olivia said. 'Even alpacas.'

Their mother shook her head. 'So we're all set for the big day, then? Excellent. I'm glad you decided on cars in the end. So much more reliable than more... unorthodox transport,' she said, and Ruby knew she was thinking of balloons.

As she looked round at their happy faces, Ruby felt a mix of warmth and excitement. It was good to have something nice to look forward to – especially when she thought back to the day the wedding invitation had landed when all she remembered feeling was dread.

* * *

After the hen night, Ruby had the best night's sleep she'd had in ages. She dreamed of a perfect day at the Bluebell. She and Hannah were drifting across a velvet green lawn behind Olivia, who was a stunning vision in her dress. The sun was shining out of a bright blue sky and the music of the sea pounded rhythmically on the beach far below.

Harry was there too, done up to the nines in a top-end suit and he was heading in her direction. 'I've always...' he began, but whatever he said next was drowned out by a wailing siren and Ruby woke up with a jolt.

She'd been woken by a text notification on her phone. Or more to the point an email notification. She glanced at it and saw it was from one of her bigger London clients – she'd looked after their art for years.

Why were they emailing her on a Sunday?

Simon began to wail and Ruby got up and went to see to him. 'Hello, my darling, did the naughty phone wake you up too?' She picked him up and cuddled him.

Ten minutes later when he was changed and dry again, Ruby

remembered the email and she took Simon and her phone down-stairs to breakfast.

She'd been eating breakfasts again for a while – oats soaked in very low-fat yoghurt and mixed with berries. Never mind what Mr B said about not needing the most important meal of the day, it worked for her. Simon ate better when he saw that she was eating too. They played the game of, 'One spoon for you, and one spoon for me.' Only when they'd finished did she pick up her phone again and read the email from her client. And when she did, her heart froze.

They had decided to terminate their contract with her and move their collection to another dealer. They felt as if they weren't getting the personal attention they'd once had from her. Emails weren't answered, calls weren't returned.

Oh my God, was that true? Ruby realised it was. She hadn't answered an email from them that had been sent a fortnight ago. She didn't realise she'd missed calls too, although come to think of it, there had been a message on her voicemail from one of the women – they were a pair of high-society trust-fund babes who had far more money than most millionaires earned in a lifetime. She didn't think she'd answered that call either.

Her first instinct was to ring them immediately. It was only eight a.m. Was that a reasonable time to phone a client on a Sunday morning? Her heart told her no. But they had emailed her.

No, more likely they hadn't just emailed. Either it had been scheduled or sent by a member of staff.

Ruby agonised. Her hands felt sweaty on her phone. The last thing she wanted to do was to piss them off even more. She decided to call them later in the morning.

* * *

When she did, she got a voicemail message. The same thing happened on Monday morning when she tried them again and on Tuesday and on Wednesday. She finally sent a long apologetic email response to their email and that was ignored too and then on Wednesday lunchtime, she got a further email.

Dear Ms Lambert,

As per our previous instructions, our new agent will be Will Bailey. Could you therefore make arrangements for the collection to be shipped as soon as possible via our office? No further correspondence will be entered into.

Olivia tried them again but was rebuffed this time by a PA who refused to put her through to her clients or talk about anything other than the shipping arrangements. They clearly meant what they said about no further correspondence.

The worst thing about it was that it was her own fault. If she'd been more on the ball, they wouldn't have felt the need to leave her and move to Will Bailey, a big New York dealer. Her clients stayed with her for the very personal service she gave them and since she'd had Simon, they hadn't been getting it. She'd been mad to think she could simply put the art world on hold while she swanned around in a paint-streaked kaftan with her baby in a papoose. It just didn't work like that.

She had made an incredible amount of money in the ten years since she had run her own company and she stood to lose an incredible amount of money too if she pissed people off. It was a small world and one disgruntled, influential customer could ruin a dealer's reputation. Ruby felt as though she'd had a very rude awakening back into reality.

* * *

She was still trying to sort it all out when her doorbell rang late Wednesday afternoon. Irritated because she wasn't expecting anyone, she went to open it and was astounded to see Harry on her doorstep.

'Erm, hi...' She tailed off, flustered. 'Did we have an appointment I'd forgotten?' She had sent him the photo of his ex and the solicitor and he'd thanked her profusely, but she didn't think they'd arranged to meet again on a professional basis. Although she had to admit she had been totally distracted.

'No, no, we didn't. I was worried, that's all. Could I possibly come in?'

'Er yes, of course. If you don't mind taking me as you find me. I've had a bit of a day. A bit of a week actually.' She felt slightly disorientated. How had he even known where she lived? Then she remembered her address was on her business card. Which, of course, she'd given him.

She led him through the big hall and into the kitchen. There was paperwork strewn across her breakfast island and a laptop open in the middle of it and Simon was on his play mat on the floor.

'Da, da, da dad,' he said as soon as he saw Harry.

'No, darling, this is Harry.' She picked up the giggling baby. 'Say, hello, Harry.' She screwed up her face. Oh goodness he needed changing. What an introduction that would be to Handsome Harry. She bit her lip. Did she still see him like that? She was so all over the place she didn't even know.

'Hello, little man. You are a fine fellow.' Harry was smiling at her son, despite the smell, and his dark eyes were soft. 'He's gorgeous.'

'He's gorgeous when he smells better. Harry, I'm just going to change him. Please help yourself to coffee. I'll be two minutes.'

When she came back, complete with a now sweet-smelling Simon Harry was sitting at her breakfast island, sipping a coffee, doing something on his phone and looking totally at home. He glanced up as she came into the room and then before she had the chance to say anything, he got up and came across to them both.

'I'm sorry to call round unannounced, Ruby, but I was worried when you didn't show up at Booty Busters last night. Also your phone seems to be constantly engaged. I did leave one message.'

'Booty Busters. Oh God.' Ruby clapped her hands over her mouth. 'I completely forgot about it. How could I have forgotten about that?'

'You've had other things on your mind?' Harry suggested.

'Yes, I have. I didn't see a message from you either, but you're right. I've had other things on my mind. How did it go? Did Becky get to target?'

He did a double thumbs up sign. 'She did. She smashed it. We all went for another celebration coffee. An official, Getting to Target Celebration.'

'I'm so sorry, I missed it. I'll text her and say congratulations.' She sighed and became aware of his eyes on her.

'Would it help to chat things through with a friendly face? I've made you a coffee.' He gestured towards the worktop.

He had, she saw, and in her favourite mug too. How had he known that?

'Possibly, but I'm not sure where I'd even start, Harry. It would take for ever.' She was only just getting used to him being in her kitchen. 'How long have you got?'

'I'm in no rush. Seriously.' He picked up her coffee and his own and came over to her. 'Shall we maybe start with drinking coffee somewhere you and Simon are comfortable?'

She took him through to the lounge, which was tidy. Her default setting was tidy and she'd barely been in there lately.

He put their coffees on the low table. 'Is that OK? Or do they need to be higher?'

'That's OK, he's not walking yet. Thanks. And he's pretty sleepy. It's time for his afternoon nap.'

When she had settled Simon for his nap and had come back into the room again, Harry was standing with his arms behind his back, looking at the painting that was hung over her fireplace. It was a nude in profile by an artist Ruby really liked, tastefully done, but without a great deal left to the imagination. Fortunately, the woman had long Titian hair that partly obscured one of her breasts, and her legs were stretched out in front of her, even as her head was tilted to one side, as she flirted with the artist.

Ruby was so used to it being there, she barely noticed it. Bare being the operative word, she thought now, feeling a little tingle run through her as Harry studied it before turning back towards her. Oh my God, she still felt it then – the chemistry of his nearness. She had thought it might have lessened now there was the reality of him standing in her own home, but it definitely hadn't.

'That's a stunning painting,' he said. 'I'm sure I've seen that model before – did he paint other portraits of her?'

'Yes, she was his wife, as well as his muse,' Ruby told him. 'It's said that they had the happiest of marriages – not that common in those days.'

His eyes darkened briefly and she thought, *Oh crap, tactless Ruby strikes again.*

But she realised he looked more concerned than anything else.

'I meant what I said just now, Ruby. I'm a very good listener. It would be a privilege if I could help you as much as you have helped me.'

There was such genuine warmth in his voice and she knew he meant it, so finally she did as he'd suggested and she sat down on one end of the two long sofas in her lounge and Harry sat a reasonable distance away so she had space. And then she told him everything that had happened that week.

At the end of it, he looked thoughtful. But he didn't speak straight away. He didn't offer any glib suggestions. Then he moved a bit closer on the settee and said softly, 'That's one hell of a week, you've had.'

'I know.' It was weird. She'd managed to recount the whole story in a flat unemotional voice – just conveying the facts and nothing more, but now suddenly she wanted to cry.

'Would you like me to tell you what I think, Ruby? Or do you just need a hug?'

Ruby swallowed tears. A hug sounded both amazing and dangerous. She couldn't remember ever feeling so conflicted about a simple question. But then, before she could stop herself, it was as if her body took matters in hand and she shifted the remaining distance along her sofa to meet him and he put his arms around her. It felt amazing. She'd been right about the chemistry. She could feel it in him too. She could feel it in the strength and warmth of him as he wrapped his arms around her and held her tight.

She laid her head against his chest and he said gently, 'It'll be OK. It might look bad now, but it'll work out. Things always work out.'

The most bizarre thing was that she believed him, Ruby thought, when she finally lifted her head from his chest and turned to look at him. His lips were just inches away. His eyes were gentle and she couldn't resist for a millisecond longer. She leaned in and kissed him and for a few seconds he kissed her back. It was the most gloriously tender and beautiful of kisses and the sparks that it set off in her tummy were immense and unstoppable.

Then he was gently pulling away. 'I'm so sorry,' he said. 'I didn't mean to do that. It was taking advantage.'

'If anyone was taking advantage it was me,' Ruby told him, meeting his eyes and seeing a longing in them that she knew was reflected in hers. 'I've wanted to do that for ages.'

'Have you? Oh God.' He blinked a few times as if he was trying to clear his head.

'Yes.' She felt wanton and reckless. 'Haven't you?'

'Yes.'

He restarted the kiss and for a long time that was all there was in the world. Just Harry. The warmth and the tenderness and the familiar scent of him, which was different and more powerfully erotic close up.

They finally broke apart again, both of them breathless, and Ruby knew in that moment that nothing was ever going to be the same again. Not for either of them. This was the feeling that had eluded her all of her life. She had suspected it for a while but she hadn't dared to give it a name. And now she did. This was love.

31

'What happened next, Rubes? You can't stop there!' It was the day after Harry's visit – he'd only just left – and Olivia's voice on the phone was all breathy and excited. 'Or is that classified?'

'No, it is not classified. What do you take me for? He's married and there's no way I'm getting caught in that trap again.'

'Yes, but he's only married in name. It's not a repeat of Scott. It's nothing like the Scott situation.'

'I know it's nothing like the Scott situation,' Ruby said, laughing out loud because she felt so happy. 'But that isn't the point. We've agreed we won't be taking things a single step further until his divorce comes through.'

'You're kidding me. A tenner says you'll never be able to keep your hands off each other that long.'

'I can't make a bet like that on my future love life. No way!'

'Yes, you can.' Olivia was laughing too. 'Oh wow, Rubes. I'm so happy for you. He sounds lovely.'

'He is lovely. I've been a bit in love with him for ages I think, but that kiss just – wow – that kiss just cemented it, and he says he feels the same. We actually stayed up all night talking.'

'About what, for goodness' sake?'

'About what I'm going to do about my client. Losing them didn't seem anywhere near as important once I'd talked it all through with Harry. It was a lesson not to take my eye off the ball and to make sure I'm fully engaged with the other clients I have. But it's not the end of the world. They might very well have been planning to leave for a while. Things change. People do come and go.'

'That's very mature and wise. You sound like Aunt Dawn.'

'That's a compliment, thank you. We also talked a lot about Harry's situation. Thanks in part to what happened at the Bluebell, with him seeing his ex out with her solicitor, he isn't going to be bankrupt. In fact, the solicitor isn't even her solicitor any more. Once they realised they'd been caught red-handed, they had a huge bust-up. Both personally and professionally.'

'That sounds like a great result.'

'Yes, karma, if you ask me. Harry's also found some evidence that the introduction she made wasn't as important as he'd originally thought. Gargantuul, his company, were already in discussions with the client. So she can't take him to the cleaners after all.'

'That's amazing news.'

'She'll still get a fair settlement. But it will reflect the very short marriage they've had so it won't bankrupt him. Harry's like that. He's really straight and honest.'

'He sounds lovely. I said that already, didn't I?'

'You did. But you can say it again. You can say it as many times as you like. I still can't get over the fact I've managed to find a lovely man – one who's kind, I mean, and loves kids, as well as being as hot as hell.'

'I take it you're bringing him to the wedding now then?'

'Yes, yes, yes, definitely yes. I've already asked him. Although he did say he'd have to buy a new suit. One that isn't too big for him!'

* * *

Harry was also walking on air. He couldn't remember ever feeling the way he felt now. Not even in the early days of Annabel. In fact, the way he felt now was nothing like the early days of Annabel. Because back then his joy had been threaded through with a massive dollop of insecurity – did she really like him? Was there something else going on?

He wished he had paid more attention to those niggling doubts, he thought now. It would have saved a great deal of heartache. But then, as he and Ruby had both agreed during the night they'd spent talking, maybe it was the fact they'd both been through so much heartache that made it so special now.

It had certainly made them into the people they were. And, by God, Ruby was beautiful. She was the most beautiful woman he had ever met, because she was beautiful both inside and out. She was also smart, sassy and, as far as he could see, supermum. She was brilliant with Simon. It had made his throat tighten watching them together. It was early days – very, very early days – but the thought that she might one day be mother to his children too was just the icing on the cake.

And talking of icing on cakes, he needed to buy a suit for her sister's wedding. He'd been thrilled when she'd asked him to go along.

'You can meet all my family in one fell swoop,' she had said. 'And if that doesn't put you off, nothing will.'

Harry knew one thing for sure. Nothing was going to put him off being with Ruby.

32

It was finally here. The day of the wedding. Ruby, Simon and Olivia had all spent the previous night with their parents. Olivia because she didn't want to see Phil the night before she married him and Ruby because it would be a lot easier, not to mention more exciting, if she and her sister woke up in the same place on the day of the wedding.

'What's the weather like?' Ruby asked, as she came into the kitchen with a grumpy Simon in her arms. He had picked up the charged atmosphere and knew something was afoot. He'd also just started to crawl and was into everything, which was easier at Ruby's than her mum's because home was more toddler-proof.

'Bit overcast,' Olivia said as she turned from the window. 'It's probably a sea mist.'

'Better for the photos then. Cloudy is better than bright sunshine.'

'Yes, that's true.' Olivia looked happy. 'I wouldn't care if it rained, to be honest. I'm just so pleased the day is finally here.'

'Have you heard from Phil?'

'He sent me a "break a leg" text first thing. I guess that getting married does have a lot in common with acting. The hair, the make-up, the clothes, the learning your lines – I mean vows!' She winked.

'It's certainly a bit of a performance,' Ruby agreed and they both laughed. Simon wriggled in her arms. She put him on to the kitchen floor and he immediately launched into action. 'You're not having any last-minute second thoughts then, Liv?'

'No, I'm not. He's all I've ever wanted and being married isn't going to change much really.' She frowned. 'I'm lying. I don't mean about the second thoughts, don't worry. I mean that it does feel different. All grown-up and serious. I have got a few butterflies about today as well. All the work and the planning and the huge expense.' She took another look out of the window. 'I'm glad we didn't go for the balloon in the end. I'd now be biting my nails worrying about the visibility.'

Ruby intercepted Simon from crawling out of the kitchen and he yelled in protest.

'You didn't go for doves in the end either, did you?'

'No. It's all pretty normal and straightforward. Midday wedding at the Bluebell, followed by sit-down lunch at the Bluebell. Followed by evening reception at the Bluebell. Followed by first night in the Bluebell's lighthouse.'

'Followed by an amazing honeymoon in the Seychelles. Oh, and Mr B doing the catering. Mr B as best man,' Ruby said with a wicked smile. 'You're not worried about that, are you? Mr B, I mean, not the honeymoon.'

'I'm not worried about him doing the catering. He's done most of it already and his staff are under threat of death if they put a foot wrong with the rest. I'm ever so slightly worried about him being best man.' She paused. 'And this flaming trick that Phil has up his sleeve for later. You know what their history is like.'

'The pranks and the wind-ups?'

'Precisely. Phil thinks he's going to have the last laugh with what he's got planned for today, but I'm not so sure. Mr B always comes out on top in the end.'

'Do you know what he is going to do?' Ruby asked, keeping an eye on Simon, who'd given up crawling out of the kitchen and was now talking to his reflection in the oven door.

'Vaguely, but not the details. He had to tell me some of it – presumably to stop me slapping them both when the shenanigans kick off. All I can tell you is that it's going to happen during the ceremony and Saskia's involved.'

'Saskia?' Ruby said, surprised. 'How did Saskia get involved? I knew you'd invited her to the reception, but I didn't know she was even coming to the ceremony.'

'Neither did I until the other day. You know, Charles Winton, Phil's agent?'

Ruby frowned. 'I think so.'

'Well, it turns out that he and Saskia have just started dating and when Charles realised there was a connection, he asked if he could bring her to the wedding as his plus-one. And Phil knows Saskia anyway from the Bluebell. Small world, isn't it?'

'It certainly is.'

'It wasn't too hard for Phil to rope Saskia into his wind-up. As you can imagine, after the shenanigans that have gone on between her and Mr B at Booty Busters.' Olivia shook her head in mock disapproval. 'They're like children, the pair of them!'

Their mother chose that moment to arrive, yawning, as she came into the kitchen. 'Who are like children? Hello, hello, hello, my scrumptious little man,' she addressed her grandson and then in an ironic voice to them, 'You two are up early. Is it a special occasion or something?'

* * *

The day began in earnest. Dad knocked up a wedding breakfast of Danish pastries and buck's fizz and Ruby decided that for the next twenty-four hours, if not the entire week, her diet was going out of the window.

The make-up and beauty ladies arrived together and the rest of the morning was a whirlwind of getting ready, punctuated by the arrival of flowers, good luck messages, phone calls and queries from people checking on last-minute details.

'Why don't they just look on Google Maps?' Ruby heard their mother yell in exasperation after one clearly tiresome phone call. 'Don't they know we're ever so slightly busy over here?'

It was chaos and Ruby loved it. She'd been messaging Harry with updates. It had been two days and three sleeps since that amazing kiss, although it hadn't really been three sleeps because they had spent most of Wednesday night talking and the time since messaging non-stop on their phones like a couple of teenagers. At her insistence, he had even WhatsApped her a selfie of the suit he had bought yesterday for the wedding.

Ruby felt as if they were both on a journey of discovery. She also felt as though she'd known him all her life. It was an intoxicating combination.

* * *

Harry was just about to leave for the wedding when the intercom buzzer for the gates went.

He opened the front door and saw with a thump of shock a familiar car on the other side of the gates. So Annabel had finally decided to rock up then. She certainly picked her moments.

Deciding that he didn't want to let her in – the last thing he needed was to be held up – he went to meet her without opening the gates.

She was alone. That at least was something. As he got to the car he had bought her, the electronic window slid down.

'Hello, Harry. How are you?' Her voice was cool and her beautiful face was almost expressionless.

'I'm just off out.' He didn't ask how she was. He had got to the stage, he realised with a little shock, of not actually wanting to know. It was as though she was some stranger he had once met. All the love he had felt for her was gone. It had been totally extinguished by what she had tried to do to him over the last few weeks. Also, if he was honest, because of the feelings he now had for Ruby.

'I wondered if we could talk some time.' She lowered her eyes, and then glanced back up at him under her lashes. Vulnerable and flirtatious. It was a look he knew so well. And, once, it would have tugged at his heart. But not any more.

'We have nothing left to say to each other. Unless you mean you would like to make an appointment to collect the rest of your belongings.'

'I... I didn't come for that. I just thought it might be easier if there were no solicitors...' Still vulnerable but the flirtatious look had gone.

Harry guessed that she hadn't yet found another pet one who would deal with her divorce free of charge. 'I'd prefer to talk via our solicitors,' he said and the flash of anger in her eyes told him he was spot on. 'I'm on my way out. As you can see. If you want to make an appointment to collect your belongings, let me know. Other than that you can contact my solicitor.'

'You callous bastard,' she hissed at him, all signs of vulnerability gone. 'I can't believe you're being like this. Let me in now.' She revved the engine and pressed the accelerator hard so the car's tyres spat gravel and Harry had to jump back sharply out of the way to avoid getting his foot run over.

She reversed back again a few feet and then revved up sharply for another go and flew forward again. This time, her car banged hard against the gates which clanged loudly but stayed shut. Harry was half afraid she was planning to use the car as a battering ram to knock them down. And he wasn't at all sure how he was going to stop her.

Fortunately, the car had stalled. Annabel was now crouched over the steering wheel, her face creased up in fury. After a moment, Harry risked coming into her hearing range again.

He didn't recognise his wife at all. But then he had never really known her, had he? He'd only ever known the mask she'd presented to him. He had only ever seen what she had wanted him to see. She'd claimed to be a hotshot solicitor – not true. She'd claimed to be a vulnerable orphan with no family – he'd done a bit of research on that and it seemed that hadn't been true either. She had a father, alive and well and currently serving time for fraud at Leyhill Prison in Gloucestershire. It was true what they said about the apple not falling far from the tree then.

'Get off my property before I call the police.' He was amazed that his voice was so calm and steady. This was not how he felt inside.

She shook her head, flung open the door, charged out of the car and flew at him like a wild thing, her arms flailing. Acting on instinct because there was no way he wanted any physical contact with her, Harry sidestepped smartly and she hit the gate with her fist instead of him. Screaming with rage, she flew at him again, and again he stepped out of range and slipped back through the pedestrian gate into the relative safety on the house side, clicking it shut behind him.

Thwarted and even more furious, if that was possible, Annabel hurled a bunch of keys at him through the gates with such force that they ended up on the gravel drive not far from the wheelie bins, where the shock of the impact broke the keyring and the keys scattered.

Annabel pounded on the bars. 'Fuck you, Harry Small.'

Ignoring her, he strolled towards the bins to gather her keys. The temptation to throw them back at her was hard to resist. But no way would he lower himself to her level. Summoning the same icy control that had stopped him from flattening her boyfriend, he handed the keys back to her through the bars of the gate.

'Get off my property. This is the last time I'm going to tell you.'

'I never loved you, Harry. I want you to know that. It was never about you. It was always about the money.'

Her cruel words, designed to inflict the maximum hurt, didn't get as far as his heart. Because he already knew that. As he stood there, meeting her furious gaze with his calm, level one, Harry knew that whatever she said or did, she couldn't hurt him any more. He'd gone past it.

And she must have seen something of this in his face because she stopped shouting abruptly, got back into her car and pressed the starter button.

Harry half expected her to ram the gates again, but it seemed she'd had enough of inflicting damage on her car, which had come off a lot worse than his steel gates.

This time, she put the BMW into reverse and backed down the drive in a series of jerky zigzag motions. Annabel had never been good at reversing and halfway down she hit a tree with a sickening crunch. He could hear her shouts of outrage as she skidded the car forward again with a squeal of brakes, managed to turn it, although not without hitting the tree again, which luckily withstood the impact, before finally screeching away out of his drive.

Then she was gone. Harry waited another five minutes just to be certain she really had gone before opening the gates, which still seemed to work, fortunately. He got his own car out and still feeling a little bit shaky – it was impossible to be totally unaffected by what had just happened – he headed towards the Bluebell as fast as he dared. He was late, but if he put his foot down, hopefully he would just about make it.

Harry flew into the Bluebell car park just in time to see the bridal party getting out of two blue and cream Bentleys decked out with white ribbons.

Shit, he thought, unsnapping his seat belt as he parked, leaping out of his Lexus and giving a startled-looking Ruby a wave before hurtling around the side of the building and into the Bluebell's wedding venue at the back. Luckily, he at least knew where he was going. He had a brief impression of a room full of light and flowers and people in their best togs as he slid into a chair at the back close to the French doors through which he'd just arrived.

This was all under the disapproving gaze of Mr B, who called him a fopdoodle and told him it was far too late to sit anywhere else, and didn't he know the bridal party had just arrived?

Harry did not want to get into an argument with Mr B. He'd had enough confrontations for one day, so he did as he was told. Which meant that he had a bird's-eye view of the door and would be amongst the first to see the bridal procession.

The room wasn't that big anyway. There were several rows of chairs, maybe five in each row, on either side of a wide aisle. At the end of each row of chairs were white candles in crystal holders with white ribbons trailing from them. There were also vases of pink flowers everywhere. They filled the room with their sweet scent, which Harry breathed in as he got his breath back. He'd been in this room before, but not while it was set up like this. It was usually a music room, he seemed to remember.

Mr B strode down to the pulpit to take his place beside Phil and the celebrant, who looked a bit like Elton John, complete with whacky glasses in the shape of red hearts. An assortment of dressed-to-the-nines women in hats came next – Harry guessed they were the mothers and aunts of the happy couple. Then, when they were all seated, amidst some flapping and fussing, the pianist, who was sitting at a highly polished baby grand piano off to one side of the celebrant, launched into the wedding march.

The congregation got to their feet, all eyes on the door.

The bride, traditional in white, solemn-faced and holding her father's arm, looked beautiful, but Harry's gaze flicked past her to Ruby. Good God, she was gorgeous. She looked absolutely stunning. He couldn't take his eyes off her. Then, as she and Hannah, the other bridesmaid, walked past him, she winked and his heart swelled with love for her.

As Harry listened to the couple exchanging vows, which weren't the ones he remembered but must have been written especially, he felt his throat close with emotions.

'I promise to support your dreams. To honour you as a person, to respect you as a friend, to love you as a soulmate and to give you all of my heart...'

Wow. Harry's mind drifted into a fantasy of a future wedding which had himself and Ruby in the leading roles. Hell, he wasn't even divorced yet and he knew he wanted to spend the rest of his life with her. He was still totally immersed in this fantasy when he heard a voice rising from the front of the church.

'Stop messing about, Mr B, and just hand them over.'

'They're not here. They were here, twenty minutes ago when I checked. And now they are not.' Mr B's voice rose in an indignant wail.

Harry sat up straighter and peered around the purple hat of the woman in front of him. Ruby had said something about the groom playing a trick on Mr B. Maybe this was it. Harry had quite a good view. Even from the back, Mr B was very tall and easy to spot. He was patting the breast pocket of his jacket and shaking his head.

'Check for yourself if you don't believe me. Some pediculous rapscallion has taken them. Or...' he leaned towards the groom, 'maybe it's you, Phil. This is the kind of caper you think is funny. Don't deny it.'

'No way would I pull a stunt like this on my wedding day.' Phil looked thunderous.

'Hmmm,' said Mr B.

'Will you two please stop messing about,' said the bride, who was looking incredibly relaxed, considering the turn events had taken.

'Does anybody have the rings?' asked the celebrant, not sounding anywhere near as relaxed as Olivia.

'Maybe they've accidentally rolled onto the floor,' Mr B suggested, bending his stick-thin body to peer under the front seats.

A couple of wedding guests in the front row, following his lead, jumped onto their hands and knees and began looking under seats too.

Ruby took the opportunity to pat the jacket of Mr B's pockets and her face screwed up in puzzlement. The other bridesmaid had started walking back up the aisle and was scanning the floor as if she thought she might find them there.

Then, to Harry's amazement, Saskia York, who he hadn't even noticed until that moment, leapt up from a seat at the front, holding a jacket that looked identical to the one that Mr B was wearing. 'Try looking in here,' she called out sweetly. 'I think you picked up the wrong jacket, Mr B.'

Mr B grabbed the jacket from her outstretched hands and with one swift movement turned it upside down and shook it. Something fell out of the pockets and bounced. Two somethings. The groom halted their roll with his foot and bent down to retrieve them.

Phil straightened up, clutching what was clearly the rings in his fist. He opened his hand. 'Here are the rings. We can carry on.' He was beaming.

Then, suddenly, he blanched as he took a closer look at what was in his unclenched hand. 'These aren't our rings. What the...'

For a few seconds, there was pandemonium at the front of the church. There were still a couple of people looking under seats. Now several more joined in. There were mutterings from the bride that sounded like, 'OK, that's enough. You've had your fun.'

'I'm not joking. I don't...'

'You can borrow ours,' a woman called out from a couple of rows back.

'Thank you,' said the celebrant in response to the offer of rings. 'That would be most helpful. Now, will everyone please sit down and let us continue.'

Everyone sat down, apart from Mr B who was still standing. 'Zounderkites, the lot of you,' he said in his imperious voice. 'Complete morosophs.' He patted the pocket of his starched white shirt. 'I have the rings right here.' He held them out to Phil. 'They must have been here all the time.'

Phil looked as though he wanted to thump him, but restrained himself. Olivia rolled her eyes and grinned. Harry wondered if that was her acting training kicking in. She couldn't possibly be as relaxed as she appeared.

Ruby looked calm too. He remembered they had known this was coming – or at least something like it. He'd no doubt get the full story later.

Mr B looked smug as the rings were finally handed over.

Harry had never been to such an eventful wedding. It all seemed to be very good-humoured despite the shouting. He didn't even want to think about the chaos that would have ensued at his own wedding if someone had pulled a stunt like that at the ceremony. Annabel would have stormed out. Mind you, that would have saved a lot of trouble. He kept remembering her face today, screwed up in fury when she realised she wasn't going to be able to twist him around her little finger as she'd done so effortlessly in the past.

He blinked away the images. He didn't want to think about Annabel. He had given her enough of his time and energy to last a lifetime.

'You may kiss the bride,' the celebrant announced, jolting Harry back to the present once more and he watched as Phil stepped forward and lifted Olivia's veil. As they kissed each other tenderly, it was as though the whole congregation held its breath before letting it out in an 'ahh' of support and encouragement. Harry felt warmth swell his heart.

Then the bridal party headed back down the aisle, followed by an enthusiastic confetti-throwing congregation, until they were all outside once more.

It had been quite misty when they'd gone in, but now the sun had burnt through it and there was an arch of pure blue sky over their heads. As the guests sprawled out across the terrace and the lush green lawns of the hotel like so many bursts of bright colour, everyone was chattering and laughing and the photographer was having a hard time getting anyone to listen to his instructions.

Ruby caught up with Harry on the terrace. She was pushing Simon's buggy and he went to meet her, pausing to drink her in.

'You look so beautiful, Ruby. Hello, Simon.' He bent over the buggy. 'What a very handsome chap you are. I am loving that bow tie.'

Simon grinned and lifted his arms for a hug and Ruby looked amazed. 'He recognises you. Already. You scrub up pretty well yourself,' she added, looking at Harry properly too and adding laughingly, 'Oh my God. That was dramatic, even for my family.'

'There are always dramas at weddings. I'm guessing it had something to do with the groom and Mr B winding each other up.'

'That's right. Long story short. Phil ordered two identical jackets for the best man so he could switch them and, of course, the rings with them. It was designed to rattle Mr B so he thought he'd lost the rings, but he somehow got wind of it and the whole thing backfired on Phil.'

'So Mr B had the rings in his shirt pocket all the time?' Harry asked.

'I'm not sure.' Ruby shook her head. 'It seems there were some plastic rings which he switched with the real ones at the last minute. I don't think anyone has got to the bottom of how Mr B found out. Let alone switched the rings back. But he does always seem to get the last laugh.'

Harry blew out a breath. 'Wow. Well, it was a good distraction from my morning. I'm so sorry I was late by the way.'

He told her about Annabel's gate-ramming activities and she looked horrified. 'Oh, Harry, that's awful. Were you hurt?'

'Not on any level,' he said, meeting her direct gaze. 'I think that other than her pride, it was Annabel's car that sustained the most damage. She managed to reverse into one of my trees on her way out too.'

'Gosh.' She squeezed his hand, her beautiful eyes concerned.

'The best bit is that I'm pretty sure I'll have the whole thing recorded on CCTV from the gate camera. That clearly didn't occur to her when she was ramming my gate. But I'm hoping that once she finds out, she won't be in quite such a hurry to proceed with her blackmail efforts.'

'Wow. Gosh.'

She was nice enough not to sound smug, Harry thought, but she did look relieved.

'Sorry to interrupt.' The photographer was standing beside them. 'But we need you for some shots if you're free?' He glanced at Harry. 'Family and close friends, does that include you, sir?'

'Er...'

'Yes it does,' Ruby said, grabbing his hand. 'Come on, Harry. There are so many people I need to introduce you to.'

'What now?'

'Absolutely now. Follow me.'

* * *

'Well, that was a baptism of fire,' Ruby said to Harry ten minutes later when he had met her entire family – who all seemed to be as lovely as she was – after a whirlwind of introductions.

'I can't wait to introduce you to mine,' he said. 'Not that it will take that long, there's only really Mum, and I know she'll love you as much as...' He broke off. He'd been about to say, 'as I do.' It was too soon and he didn't want to scare her off by being too heavy. He'd been accused of wearing his heart on his sleeve before.

But he could see that Ruby knew exactly what he'd been about to say and the look she gave him warmed him through and through.

The sit-down reception was amazing. Harry had known the food would be superb, that went without saying, but his limited experience of weddings was that the speeches tended to be boring. Not so for this wedding. There was a lot of banter, both in Mr B's best man speech and the bridegroom's, and Olivia's father was clearly the proudest dad ever as he spoke from the heart about how much it meant to him to see his daughter so happy.

The wedding cake too was breathtaking. It was, without doubt, the most spectacular cake Harry had ever seen. It had four tiers and the top one was fashioned into the shape of a fairy castle, with towering, ivory turrets, windows that looked as though they were lit from inside, and cascades of roses. A miniature bride and groom twirled in front of the castle door. It was a masterpiece of intricacy, from the elaborate detail of the ivory turrets down to the cascade of pastel roses at its base. Harry had never seen anything like it – not even in the pages of the celebrity magazines that Annabel had left lying about the house.

'Our Aunt Dawn made it,' Ruby told him proudly. 'Isn't it stunning. A true labour of love.'

* * *

Much, much later when they were in that limbo period between the daytime reception and the evening one, Ruby asked Harry if he fancied a stroll in the bluebell woods.

'It's what the Bluebell Cliff Hotel is named for,' she told him. 'Not that there are any bluebells in August.'

'I would be delighted,' he said to her. 'Are we taking Simon?'

'No, we're not. He's with his Auntie Olivia and his Uncle Phil. He's their excuse to escape from the madness for a while. Not that I don't think they're enjoying their wedding day, but it's quite a long day, isn't it, when you're the focus of everyone's attention?'

'Indeed,' he said. 'Er, are you planning to go in that dress?'

'I am. Why?'

'Oh no reason!' That sparkle she'd first noticed about him was back in his eyes as they set off.

Although it wasn't the dress that was the problem, Ruby

thought, hitching it up as they reached the uneven ground that fronted the path at the beginning of the woods. It was the shoes! Ballet pumps were not designed for walking over rough ground and tree roots and she knew her face was giving her away as she stumbled on a sharp stone.

'Are you OK?' Harry paused and held out his arm and, after a moment's hesitation, she took it. The familiar tingle of his touch sparked through her and she let out a breath. 'I'm so glad I met you,' he said as they went under the canopy of shade offered by the leafy silver birches overhead. 'I'm so glad I came to Booty Busters.'

'I'm so glad I met you too,' Ruby said, pausing and drawing him to a halt beneath the trees. The woodland, which wasn't much more than a copse with a path leading through to the clifftop, wasn't very big, but after the brightness of the day, it was dim beneath the trees and very peaceful. There were just the sounds of birdsong and rustling leaves and the distant pounding of the sea below the cliffs.

They stood for a while in the dappled sunlight and Ruby knew that she had never been so happy. Olivia and Phil were finally married. With luck and a little bit of help, Olivia would very soon be pregnant. She had met the man of her dreams and she was here at her sister's wedding with him.

Even Phil and Mr B had sorted out their differences and had been laughing over lunch about the ring fiasco, which Phil had instigated, but which had backfired so spectacularly, thanks to Mr B's sleight of hand.

During the after-dinner speeches, Mr B had proclaimed that he was going to give up being a world-class chef and become a world-class magician instead. Turned out he'd known for ages about the wheeze – ever since the wedding hire shop had let slip that there were two best man jackets. After that, it had been fairly easy to swap the real rings in the identical jacket for the plastic ones whilst knowing that Saskia had been watching his every move.

'Penny for them,' Harry asked Ruby now.

'I was just thinking that I haven't felt so happy for years,' she told him, looking at his face in the dappled sunlight. 'I'm so glad we've had the chance to get to know each other as friends before...' She felt suddenly shy. 'Before taking it any further.'

He smiled.

'Also, Harry, you were right. I shouldn't have worn this dress because I've got a moss stain on it already. Or these shoes,' she added with a frown. 'They're not very suitable footwear for walking through woodland.'

'I could carry you back out,' he offered. 'If that would help?'

'I'm quite heavy. Although I guess I'm a lot lighter than I was.' She glanced up at him in a challenge.

'You're as light as a feather,' he said, picking her up and puffing only slightly as he took a few steps.

'Don't tell lies, Mr Small. Promise me that's the last lie you'll ever tell me.'

'I promise,' he said, and they both laughed as he put her down, breathlessly, then caught her hand and bent to kiss her.

Another amazing kiss, Ruby thought, which sent her head spinning into orbit and beyond, not just because of this moment but at the promise of what was to come. It had taken them both a few mistakes and a lot of heartache, she thought, but they'd finally found each other. And their love was all the sweeter because of what had gone before.

Then, still smiling, and with the uneven ground forgotten, they both ran, hand in hand, out of the woodland and into the afternoon sunshine.

EPILOGUE

The official first dance was supposed to be to Ed Sheeran's 'Perfect', but Mr B had, by some sleight of hand, switched it to the 'Birdie Song', which caused some uproar and a lot of laughter. Especially when Phil and Olivia rose to the challenge and performed a fault-less rendition of cheeps, elbow flaps, wriggles and claps, as effort-lessly as only two professional actors could, while Mr B watched open-mouthed from the edge of the dance floor.

* * *

Ruby discovered after the wedding, via Phil, that Mr B tried to join the magic circle but was thwarted at the first hurdle. Rumour has it that he's still trying and is also thinking of writing a book called Foodie Magic.

Phil also told Ruby that Saskia York has enlisted Phil's help to plot the ultimate caper to play on Mr B. This time, they are deter-mined to keep it top secret. Watch this space.

* * *

Becky went on her once-in-a-lifetime holiday to New Zealand with her husband and was thrilled to have the energy to play with Maisie on the beach as well as the bonus of being 'bikini ready'.

* * *

Ruby is still friends with Becky and Dana and they meet regularly for coffee on the Bluebell Cliff's terrace with Simon and Maisie. The Bluebell Cliff was also the venue for Harry and Ruby to have their celebration caramel latte with chocolate sprinkles, although they kept that little transgression to themselves!

* * *

Olivia fell pregnant without ever needing Ruby's wedding gift of IVF and she and Phil are expecting their first child nine months to the day after their wedding ceremony.

* * *

Marie and James are over the moon with the prospect of a second grandchild to look after although James has no plans to retire completely, just yet.

* * *

Aunt Dawn and Mike are also expecting a new arrival in the form of a baby alpaca and they're going to call it Arty, short for Moriarty.

* * *

Harry's divorce finally came through and Annabel left the marriage no richer than she was when she came into it, but a lot wiser! Her car hasn't been the same since she drove it into Harry's gates and her insurance premiums have shot up shockingly too! Apparently the insurance company couldn't understand how an accident that she claimed wasn't her fault and involved no other vehicles had damaged both ends of her car.

* * *

Harry kept his Banksy and his Damien Hirst, which he and Ruby plan to pass on to their own children when they have them. They are planning a brother or sister for Simon before he gets too much older. But currently they are living very happily in sin and making up for all the time they lost before they found each other.

* * *

NB. Harry caught Olivia's bouquet!

* * *

Ruby thinks she has sorted out her life/work balance but has come to the conclusion that this will always be a work in progress. No one has a perfect life. Or indeed perfect balance. And, quite frankly, she's seen enough scales to last her a lifetime.

On that note, Ruby and Harry are both still at their target weight. But they also indulge themselves fairly regularly, secure in the knowledge that Mr B is a far better chef than he is a magician, whatever he might claim.

They are also in the privileged position of knowing they fell in love with each other because of what was on the inside, not the outside.

And that – they both agree – is absolute magic.

ACKNOWLEDGMENTS

Thank you so much to Team Boldwood – you are amazing. As always, my special thanks go to Caroline Ridding, Judith Murdoch and Jade Craddock.

Thank you to Jennifer McCormick for her knowledge and expertise of the art world. Thank you to my brother, Mark Parkhurst, for his knowledge of the corporate business world.

Thank you to Meena Kumari for naming my alpaca, Mr Holmes, and to Sheila Mclean for providing the name Arty, for my baby alpaca. Much appreciated.

Thank you to Gordon Rawsthorne for his enduring support. He endures a lot!

Thank you, perhaps most of all, to the huge support of my readers – without whom it would be pretty pointless writing novels. I love reading your emails, tweets and Facebook comments. Please keep them coming.

MORE FROM DELLA GALTON

We hope you enjoyed reading *Confetti Over Pebble Bay*. If you did, please leave a review.

If you'd like to gift a copy, this book is also available as an ebook, digital audio download and audiobook CD.

Sign up to Della Galton's mailing list for news, competitions and updates on future books:

http://bit.ly/DellaGaltonNewsletter

Sunshine Over Bluebell Cliff, another glorious escapist read from Della Galton, is available to order now.

ABOUT THE AUTHOR

Della Galton is the author of 15 books, including *Ice and a Slice*. She writes short stories, teaches writing groups and is Agony Aunt for Writers Forum Magazine. She lives in Dorset.

Visit Della's website: www.dellagalton.co.uk

Follow Della on social media:

facebook.com/DailyDella

twitter.com/DellaGalton

instagram.com/Dellagalton

bookbub.com/authors/della-galton

ABOUT BOLDWOOD BOOKS

Boldwood Books is a fiction publishing company seeking out the best stories from around the world.

Find out more at www.boldwoodbooks.com

Sign up to the Book and Tonic newsletter for news, offers and competitions from Boldwood Books!

http://www.bit.ly/bookandtonic

We'd love to hear from you, follow us on social media:

facebook.com/BookandTonic

twitter.com/BoldwoodBooks

instagram.com/BookandTonic

Printed in Great Britain
by Amazon